in the
SEASON
of the
DAISIES

IN MEMORY OF ANNIE AND JOHN
TO PAT AND JOE AND MIKE WITH LOVE

in the
Season
of the
Daisies

★

TOM PHELAN

THE LILLIPUT PRESS

First published in 1993 by
THE LILLIPUT PRESS LTD
4 Rosemount Terrace, Arbour Hill,
Dublin 7, Ireland.

A CIP record for this
title is available from
The British Library.

ISBN 0 946640 97 1

Acknowledgments
The Lilliput Press receives financial assistance from
An Chomairle Ealaion/The Arts Council, Ireland

Set in 10 on 12.5 Trump Mediæval by
mermaid turbulence
Printed in Dublin by
ßetaprint Ltd of Clonshaugh

GUARD McSWAINE

It's only when I begin listening that I hear her, even though the sound of her has been there for a while. She wasn't even at Madden's Bridge when she was in my head without me knowing it. That's what started the stirrings in my trousers.

Isn't that a curious thing! The way she's always dressed is one reason – with the tight white trousers on her. Another is the moves of her – that non-stop up and down on the horse. And then the shape of her arse in the skin-tight trousers. Every time she goes up with the horse's trot the outline of her is plain to see. I wonder if she feels anything when she goes down on the saddle. God she must! Up and down. Oh Jesus, I'd better straighten myself out.

No sign of anyone. I'll turn my back to the street and face Hubey Sherlock's jewellery window. Ah! that's better.

Now the hoofs sound different because the Church is set back from the street across from the Dummy Cashin's. She'll look in at the Church going past to see if all the scaffolding is gone, and all the wheelbarrows and the other stuff that the builders used. They were still gathering it up when I was down there around six.

I can see her now, passing Jack Quinlan's forge. As usual, she's dressed in her riding cap and jodhpurs. The crop is in the heel of her hand, brushing the horse's flank every time she goes down on the saddle.

I face straight across the street at the Cinema, my eyes twisted sideways in their sockets looking at her.

The get-up of her! Only a Protestant would dress like that. By Jesus! if a Catholic came riding through the Town got up like that, the rest of us would throw rocks at him. But not at Miss Bevan! It's Miss Bevan this and Miss Bevan that, and good day Miss Bevan and how are you Miss Bevan!

But then they have to clean themselves by turning to whoever's nearest them and saying under their breaths, 'Bloody Protestant bitch.'

On she comes, clipping and clopping, and I squint into her tight-covered crotch, as it rises and falls. When I know she's seen me, I look away. That hatchet-like face of hers is always a bit of a disappointment.

She's past Maxwells' fish-and-chip shop now. I can see her smelling the vinegar they sprinkle on the chips. Just chips. No fish. Never sold fish. Fish and chips! Jack Maxwell wouldn't know a fish if it fell on him. It's the brown mare with the star she has out tonight. A grand-looking animal it is, and it never shies at anything, not even blowing newspaper. She looks like she's completely in charge up there, but she has respect for the Law.

As she passes between me and the Cinema lights, Miss Bevan lifts the crop to the peak of her riding-cap.

'Good evening, Guard McSwaine,' she says in that almost-English accent of hers that sounds hard, like a voice used to giving orders without thinking.

The Bevans fatten their pigs on broken biscuits from their factories in Dublin.

'Evening, Miss Bevan.' I bring two fingers to the shiny peak of my cap. I'd love to give it to you now, Miss Bevan.

'Are you all ready for tomorrow?'

'As ready as we'll ever be,' I call after her. And I'm ready for you Miss Bevan. I'm always ready for you.

She trots away as if the answer to her question doesn't matter.

You won't be so high and mighty tomorrow, Miss Bevan. You won't even show your face.

Her mare trots up the street, the hoof beats fading. She and the mare are fading too, because of the dark. Clip clop, and she going up and down. Clip clop fading away, and I'm beginning to shrivel.

All quiet now, not a sinner anywhere. Anyone else who's awake is in the Cinema. If Father Quinn hadn't built the Cinema the street would be quiet till morning. But they're all in there, all looking at the screen with their mouths open, mostly big lads from the country with cowshite on their wellingtons; big bad-toothed buggers who never clean their teeth. They wouldn't know what to do with a toothbrush. There's the few respectable ones from the Town scattered around in the plush seats, as far away from the smell of the cowshites as they can get. The townies have shoes on, shining from the polishing they got last Saturday night for Sunday morning mass.

Still, it's from the country ones I get a bag of spuds for the pigs, or a bundle of rhubarb, or a few apples for the Missus to make a nice cake with. I can always find something wrong with a farmer's bike; no headlight, no tail-light, a loose mudguard – I can tell them anything and they believe it. It's killing the two birds with one stone, as they say. They don't get a summons and their name in the paper, and I get potatoes for my two pigs. Big John Joe Grimes is in there, tonight. He's always good for a bit of bran or groundmeal. A bit of meal and the pigs would put on three or four pounds overnight. By the end of October they'll be ready for selling.

One pound and five shillings was the going price at Walls today; dead weight. By the time the small one is fourteen stone, the big one'll be sixteen. That'll be nearly forty pounds for the two of them. When I show that to the Missus, she won't be smelling the pigshite in the back garden. The last time it was nearly thirty. That kept her smiling for a couple of months and the smell of the pigshite away too. And, by God! it made her easier in the bed for a couple of weeks. She gets reluctant again once the money is gone. If I could fatten one a week, I'd have her every night! The hot wetness of her! Oh! But once the money is gone, I have to be content with the hand under a bush, and you never know who's going to walk up on you.

That little bastard last week! Me in the hedge at the railway bridge up on McDonagh Street, pretending to be taking a leak. It was shooting out of me when that young whelp of Jack Quinlan's let out a screech about the size of my mickey, only he called it a parsnip. How the hell he ever crept up on me! and me sawing away with my eyes closed.

Then there's Father Quinn when you go to confession! All the questions he asks, it's embarrassing. It takes all the excitement out of it, knowing I'm going to have to tell him. It's the strangest thing. The one minute nothing could stop you, but Jesus, once it shoots out all you can think of is Father Quinn while this thing shrivels in your hand. There he is in the dark behind the grille asking all his bloody questions. Did you do it by yourself? Are you married? Do you have conjugal relations with your wife? Conjugal! I hate that sound. It's the sound of Father Quinn seeing me on top of the Missus, the tail of my shirt not covering the crack of my arse, going up and down. If anyone saw me then! I'd never get my authority back.

Jesus! There's a car stopped between myself and the Cinema, and I hadn't noticed a thing. Of course it's Father Quinn in his bloody Peugeot. No car should be as quiet as that. A person could get killed and not know what hit him.

And what is Father Quinn doing out here anyway? He should be at the pictures, like he is every night of the week. He's been off someplace else and I knew nothing about it. I feel like walking over and kicking a dent into the door of the car. Where could he have been? Maybe someone's sick, but if anyone was sick enough for a priest, I'd know about it. Still, I'll show my respect in the usual way. I always give him my best salute; shoulders up and belly in, like we were taught in the Barracks in Dublin.

The car is so modern that a light goes on inside when the door opens. When Father Quinn steps out, it's the rubber boots flapping around his knees that give him away. It's in the training to notice things. Fishing! At least now I know where he's been.

'Good evening, Father Quinn.'

The priest is short and round – a stretched-out ball with legs and a head. Fussy little man, always jerking around in a state of agitation like a child who's dying for a piss but won't waste the time doing it.

4

'Good evening, Garda.'

Garda! Father Quinn is a great one for the Gaelic, a great one for showing respect for the Law.

'Did you catch anything, Father?' Let him know that I miss nothing.

'A few trout,' he says, feeling around in his pockets. Stop fussing for Christ's sake, you'd give anyone the itch.

But I see the connection now – this will impress him. The President and Eamon de Valera are coming tomorrow for the opening of the new wing of the Church. They'll be eating at Father Quinn's house.

'Will Miss Dixon serve the trout for the president?' I have to smile at my cleverness. It's not everyone can carry on a conversation with the priest.

'It was to send home with them, not to eat tomorrow. I was hoping for salmon,' he says, sinking his thumbs into his waistcoat pockets, still searching. 'I almost got a good one,' he mutters. 'I had him on the hook.'

'A salmon!' I put plenty of admiration in my voice.

'A salmon,' he says. He does up his coat, the short fat fingers fumbling and fussing with the buttons. 'I think I lost my penknife though,' he adds, starting to pull off one of his big boots, using the edge of the footpath against the heel. I hold my hands out to him, like I would to a doddering old woman. Father Quinn is seventy-one, after all.

'Can I help you with them?'

He doesn't hear me. He fusses his feet into a pair of slip-on shoes, as shiny as my boots. My boots are black too, but they're plainer.

'I'll put the boots in the car for you, Father,' I offer, but he wants to do it himself. What has he in the car that he doesn't want me to see?

'Are you going to have a look at the picture, Father?'

He flicks me a glance.

'It will be over soon,' he says, 'but I'll look in anyhow.' Closing the car door he asks as if the thought has just struck him, 'Did Mr Sheehan go home yet, Garda?'

'No, Father, he didn't. I saw him a while ago on the steps,

out for a bit of air.'

Why does he hate the Cinema manager – and him one of his teachers too, taught every man in town under the age of forty. The Chief! But no one would ever call him that to his face, any more than they'd call me Baggy.

'Good night, Garda.'

'Good night, Father.' He's turned away before he can see my salute.

I bring the saluting hand down to my side and look in through the car window. All I can see is the reflection of the Cinema lights.

FATHER QUINN

McSwaine sticks out his chest, pulls up his shoulders and sucks in his guts. He sees my back. He gives the salute anyhow, with the hand that milks his parsnip in the bushes at McDonagh Street railway bridge.

Parsnip milker! That's a new one.

Jack Quinlan's wife asked me to speak to the garda about it. What should I say to him? Don't milk your parsnip in public, you big eejit. The next time he comes to confession, I'll ask him where he does it. Then I'll ask him if he's not afraid some young person might see him. That should give him the hint. Then again, a wink is as good as a nod to a blind horse.

I should have got him to tell Butler-the-Butcher about the meat, but I can't bear the look on his face when I ask him to do something; like a sick pup. When I get home I'll telephone his wife and let her pass on the message.

I wish Sheehan had gone home.

7

GUARD McSWAINE

I can see Father Quinn in the car window, growing smaller as he shuffles towards the Cinema steps. It's a pity he never waits for the salute, that he never sees it. It's my way of showing him respect for calling me Garda. I love that – Garda, from the parish priest.

Back across the street in my position at Hubey Sherlock's window, I can see him slowly climbing up to the glass door. The lights silhouette him and light up his hair like a halo.

Yes, it is nice to be called Guard and Garda. It's like being the priest. Good morning, Father. Good morning, Guard. The priest and the doctor and the guard and the teacher! Big shots in the Town. They know everybody and everything that goes on. But none of them knows as much as me. None of them knows what goes on at the Ploverlegs Dunne's house every Tuesday night. It was pure luck stumbling across that. How the two of them ever put it into that woman I'll never know. She is the ugliest woman, and the legs of her! No wonder they're all called Ploverlegs. And the husband in the kitchen looking into the fire while she's at it in the next room. He collects the ten shillings from them on the way in, and I collect the bags of spuds on the way out. I couldn't get anything out of Dunne; said he didn't give a tinker's curse who knew about it. But the other two eejits! Two bags of spuds a week. If I had a few more regulars, I wouldn't have to be here every night waiting for the pictures to be over, waiting to catch a farmer with no light on his bike.

Father Quinn's gone left to the ticket window to ask Joey Bannon how much has been taken in. Mister Sheehan must be patrolling inside the Cinema. If he was in the ticket office Father Quinn wouldn't go near it. They say Father

Quinn is a genius with figures. He can divide three different prices into three different totals in his head, and know how many tickets were sold before Joey Bannon can tell him. Three different prices to see the same picture, I ask you! The Protestants and the lads who want to do a bit of heavy courting in peace in the dark, and don't want orange and banana skins thrown at them, go up to the balcony. The ones who shouldn't be going at all, the poor ones, sit up in the front under the screen and they all come out with big eyes, like they were looking into the sun for two hours. The townies and the better-off farmers sit in the parterre, if you don't mind! That's a French word, Paddy Lemon told me.

No matter where they sit they have respect for me. I am the Authority! If I face Hubey Sherlock's window, and with the Cinema lights behind me, I can see my shape among the rings and watches and necklaces in the glass.

If I pull down my tunic and pull in my paunch a bit, I look grand. Six foot three, peaked cap, silver buttons and navy blue uniform; shoes shining.

Hubey has a daughter as ripe and juicy as an apple after the first frost. Red hair. I wonder what's it like to do it with a Protestant. A Dublin lad told me one time that they go across and not up and down. Shite! There's someone coming. Did he see me? I'll walk on a bit as if I was just passing the window.

Scutter! It's only Seanie Doolin. I should have known by the way he's limping along against the houses. Watch him now! Instead of walking past, he'll go into the Cinema yard, limp all around by the wall, limp up the steps, limp down the steps, around by the other wall and back out onto the footpath. Quare in the head, with an eternal drip at the nose. Everlasting snuffle. He'd sicken your arse. When he comes out of the yard, I'll frighten the shite out of him with a roar. He's the hungriest, the most starved-looking fellow I've ever seen. He looks like a greyhound with a broken back walking around on its hind legs. He hasn't got the blanket with him. Stinking blanket! They say he's had it for thirty years, and that it's never been washed.

Will you look at him! Up on the steps and he looking in. All he can see is a blank wall with a shut door in it. It must be a curse to be so thick. Around the wall he's coming, sloping, limping. I'll walk back slowly past Sherlock's window and make him jump out of his drawers. Look at him! The twisted head of him and he dragging something over the pebble-dashing on the wall, making a noise. It's a piece of metal. When he gets to the end of the ...

'Hey! Blindeye!'

Heh heh! He jumped, and look at him squinting around. He hasn't seen me yet.

'Hey! Blindeye!'

Now he sees me, wiping the drop off his nose, the blind blue eye pointing up at the sky.

SEANIE DOOLIN

It sounds like a motorbike, the blade against the pebble –
dashing, dashing from pebble to pebble, making a sound like
a motorbike dashing. Ber umb ber ump bee beep ber ump.

I saw the knife falling and the Priest didn't, when it fell
with the salmon falling back into the water, falling into the
grass at his feet, with a splash and he shouting *Camarawn!*
Camarawn! dancing on the grassy bank with his big boots
flopping around his knees like fish.

Camarawn! Camarawn!

Ber ump ber ump ber ump.

The knife fell in the long green grass when the salmon
splashed in my ears, because my eye was on the spot where
the knife went down into the long green grass.

'*Camarawn! Camarawn!*' the Priest roared with crossness in the sound, my eye on the spot and the splashing
salmon in my ears. I was hiding in the big clump of blackberry briars for so long I was them. Not even God could
have found me.

He caught four trout while God was looking for me and
couldn't find me in the blackberry briars, while I stared at
the spot where the knife had fallen into the long green
grass. *The life that I have is all that I have, the life that I*
have is yours; the love that I have for that life that I have is
yours and yours and yours, Willie in the long green grass.

My eyes never moved off the spot on Willie's forehead,
them holding him down, and that thing pressed into his
forehead. '*Camarawn!*' the other one shouted – the short
one, 'give it to me and I'll do it,' and Willie's eyes – Willie's
eyes – Oh God! – Willie's eyes were bursting out of his –
Oh! Daddy Daddy save Willie! 'Hold his fucking head!' the
short one screamed, and then he put the thing on Willie's

11

forehead, pressing it down, and it went white with pain, Willie, poor Willie screaming, 'Seanie! Seanie! Seanie!' But my mouth was terrified dry, and then the shot, like a gun, shooting his legs, shooting out straight in the long green grass like he was kicking something away with his heels. Daddy Mammy. Poor Willie – poor poor poor Willie – wet himself then.

Ber ump ber ump ber ump ber ump BER UMP BER UMP.

The big flopping boots moved away from where the falling knife had gone down with the splashing salmon. When the flopping boots moved, it was hard to keep my eye on the place in the green grass. But I did, in the blackberry briars while God was looking for me, and couldn't find me, all over the Bottoms. *I fled him down the nights and down the days. I fled him down the arches of the years. I fled him down the labyrinthine ways of my own mind, and in the mist of tears I hid from him, and under running laughter.* I was a blackberry briar.

Ber ump ber ump ber ump bee beep.

Oh! Jay! What's that! What a fright and I skinned my knuckles off the pebble-dashing with the fright. Oh! Jay! Again. Where is what is? My wind goes in and out real quick, and my heart is shaking in my chest. What was ...

There! On the other side, near Sherlock's shop window, is a black shape and upstairs over it the window is open. Hubey Sherlock's daughter's head with the red hair is in it, but the hair looks black now in the near night. She is looking down on the black shape, and the same sound comes again, only now I know the sound. By the shape of the shape, I know it's the Guard, frightening me. Every time he sees me when there's no one around, I get frightened.

The Guard calls from the other side of the street about what I'm doing. I'm doing nothing, and I push the knife down into my pocket, down through the hole and into the lining of my coat.

He calls again from across the street about what I'm doing, about what I was making the noise on the wall with. I tell him a stick, and he starts across the street to me.

'Playing motorbikes, are you!' he says in a funny voice that's hard to understand. 'Motorbikes. What did you put in your pocket?' He steps onto the footpath and looks down on me. He is tall and he has a big belly and a big backside and big feet and a big red face.

I tell him, I only put my hand in the pocket, sir. He walks to my side where the pocket is, and I can see his backside real close, like he has a bag of potatoes in the seat of his trousers.

'Yab yab yab yabby yab yab yabby,' he says in that funny voice, and before I know it, he has his hand in my pocket. I can feel his heaviness pulling my coat down at my shoulder. Then he says: 'Hummmmmm. A hole. Maybe your hand fell through the little hole.'

I point across the street to where Hubey Sherlock's red-headed daughter, like the statue of the Blessed Virgin Mary in the Church, is looking at us with black hair in the near night. When the Guard looks at her, he tries to pull his hand out of my pocket, but it's like he's trying to pull his fist out of the jar with a sweet in it. The pocket won't come off his hand and he has the side of my coat up at my head. He catches the coat with his other hand and pulls out the first hand. At the same time he whispers in a hiss: 'You scrawny little fucker. I'll break your arse with a kick,' and he turns to Hubey Sherlock's daughter in the upstairs window.

'Good evening, Miss Sherlock,' he says, and he starts across the street. He touches his hand to the shiny peak of his guard-cap. He doesn't know he is at the edge of the foot-path and he stumbles like Doctor McKenna when he's drunk. Hubey Sherlock's daughter twitters *like the swallow twittering in a straw-built shed, the cock's shrill clarion or the echoing horn, no more shall rouse them from their lowly bed.*

I slip into the dark spot that the Cinema wall makes with Bennett's Lane.

I have a million hiding-places and before the Guard is across the street and onto the other footpath, I am the shadow in Bennett's Lane. God starts looking for me in the

13

back yards behind the houses along Dwyer Street like in the briars. The Priest owns the biggest house on Dwyer Street, and I know where the Housekeeper throws the bottles when they're empty.

The Guard is looking up at Hubey Sherlock's daughter's head in the window, and she is looking down at him. It is almost dark and I can hear their voices. The Guard's voice is changed because it's coming out of him looking up. She is like the Virgin Mary in the Church. Hubey Sherlock's daughter once appeared to me in the window with the watches and chains and pearls and diamonds, when it was late and they were doing it to Willie again and I couldn't look away. She was suddenly there with watches and bracelets moving through her. The only light was from the pole light near the Cinema. But she was there. She was. *She was a Phantom of delight when first she gleam'd upon my sight; a lovely Apparition, sent to be a moment's ornament.*

There were watches all across her chest, and lower down there were strings of pearls in her, and her feet were in two alarm clocks. Slowly so soley slow oley her hands drifted up along chains of gold and silver. The watches began to move around in the backs of her hands as she moved them so soley slow on her chest. She floated in the window and she was full of watches and necklaces and chains. One hand left one side of her chest and came slowly down and down. She was moving around in a slow so slow circle. I saw her with all the gleaming and shining things moving around in her. Her slow knees were like weeds at the bottom of lazy water moving through strings of pearls, and up along her legs were silver things for going on women's wrists. All of her moved then, like tall golden wheat moving in the August wind. So slowly so lovely moving and moving oh so lovely it was the way she appeared in the silver and gold and diamonds and pearls, all moving through her as she moved and waved, and her hair slowly came over her shoulders as she bent her head, down down so gently onto her knees she went. She shuddered and shook when she leaned forward and put her red-haired head on the floor. She had nothing on her.

Oh! the beauty of her in the window made me want to dance around the altar in front of all the people at Sunday mass; to dance with my arms going any way at all, trying to keep up with my mad legs that buckled and bucked and jerked; my head held back, my face to the ceiling of the Church looking straight into the face of God; glad gladness gladdening me while I dance for God, in an outburst of magnificent joy, because the thing being joyed at is magnificent. *Magnificat anima mea Dominum* they sang in the nuns' golden evening garden full of daffodils and tulips when I was an altar-boy at the Children of Mary Sodality. I could dance to the memory of that. They all looked so lovely in their white dresses and wide light-blue scapulars. They were so lovely in the tulips and the daffodils. *And daffadillies fill their cups with tears to strew the laureat hearse where Lycid lies.* Fill their cups with tears. Poor Willie. They cried for poor Willie. Poor poor Willie. The daffodils cried for him.

I hear their voices across the street again, the Guard's and Hubey Sherlock's daughter's. The voices are clear, but I cannot hear the words. They sound like whispering sounds, like voice-sounds that are not meant to be heard. When we heard the sounds Willie caught me by the elbow in Carther's Bottling House. In the dark we stood without moving, without hardly breathing in the middle of the bottles and the barrels, and I could hear water dripping from a tap. Then there was the whispering again outside the door. Willie put his mouth to my ear. In the dark I could feel his breath in the porches of my ear before I heard his words. In the dark he said with hot frightened breath, we would hide in the space between the bottle-crates and the wall. The door creaked as if someone had leaned against it, and there was the whispering again. I caught Willie's sleeve, and he led the way to the space between the wall and the pile of crates. Just as we were sitting down, we heard a window breaking. I thought for a second that we had ... we had ... My heart went like mad and I held Willie's hand Willie's hand! Willie Willie! We had come in to steal six bottles of ale from Carther's Bottling House like we did every Tuesday night.

I hear the sound of a window closing. When I look over, Hubey Sherlock's daughter's head is gone. The Guard is pulling down the front of his uniform so that it's stretched against his puffed-out chest. He turns sideways in front of Hubey Sherlock's window and runs the palm of his hand down his front. He touches his guard-cap as if it needs straightening.

GUARD McSWAINE

When she says, 'Good night, Guard,' she lifts her arms up over her head to pull down the window. Her blouse pulls up and hangs out from her. If it was only a bit brighter! But I can see them anyhow, the shape of them, young and sturdy, sticking out from her. What a sight! As she closes the window she looks down at me through her arms and over her chest and smiles. My mouth is dry.

When I catch my reflection in the window, I realize she's attracted to the physique of me, my physique and my authority. All the questions she was asking me! and I having to make up half the answers. What's the new wing like? What will the bishop do? Why is the President coming? She was only thinking up questions so she could talk to me, so she could look at my physique in the uniform. Even the Protestants know Father Quinn was in jail with de Valera that time of the English. IRA, the two of them.

The way she was looking at my chest! If I had her for a few minutes in the bushes at McDonagh Street railway bridge I'd give her a look at my chest!

I could have killed that little bollicks, Doolin, when I fell off the footpath; little fucker, and she sniggering up in the window. She saw me with my hand in his pocket and trying to get it out. The next time I see the little bollicks I'll give him such a kick up his arse he won't be able to take a shite for a week. Where did he disappear to all of a sudden once I started talking to her?

Bennett's Lane! He's probably over there in the dark of the wall watching me, the scut. I'll amble across and pretend I'm minding my own business.

Maybe Hubey Sherlock's daughter is still looking at me with the light out. Jesus! The thought of her! The hair of her fork must be red, too.

There's not a sound from the lane, but he's in there in the dark. Eleven o'clock starting to strike. I've a few minutes before the lads come out of the Cinema. At least I can frighten the shite out of him.

I go into the lane and sing out softly, 'Hey, Blindeye!' and stop to listen.

I hope I don't step into a fresh cowshite. The Bennetts let the cows out around six, after the milking, so the cowshites should be fairly dry by now.

Deeper into the lane I go and there's still nothing to be seen, only the line of the top of the wall against the Cinema lights.

'Hey, Blindeye!' I call out again.

Holy Jesus! I hear them all coming out of the Cinema on the far side of the wall! While running back I slip in a wet cow dung, and stumble into the light at the end of the lane.

'Keep an eye out for Baggy McSwaine, lads!'

I stride out into the footpath with all my dignity in the chest of my uniform. If I could tell which fucker called me Baggy he'd be feeding my pigs for a month of Sundays. But there's a big flock of them in the street on their bikes, all with their arses in the air, sawing from side to side, getting away as fast as they can. Then, like a miracle, here comes John Joe Grimes and he pedalling like a hure. He has no light on his bike, and I know for sure I have a bag of ground-meal for the pigs. I calm myself, take the running out of my breath and when he draws level with me I let out my best guard tone of voice.

'Where's your light, John Joe Grimes?'

'Up my hole,' he yells from the safety of the crowd.

He keeps pedalling, while all the other thick fuckers let out a roar. But quick as lightning I see how I can have the last laugh.

'That it may burn the arse off of you!' I shout at the top of my voice.

I stand there with my hands on my hips, and across the street in the upstairs window over Hubey Sherlock's shop window, I see a face moving away and the curtain falling across the glass.

In front of the Cinema Father Quinn looks like he has stopped getting into his car. Mister Sheehan is walking towards me across the yard with the bag of money in his right hand. A few townies are going past me on their way home. I hope none of them heard me shouting at John Joe Grimes. Not that I give a shite, but it doesn't sound good to have to raise your voice to exert your authority.

Grimes knows enough to bring at least a bag of spuds into town with him on Saturday.

The next time I see that scrawny little gobshite with the crooked neck I'll kick his arse off. On his account I missed getting that ground-meal.

MISTER SHEEHAN

It's not as a reward for the work I do that I'd like Father
Quinn to talk to me, to be pleasant to me. It's discouraging
that he will not bid me the time of day. I teach in his school,
I manage his cinema without pay, I have sold most of the
tickets in every raffle he ever thought up. He trusts me to
take this money home with me every night, but he won't
talk to me. Oh, now and then he'll ask for a piece of infor-
mation, but there is never a word of thanks. I know I
shouldn't expect thanks, it's just that it's awkward. It's a
hurt that he's not even decent to me.

It hurts that he hasn't invited me to the dinner with de
Valera and the president tomorrow. I was looking forward to
meeting a great man, an historical man. I can see the surprise on people's faces when they ask me if I'm going, and I
have to say no. They know, he knows, that no one has
worked as hard as me for the Church Building Fund for the
last twenty-seven years; for the twenty-seven years since he
got it into his head that the Church had to be expanded,
since he decided to build a monument to himself. God forgive me, but I have often thought that. Every Sunday, for
twenty-seven years, we have heard about the Church Building Fund from the pulpit. Will he be able to give a sermon
now without mentioning it?

That is unkind of me; mean-minded.

There he is now getting into his French car.

I will have to accept it as a cross to be carried, the fact
that he won't speak to me. I would do the same again today
if I had to, even though I now know the consequences. It
was my duty to tell him he was wrong. It was never my
intention to ...

What's that shouting? A fight! Father Quinn has stopped

20

getting into his car and he's looking towards Bennett's Lane. It's Guard McSwaine.

'That it may burn the arse off of you!'

The big men from the country must be tormenting him. That poor man has dug himself into a hole, and he'll never climb out of it. He's in a mess of his own making, and he'll be crucified if he continues to demand bribes for every minor offence.

The crucifixion of any man is a terrible thing to see, but every corrupt official ought to be crucified. God forgive me. No man ought to be crucified.

Carthage must be destroyed – *delenda est Carthago* – perfect example of the ablative absolute.

Father Quinn gets into his car and drives away. He must have been coming from somewhere when he came in tonight, he never drives to the Cinema. He looks straight ahead, even though he's passing within ten feet of me. While it does not come easy to me, I say a Hail Mary for the priest, for his well-being.

Guard McSwaine snaps off a military salute as Father Quinn drives past and, by the time I've finished my prayer, I'm nearly up to him. He has his big hands on his hips, and he's looking up the street after the bikes. He knows I'm coming up behind him. His stance of authority is his little show for me. He should have been hatched in a peahen's nest, God forgive me.

'Good evening, Guard.'

I silently say a prayer that he won't start one of his interminable one-way conversations.

He looks around, as I knew he would, with a look of surprise on his red face. He touches the shining peak of his guard's cap with his right index finger.

'Mister Sheehan, sir! Good evening!'

The buttons on his tunic are straining against their threads.

There is a strong smell of cow dung. I keep walking and I speak to him over my shoulder.

'Are you all set for the big day tomorrow?'

21

'Everything's under control, sir. Six guards and Sergeant Keogh are coming from Queentown to control the traffic.'

There's only six cars in the Town, I think to myself, and only two thousand people.

'Of course the President will have his own men. Body-guards! Big lads, sir. Himself', Guard McSwaine inclines his eyebrows at the fading tail-lights of Father Quinn's car, 'was trying to catch salmon for the President and Dev to bring home with them. All he caught was a few trout. Miss Dixon might cook them for you at the big dinner tomorrow.'

Miss Dickingson would correct the guard if she heard him. She imagines her name is several classes above Dixon.

I do not tell Guard McSwaine that I won't be eating anything at Father Quinn's tomorrow.

I keep walking but I am almost walking backwards. It's important to keep moving. One time he buttonholed me for an hour when I asked him how he was. 'I'm sure you will make good account of yourself tomorrow, Guard.'

'I will, at that, sir.'

'Good night, Guard.'

'Good night, sir.'

Ahead of me, Father Quinn's car bumps up onto the pavement and seems to disappear, nose first, through the wall of his house. In my angle of vision I can't see the high, arched doorway.

The Christ-like thing to do would be to liberate Mc-Swaine, rather than assist in his crucifixion from the side-lines, by saying nothing. But who am I to approach him and tell him his little scheme is wrong, that it will backfire on him? I imagine he would deny ever having taken a bribe. He would probably interpret his system as a means of helping people to avoid a summons. Am I seeing myself as a beacon of integrity? I hope not.

That's what Father Quinn asked me at the foot of the wide stairs in his big house, he standing two steps off the floor looking me straight in the eye. 'Are you a beacon of integrity, Mister Sheehan? Beacons of integrity are suscepti-ble to galloping spiritual death from pride.' As things turned out, he was taken in by the oratory of a lunatic. That in itself must make it more difficult for him to look at me.

It's almost ten years now since he accidentally heard Hitler at Nuremberg, ten years since he was swept off his feet into a whirlwind of patriotic zeal, as if he hadn't already been zealous enough; as if he didn't already know, and had the scars to prove it, that that kind of maniacal zeal bears nothing but pain and imprisonment. He came back to the Town as if he'd been in Jerusalem on the first Pentecost. He pounded the pulpit; he salivated and roared out his newly baptized hatred. Over and over he quoted Hitler, paraphrased him so often that the people knew the words by heart, the lads in the back pews mouthing them to each other with smirks and winks.

He was as mad then as the Reverend Hightower in that book of Faulkner's I couldn't understand; Hightower forever hearing the clatter of hoofs; his grandfather forever charging into Jefferson, forever getting shot out of the saddle. Father Quinn was forever seeing Cromwell in the perpetual act of laying siege to Drogheda, while the people inside went mad with the hunger and ate their own children; forever the Red Coats were in the act of throwing babies into the air in Wexford and spiking them on their bayonets as they fell; forever the potato famine went on, the skeletal hungry people green in their faces from eating grass, while the riches of the harvests were sent to the absentee landlords in England; forever the English were hanging and drawing and quartering.

His fervour has cooled somewhat – nobody could sustain that forever – but the feast-day of Blessed Oliver Plunkett, falling as it does on the day before the Twelfth of July, gives him the opportunity to blast the English, Protestantism in general, and the Protestants of the North of Ireland in particular.

Year in, year out, the English hang, draw and quarter the unfortunate Bishop of Drogheda. Every year, on the Sunday closest to the feast-day, we feel the rope cutting into the flesh of the neck until the face turns black, the eyes and tongue protruding. While the air passages are strangulated, the congregation holds its breath and waits for Father Quinn to cut down the jerking victim. The whole church draws in air when the noose is cut, and the bishop is given the chance to recover consciousness by his tormentors.

At the first sign of recovery, Plunkett is pulled back up on the scaffold, feet first, and the executioner steps forward with a sharp knife. He slits the blessed belly from groin to breastbone. Gloriously, Father Quinn describes the glistening visceral outpouring and the church groans and gags as the precious intestines slither down onto the ground, steam rising up out of them. Again the victim is cut down, this time with no concern for his recovery, and everyone feels the skull-splitting thump when the rope at the feet is slashed.

The congregation gapes with gushing saliva as the axeman steps forward, spits on his hands, shakes the cloying human entrails from his boots, and hacks the body into four separate pieces. Finally the head is severed and the whole mess is left for the dogs. It is only through the bravery of some pious and patriotic souls that the head is saved, and can still be viewed, in its glass case, in Drogheda Cathedral.

The people come reeling out of the church queasy and pale-faced, the anticipation of Sunday dinner swept from their minds.

I saw the head of Blessed Oliver Plunkett once and, God forgive me, I felt sick.

Just ahead of me the two big iron doors of Father Quinn's driveway clang shut. I hear the rasp of the iron bar that secures them.

Six months after he came back from Europe, when Czechoslovakia was invaded, the priest started his weekly summaries of German war broadcasts from the pulpit. On the Sunday after the evacuation from Dunkirk, the parish choir sang the 'Te Deum', while Father Quinn praised and thanked God for the revenge he had meted out on that black Protestant race, which had sprung from the heretical and diseased loins of Henry VIII, and which had been robbing and killing the Irish for the past seven hundred years. 'Oh! God be praised!' he shouted out at the end of the mass and, God forgive me, it was the first time I had heard him utter a prayer with sincerity.

Someone had to talk to him. Someone had to tell him that it wasn't hatred that should be preached from the pulpit. I didn't want to, but someone had to do it.

As I pass it, the wicket door in Father Quinn's gateway opens. He's going to ask me to the dinner tomorrow, after all my unkind thoughts.

But it's not him. The emerging shape is boyish, maybe a boy running from something or somebody.

'Hello!' I say. I see the dim street-light shining like the yellow flame of an oil-lamp in the boy's hand.

It's Seanie! He makes a sound in that strange, shy, childish voice of his that should have been a man's voice long ago.

'Hello, Seanie,' I say, as he comes towards me, the reflection of the street-light dancing in the blade of the knife in his hand.

FATHER QUINN

I'll have to write to Dublin about that McSwaine. He's lost his command over these people, and he'll never get it back. It's better to get rid of him.

There's Sheehan, looking over at McSwaine. Maybe he'll give the garda a lecture about his familiarity with the peasants. Sheehan is good at giving lectures. He'll never give me a lecture again, I'll tell you!

That salmon was so close, damn it! Just another few inches and I had him.He had to be fourteen pounds! What a present that would have made for Eamon, and to be able to say I caught it myself. Damn! It would've been like the old gentry telling their guests where they shot the pheasant and grouse.

Sheehan has passed McSwaine. No lecture tonight.

The money-bag is pulling down Sheehan's right shoulder. He doesn't know it yet, but in that bag is forty-seven pounds, twelve shillings and eight pence. Sheehan counts the money. I keep account of it. He has never been a penny short. He's honest. Like all saints, a pain in the neck. Not being asked to tomorrow's dinner must have sickened him. No doubt he'll use this as another cross to bear.

The knife is annoying me. I know I had it in my waistcoat pocket. I must have dropped it when I was trying to pull in the salmon. I know exactly where I was. First thing in the morning I'll go back and look in the grass. Odd that I lost it the day before Eamon is coming. I was with him in Geneva when he bought it for me.

Anyway, it will have to be a box of steaks each for them from Butler-the-Butcher's shop.

Damn it! I have to call McSwaine's wife on the phone. I almost forgot.

SEANIE DOOLIN

It is still twilight but nearly dark.

In the dark of the Cinema wall I am a piece of darkness. I am two eyes looking out of a shadow, looking across the street, looking at the Guard looking at himself in Hubey Sherlock's looking-glass window.

Darkness is killing the twilight, and I hear the bell striking in the Church tower. The sound is soft and yellow. *Twilight and evening bell, and after that the dark! And may there be no sadness of farewell, when I embark.* In the terrible dark between the wall and the bottle-crates we held each other's hands. It was black dark and we could only hear the sounds of whispering, but we were waiting for something to happen. Willie's hands were shaking like the hands of an old man putting tobacco in his pipe. When the window broke, Willie made a noise of fright like a kicked dog. Poor Willie. His breath began to shake like his hands. His teeth were chattering, and the glass kept falling on the floor, making dangerous noises. He was holding my hand and hurting it. He jumped when another pane of glass was broken. 'Oh! Seanie,' he said. He was so frightened, and so was I.

Poor Willie. Look what they're doing to him.

Willie! Willie!

When we heard the footsteps, he put his arms around my neck, and real tight he squeezed me. In my ear he said we have to steal out. *Oh! God let me steal from the world and not a stone tell where I lie.* The footsteps came closer. There were a whole lot of footsteps.

There is whistling, and when I look out the Guard is walking across the street, as if he's taking a stroll. He is whistling through his teeth a song Miss Groom taught us –

27

the way she used to wave the stick to keep us all together. *We are the boys of Wexford who fought with heart and hand.* He stands near the wall with his hands behind his back, swaying from his toes to his heels.

I am very close to him. He suddenly turns and walks into the lane, and Willie's arms squeezed my neck and he said desperately we should steal out. Just as he passes me, the Guard sings like a priest singing at mass.

'Hey, Blindeye!' he sings. Then he stops, and I hold my breath. I thought he was just coming in to pee in the dark. He starts to walk again like a man putting his feet down carefully. Then he whispers again, quietly, like a small girl calling a kitten.

'Hey, Blindeye!' He stands and I can see his cap against the Cinema lights at the top of the wall. Then all of a sudden he frightens me because he almost shouts.

'Holy Jesus!' and he starts to run back to where I'm hiding. I get ready to be hit or kicked; scrunch myself up in my arms. But he passes me and slips. He throws his arms around to keep his balance.

Then out on the street there is a shout.

'Keep an eye out for Baggy McSwaine, lads!'

I would not like to be the man who said that if the Guard gets his hands on him.

When he gets his balance back, the Guard walks out of the dark onto the footpath. His chest is as big as the big drum in the Pipe Band. I hear him shouting.

'There's a fight on in the mornin.'

Then I hear from the street: 'Upon my soul.'

The Guard shouts: 'Cratchit and Mary burn the arse off of you.'

God bless us everyone.

The Priest's car goes by the lane, and I feel in my pocket for the knife. I find it in the lining near the back, and I push it out through the hole in my pocket. The Guard puts his hands on his hips and looks up the Town towards the Priest's house.

Just then Mister Sheehan walks by the lane carrying the

bag of money. He says something to the Guard, and I know if I run down the lane, jump over the gate and into the field, run along the back of Bennetts, Crawfords, and Ditkoffs, climb through the barbed-wire fence and the privet hedge into the Priest's yard, and come out through the wicket door in the big gate, I will be able to catch up with Mister Sheehan and not let the Guard see me.

In the shadow of the wall I run, the full feel of the knife in my hand. I could run along Bennett's Lane with my eyes shut, I know it so well. It's one hundred and forty-three running steps long, and at the end there's the red gate made out of hollow tubes of iron. It's a nice gate to climb and to sit on with the sun on your back, unless one of the Bennetts sees you.

When I grab at the bars with my two hands, the man with his arm around my neck squeezed until I choked. I felt my eyes swelling, and the man on the far side of the gate was trying to pry my fingers off the iron. He had wild eyes, as if he was doing something terrible that had to be done, but that he didn't want to do. The one who was choking me screamed in a whisper into my ear: 'Let go or I'll fucking choke you,' and he tightened his grip on my neck. Everything turned red, and when the red went away the man on the other side of the gate was tying a sharp rope around my wrists. My tied hands were on one side and I was on the other. When the man who tied the rope went away, I saw Willie lying on the grass on his back. He was crying loudly and saying my name, 'Seanie Seanie Seanie,' as if he was calling me to help him.

The sun was white bright in my eyes, the way the new sun is in the morning. I started to cry. Big gulping wet sounds came out of me. I tried to say his name his name his name his name. Willie I can't say your name because I can't make my body do what I want it to do. And he cried out again. 'Seanie! Seanie! Seanie! Seanie!' And because I can't touch him or help him or say his name to him, I do it in my trousers, front and back, and there's a terrible scream. Poor Willie Poor Poor Poor Poor Poor Poor Poor Poor Poor Poor.

They are all around him, like a crowd of men around a big bull that's going to be castrated.

In the dark I land quicker than I expect on the far side of the gate. The jolt cracks all my bones together. My neck is shocked. My jaws make a snapping sound, like a dog in summertime trying to bite flies.

There are no lights back here, but that's alright. Willie and I used to come to the Town this way, except when The River was over the stepping-stones at Saint Fintan's Terrace. I hated it when there was a flood and we'd have to walk all the way down to Madden's Bridge, and then back along the other side to get to the Town. So many people used to take the short cut that the Bennetts put up a stile on each side of the field. *There was a crooked man who walked a crooked mile he found a crooked sixpence beside a crooked stile he had a crooked cat.* A crooked track was worn into the grass across the field from one stile to the other. You had to stay on the track or the Bennetts might see you and shout. Willie used to pick the cowslips in the summertime that grew near the path. He would bring them to Mrs Sheehan when we went there to learn. Mrs Sheehan loved Willie. When he'd want to run out after the learning, she'd say: 'Stay a while, Willie. Stay a while and talk to me.' *Stay until the hasting day has run but to the evensong: and having played together we will go with you along.*

I run past the end of Crawfords' garden. In the summertime they had swings hanging from the branches of their trees. One day the three children, little girls, were swinging in there. Willie and I were young then, and we sat under their hedge. We stared for hours and the swings in silence went back and forth. Mrs Crawford came out and every time her swing went over to the left, a ribbon on her hat hung in the air behind her head. It was pink. She was beautiful, like a saint in the window of the Church. Now she is dead.

The hedge of the Ditkoffs' garden has gooseberry bushes in it.

The Priest's hedge is just a line of big bushes that don't match. They are high and wide. On sunny days full of flies, the cows come to them. The ground around the bushes is black and soft and wet and dungy. I feel my way with my face bent so as not to get slapped in the eye with a branch. Then I feel the wire, and I get through the bottom two strands without getting the second one caught on the back of my coat.

The Priest is shutting the second big door. It makes a clang, and then he pushes the bar that locks them together. On my right is the small shed with the black-tarred door where the Housekeeper throws the bottles. Without a light, the Priest goes to the back door. I hear the latch when he puts his thumb on it. When he shuts the door, I run across the yard and feel around for the handle of the wicket door. I step through and Mister Sheehan is outside on the footpath.

'Hello!' he says.

I can't think of the word that I wanted to ...

'Mister Sheehan,' I say, and the word is there in my head, but it has slipped down somewhere and got lost.

'Hello, Seanie.'

I'm still looking for the word and I know I will find it, but I'm afraid he might leave. But then I remember he won't. Mister Sheehan is not like the others.

'Mister Sheehan,' I say again, and the word was just there. My tongue had it. My tongue was going to say it. My tongue found it and let it go again.

'Yes, Seanie,' Mister Sheehan says, and his voice is not full of glass like the top of the wall around the Workhouse.

'Mister Sheehan,' I say, and I step closer to him. '*Camarawn Camarawn Camarawn Camarawn*,' I say, and terrible hot tears are burning me because Willie was being hurt. One of them was standing, one sitting on his legs, one lying over his chest holding down his arms, one kneeling – holding his head with an ear clenched in each hand. I could see it all through the gate. 'Seanie! Seanie! Seanie! Seanie!' Poor Willie, and the short one shouted: '*Camarawn*! Give it to me and I'll do it.'

31

GUARD McSWAINE

Sheehan smelt the cowshite on me. I knew it; the way he
backed away. I wish I could see where it is. Everything looks
the same colour in the light of the street-lamp.

Shite, it's all over the leg of my trousers. That fucking
hure, Doolin! I've rubbed my fucking sleeve in it too. Now
what the hell do I do! I'm supposed to be at Ploverlegs
Dunne's house in ten minutes. I'll have to run in home and
change my trousers and wash myself. God damn them fucking farmers and their fucking cows and their fucking cowshite. How do they put up with the smell of it day after day?

Jesus! I can't ride my bike with this stuff all over me.
What will I wipe myself with? There's not even a piece of
newspaper in the gutter. I'd better pretend nothing is wrong
in case Hubey Sherlock's daughter is in her window with
the light off. And of course my bloody bike is lying up
against the wall of her house. What else can I do!

I hold my breath crossing the street, put my feet down
gently to stop my heels clattering, keep my arms out from
my sides because the rubbing serge sounds loud to me. I
take hold of the handlebar and start out for home, wheeling
the bike.

God! It's a relief to breathe, and it's a relief to let my heels
down. She must be in bed by now. The shapes of her! The
smell of this bloody cowshite! I hope I don't meet anyone.
There's nowhere to go, with the row of shops and houses on
each side of the street. And I'll have to listen to the Missus
about it. It's worse than the smell of pigshite. Bloody John
Joe Grimes! When he gives me the bag of spuds on Saturday,
I'll tell him I want a bag of cornmeal too. Big bugger with his
smart answers! Up my hole, he yells in front of all them

other hures, and Father Quinn and Mister Sheehan, too. I'm glad Mister Sheehan didn't stop, with the smell of the cowshite so bad. I don't like having to talk to him. I feel like a boy meeting his teacher during the summer holidays.

Jesus! There he is across the street talking to someone. I'll go on as if I didn't see him. I'll be out of the next streetlight when I'm passing him. Who is it he's talking to? Christ, it's Doolin – the little ... How did he get up here if he was in Bennett's Lane a few minutes ago with me standing in front of it? I wonder does Sheehan understand him talking. I never know what the eejit is saying. It's all blab blab to me. And he looks at you like you should understand him. They say he was brought up in the Workhouse. His mother must have taken one look at him and left him at the front door.

I can feel the cowshite drying on my right hand, where I touched my trousers.

Mister Sheehan has his back to me. The way I feel when he looks at me! Like I had done something wrong. And then I can't stop talking when he asks me something, like I'm stopping him from saying something I don't want to hear. Doolin there looking up at him – it's hard to believe that he's nearly forty.

Course, just as I'm passing, wouldn't you know, Sheehan looks around as if he knew all along I was trying to sneak by. Maybe Doolin, the hure, told him I'm here. I decide real quick to get the jump on him and, quick as lightning, I say, 'Good night, Mister Sheehan.' I wouldn't please him to think I was trying to sneak past. But before I'm finished saying it he says something to me and our sounds get fuddled up in the middle of the street. I say, 'Right you are, sir,' in case he is saying, 'It's a nice night.'

Nice night, my arse! Doolin is looking across at me, too. I can see his face in the light like a dim moon. Nice night, my fucking arse! I missed my bag of meal, and stepped in cowshite. It was going great for a while there with that look I got at Hubey Sherlock's daughter's tits.

Whatever Sheehan just said is annoying me, even though

I didn't hear it, clashing as it did with my own words.

I'd better hurry if I'm going to collect them spuds up at Ploverlegs Dunne's. There's so many Dunnes in this fucking town that they all have nicknames. There's four Joe Dunnes. Joewhat, Bigjoe, Fatjoe, and Longjoe. There must be six Mick Dunnes. Chickenchoker, Turkeytoes, Skee, Mickeydogshite, Mickeydee and Ploverlegs Dunne.

That's what he said! Sheehan! The bastard. How could he know? He couldn't know where I'm going, but that's what he said alright. 'Say hello to Mr Dunne for me, Guard.' And I said – Oh God! What did I say? – 'Right you are, sir.' I admitted I was going there.

Fuck this cowshite! Fuck this town. Fuck Sheehan. Does he think I enjoy waiting outside the Ploverlegs' house, waiting for them two scrawny eejits to give me a few spuds for my pigs!

Say hello to *Mister* Dunne for me, Guard! Mister! Mister indeed, and he sitting all hunched up over the fire with the ten shillings in his hand, listening to the sounds of them two scrub bulls humping his wife. He's as bad as her. Another man would give me five shillings, at least, for casting a blind eye in his direction. Bloody Sheehan, up eating the altar rails every day.

There's a light on in a shop window up ahead. It's either Miss Lalor's or Peetie Mahon's. I'll cross over to the other side, just in case someone comes out to talk to me. It couldn't be Miss Lalor. She's in bed every night by nine, in her bed by herself.

No sign of Sheehan behind me now, so I can cross. The bloody bike rattles going down over the kerb into the gutter.

It's Peetie Mahon's shop window that's all lit up, but he has the shade down. It's curious that he would be in his shop at this hour. Maybe he's counting all that money he's making selling ice-cream and sweets to the children. And cigarettes and papers and all kinds of knick-knacks that look like souvenirs of the Town, but are cheap imported junk. He rakes in the money. If you're mean enough and clever enough, you'll get rich enough. I'm not mean enough. But

Peetie is. That man would take the eye out of your head and then come back looking for the eyebrow.

If I wasn't covered in cowshite I'd go across and peep in to see what he's up to. Maybe I wouldn't see him at all. Maybe I'd see a crook stealing the stuff. By Jesus! Wouldn't that be a good one if there was someone in there robbing the place and me, the representative of the Law, standing here on the other side of the street looking on. I'd better make sure. If it was a crook and I caught him, it would be a great feather in my cap, so to speak.

I lean the bike against Dalton-the-Undertaker's wall and go across, walking on my toes, holding my breath, arms out. My right hand feels peculiar with the drying cow dung.

The first hole in the shade I try is too high and too far to the side of the window. I try a lower one, bending down to look in.

Peetie Mahon is in his shop, and he's not counting his money. He's taking things out of the glass cases and putting them back in again. It takes me a long time to figure out what he is doing. There's a pain in my eye from looking in through the little hole. He's cleaning all his stuff, because he knows there will be a big crowd in the Town tomorrow for the opening of the new wing. Everyone will be in the shop, and the bold Peetie is getting ready for them. He's clever and rich and as mean as a hure's melt.

The eye that's looking through the hole gets all wet and, when I raise my hand to wipe it, I touch the glass with my knuckle. Peetie Mahon looks over at the sound and I jump up straight. Right then I hear a noise behind me and, quick as lightning, I know I'm safe. There's a dog coming down the street dragging a big bone. He's growling and looking sideways at another dog, who is waiting his chance to grab the bone. I make chasing noises at them, so Peetie Mahon will think that's what he heard. A bright square of light appears on the footpath beside me. I know Peetie Mahon has raised the shade on his shop door. When I look around he's turning the lock.

'Is everything alright, Guard?' He has his face between

the jamb and the edge of the door.

He's not coming out and he'll not be asking me in, so I don't have to worry about the smell.

'Oh! Good night, Peetie. It's just an old dog. I didn't want him dropping his bone out here in front of your shop.'

'Unsightly things. I wish someone would tell Butler-the-Butcher to do something better with his bones than just throwing them into a hole.'

'It's hard to keep dogs away from the smell of meat, Peetie.'

'There's no meat left on a bone when Joe Butler is finished with it, Guard!'

'Aye, Peetie. Are you getting ready for tomorrow?' I ask.

'Tomorrow?' he says as if he's surprised. 'Oh! Tomorrow! The big day. At least we won't hear more about the Church Building Fund. I'm tired of paying into that every week.'

Peetie Mahon never paid into the Church Building Fund, or any other fund that didn't have his name on it. That's why the rich are rich; they know how to hold onto their money. Mean and rich.

'It's all over bar the shouting, and the shouting will be over tomorrow,' I say. I want to get on my way or I'll be late for the spuds.

'Did your bike get punctured?' Peetie Mahon asks.

'Ah, no. I just got off here to let them dogs go on down the street. I'll see you tomorrow at the parade, Peetie.' He won't be at the parade. He'll be selling, and getting rich.

'Good night, Guard. Can you smell cowshite?' Peetie Mahon closes the door and stands there behind the glass looking out.

I have no choice but to walk across the street and get up on my bike. I'll get cowshite all over everything.

MISTER SHEEHAN

The street-light in the blade of Seanie's knife, the knife that moves in the jerking hand as if the jerking hands, the jerking body, will loosen the words stuck inside him. Streams of Milton's words, and Wordsworth's, flowed freely out of him twenty-seven years ago, and now he can't say his own name. The effort to speak contorts his face, leaving grooves behind like the marks of a stirring stick in a pot of boiling gruel. When the sounds do come out, there is a look of intelligence, or maybe pleading, on his face, suggesting that the noises he makes are heard differently by Seanie than by anyone else. Now and then I think I hear something that may be a word, but the rest is unintelligible. His sounds are like the urgent barkings of a small dog, almost yelps. I wonder can he write anymore.

The flashing knife in Seanie's spasmodic hand holds my eyes as he struggles with his words. When I look back at his face, there is desperation, almost anger, as if he were reproaching me for not paying attention; as if he were afraid I would go away without waiting to hear him. He puts his free hand on my arm to keep me there, to stop me from walking away.

To reassure him, I reach out and touch his arm above the elbow, this thin, bedraggled, tortured boy.

Sometimes when alone, I have cried out at what fate has meted out to this one person, almost my son. It was fate, not God, who dealt him his fortune. Or men. God is not that cruel, I hope. Seanie Doolin was the brightest child I have ever taught. He and his brother, Willie. They were almost identical in looks and intelligence. Twins.

Beneath the soiled cloth of his torn jacket, I can feel the muscles pulling together in an effort to eject the urgent sounds. Suddenly, over trembling jaw, the words spill out, one word repeated several times. The look on his face, the pleading in his eyes tell me that he hears an intelligent word, but all I hear is something that sounds like *Camarán* – a Gaelic word that he wouldn't know.

'*Camarán Camarán Camarán Camarán*,' Seanie says.

His knife is pointing across the street. I look over, and there is Guard McSwaine walking with his bicycle along the far footpath. It looks as if he is trying to slink past without being noticed. A sudden rage takes hold of me, and may God forgive me, I give expression to my anger.

I know where Guard McSwaine is going, because it's Tuesday night. And as he is trying to sidle silently past me, Seanie is pointing an accusing finger at him, saying over and over the word Guard McSwaine has used to hurt him. *Camarán*! It is a derogatory word that could mean any of several things: stupid person, coward, dog-dropping. It's not a word that the casual Gaelic-speaker would know, only a person from a Gaelic-speaking area, and McSwaine is from west Clare.

I shout across the street in a sarcastic tone: 'Say hello to Mr Dunne for me, Guard.' With the defiance of an arrogant adolescent, he calls back to me: 'Right you are, sir.'

I am astonished. In my astonishment, the decision is suddenly made: I will confront the guard tomorrow about his bribe-taking.

I turn back to Seanie and ask him, 'Did he hurt you, Seanie?'

But Seanie has the strange agony on his face that I first saw when he came to me at Willie's grave and I, so foolishly, told him things that were better left unsaid. It's as if he is someplace else, seeing something that I'm not seeing. There are no tears at his eyes, but he is crying on the inside, crying in the past. And now he says the sound again that's like *Camarán*, only now he is saying it without knowing. The fingers of his empty hand are pulling down on the flesh of his face, distorting it into a mask of pain and sadness.

I touch his upper arm again and squeeze softly. Then I

shake him gently. He looks up at my face. All I can say is: 'I'm sorry, Seanie. I'm terribly sorry.'

I know my words have no value, no healing power. How can that be healed which has been killed? This town killed Seanie Doolin. He is still walking around, but this place damaged him more than it damaged Willie – and it killed Willie. May God have mercy on those who did the deed, and on those of us who made the doing of the deed easy.

'*Camarán?*' He is asking me a question with the sound of his voice.

'Did Guard McSwaine call you a *Camarán?*' I ask. To my surprise he shakes his head and makes a noise that sounds like 'nath'. I have wrongly accused the Guard.

'Who called you a *Camarán*, Seanie?' I ask. The money-bag from the Cinema is hurting my arm. I want to change it to my other hand. But if I do that, I will have to take my hand away from Seanie's arm and break whatever little connection there is between us.

He mouths the word with difficulty again, and the frustration on his face tells me I am not understanding him.

'*Camarán*,' I say. 'Is that the word you are saying?'

The sound that comes out to accompany his nodding head is meaningless.

'You want to know what *Camarán* means?'

He nods; I decide to give him the least offensive meaning.

'It means a weak person, Seanie,' and he is gone again to someplace I can't go, to his place of agony. It's exactly the same as when he came to me in the Paupers' Cemetery, when I foolishly told him that it was Willie who was in the grave.

With his mouth open, and a drool beginning to spill over his lip, he glides out of my grasp. It's exactly the same! He slipped from my grasp at Willie's grave, stole away into his own mind where he sees something he can't escape from. Miss Bevan was right. Seanie would come to us, she said. He came alright, but when he did I told him too much too soon and drowned him. Now, he falls away again and disappears into a shadow before he has taken ten steps.

I change the money-bag from one hand to the other.

'Good night, Seanie.' I start off towards home again, crying.

Seanie was robbed of his nights years ago. The stories that were invented then! He had seen a banshee. He had killed his own brother. He had seen the ghosts of his father and mother. The twins were drunk, the smell of porter on the two of them – Enda McKenna said – and Willie had fallen while climbing over the Cemetery gate. One of the spikes stuck in his head. They still say he killed his own brother. The Town has officially adopted that story.

Seanie is our sacrificial goat, except in the biblical community the sin-laden animal was driven off into the wilds. Seanie never went away. His presence keeps the truth – our sins – before our eyes. He won't be driven off. He has no place to go, only the Paupers' Cemetery. So he is continually abused by the adults and the children. And those who don't abuse him shun him.

I don't even know if he realizes that someone loves him.

The same flu that killed fifty million people in 1919 killed Seanie's and Willie's parents. It also killed my – our – two girls. Deirdre and Eileen. Oh God! They were eleven and twelve and they were laid out in their confirmation dresses. White coffins, as if the colour could make any difference. Dear God! That was a time when blasphemy brushed my lips. Caithleen descended into a black place.

It was two days after Eileen's funeral that I went back to school. My sadness wasn't unique. Nearly every family in the Town had a funeral that year. The resilience of the bereaved boys in my classroom was contagious, and my spirits were lifted.

There were two new boys in my room that morning. The moment I saw them I knew they were orphans, knew they were from the Workhouse. Their heads were shaved except for a small fringe. It was a cruel hairstyle, but then, everything about the Workhouse was cruel. These two eleven-year-olds were terrified strangers from another town; before they could even see their parents buried, the local authorities had bundled them off to the Workhouse.

Workhouse; the Union; the Century House; the Poorhouse. No matter what the name, the Workhouse was what the privileged imagined was a good place for the wretched to live in, as if the privileged ever had an imagination as far as the poor were concerned. Even the window sills on the inside of the Workhouse were sloped downward, so the inmates could not sit on them. The thing that set the two boys apart the most was their pauperism. Paupers! They would have been treated better had they been lepers, because they would at least have evoked pity. But as paupers they were fair game for anyone who wished to abuse them. They sat close together in the crowded classroom, as if they were ready to grab each other. Several times during that first day tears were on their faces, but they cried silently and kept looking forward. They touched their bald heads with their fingers, and they knew they were different. During the lunch-break I saw them with their backs to the school wall, and the taunts and jeers were loud. In the classroom again I saw them surreptitiously touching each other, reassuring each other. That night when I cried for Deirdre and Eileen I cried for the Doolin twins.

Every night this money-bag gets heavier. I wonder would it be as heavy if Father Quinn had invited me to the dinner tomorrow. Now I won't be able to give up The Cinema, because everyone will think I'm doing it out of spite or revenge. I'll have to do it for another few months. It will be nice to have the evenings free after all this time. If Caithleen hadn't died, I would never have taken on the job, but without her there was nothing to do.

Caithleen! First it was Deirdre and Eileen. Their dying broke her. Then it was Seanie and Willie, the day before we were to adopt them. They would have used the girls' room, the girls' beds. But Willie was murdered, and Seanie went mad the same night. Caithleen died, too, when she heard. She cried till the end. Oh dear God in heaven! It was too much to ask. Too much!

The water in my eyes fractures the lights on the street

poles. I remove the glasses, and with the back of my hand, wipe away the itching tears. Deirdre and Eileen and Willie and Caithleen – and Seanie's mind shattered. I feel sorry for myself, because Father Quinn should have asked me to the dinner with de Valera tomorrow.

Big gulps of grief hurt my throat. I have to stop and put down the money-bag so I can blow my nose. It's something I could never do with one hand. The glasses I fold and put away into my breast pocket.

A noise, up ahead on the street, raises the hair on the back of my neck. It's a fiendish sound, growling and scraping. I fumble for the glasses, and, peering into the darkness, I can see someone near Peetie Mahon's shop. Then two dogs trot into the light. One has the thigh-bone of a cow in its jaws, the shin-bone dragging along the road, the hoof still attached. The second dog is behind and to the side, waiting for the opportunity to grab the bone and run; a stupid opportunist, because the hole in the field behind Joe Butler's shop is full of bones; bones and rats in winter; bones and rats and flies in the summer; bones and rats and boys with catapults in the twilight any day; bones and the rotten smell of decaying flesh all the time.

The big hip-bone will be dragged and kicked around the streets of the Town until one of the street-cleaners throws it into his cart and curses Joe Butler yet again.

I can see that Peetie Mahon's shop is lit up. Peetie's outside, and it looks as if he has his face against the shop window. Just seeing him does something to my insides. Peetie Mahon! If I am damned to hell when I die, it will be because of my inability to forgive that man. He robbed me of my last chance of happiness in this vale of tears. But I will pray for him.

Hail Mary, full of grace, the Lord is with thee; blessed art thou among women and blessed is the fruit of thy womb, Jesus. Holy Mary, Mother of God, pray for us sinners now, and at the hour of our death. Amen.

Peetie Mahon is going back into his shop. I won't have to greet him.

PEETIE MAHON

You'd think a cow had made a scoury shite outside the door. I'll take a look when that big, fat fuck of a guard goes away. Telling me he was hushing away the dogs, and his bike over there against Michael Dalton's on the far side of the street! Peeping in at me through the hole in the blind, he was. Stupid arse of a man. Just to rattle him a bit, let him think I'm accusing him of being smelly, I tell him there's a terrible strong smell of cowshite. It crossed my mind to say pigshite, but that might have been too direct, might have penetrated even his thickness. Him and his pigs! Wait till tomorrow!

He pushes the bike across the footpath and lets the wheels jolt into the gutter. His right hand is dirty, and I wonder what he's been up to. He's the queerest guard I've ever come across. And talk about mean! Stupid and mean! He's mean in little things and that's why he's stupid. A few potatoes or apples; a bit of bran or ground corn. He wasn't in the Town a week when he came in here for a bag of sweets and, the stupid fuck, he had the nerve to walk away without paying. I didn't give a shite. 'That'll be eight pence, Guard,' I shouted after him in front of everyone. He went from red to purple to blue, and stuttered a few words about forgetting to pay. He never came back since. Forgot, my arse! He thought he could come in here for a hand-out any time he felt like it. I nipped that one in the bud.

He's going to get a land tomorrow at the Church in front of Quinn and Dev and the whole town. I'd love to be there to see it. After that, I'd say, he'll be sent to another town. Dev is bound to ask questions when he sees what's going on. But then, Dev is half blind so he mightn't see anything. Quinn will see it. All he has to do is write a letter and Mc-

Swaine will be packing his bags.

He must be out of sight by now. I'll take a look outside.

There's no sign of a cowshite. Even the smell is gone. I wonder how did I get it before? It was hardly on McSwaine's boots. Even he has sense enough to wipe cowshite off himself.

There's two holes in the blind and he was probably looking through the higher-up one. He couldn't have figured out what I was doing. He'd have seen more if he'd looked through this lower hole, but he'd never go to the trouble of bending over to spy on me. His belly would get in the way. Funny that he didn't try to find out what I was doing. Maybe he did have cowshite on his boots and didn't want me to see him up close. That could have been cowshite on his hand.

Of course! It's Tuesday night. That's where he's going – up to the Ploverlegs Dunne's to pick up his bags of spuds from Regan and Flanagan, with their sticky mickeys hanging after humping the Ploverlegs' wife. That pair will be relieved after tomorrow. They won't have to pay the guard, as well as the husband, for their little secret fucks that everyone knows about. Everyone! Baggy McSwaine, stupid shite that he is, thinks the Ploverlegs has only two clients. Even the nuns know the names of the twelve regulars; two every night except Sunday. 'No Sunday fucking allowed,' said the Ploverlegs one time to a lad with a bulge in his trousers on a Sunday night. Twelve humps a week at ten shillings a hump. Six pounds a week, which is more than the average man earns. Ten minutes they're allowed and after that the Ploverlegs is standing in the doorway telling them the time is up. 'Get down offer,' they say he says, and sometimes he slaps an ash-plant against the door. That would knock the steam out of the randiest humper.

Ten shillings for ten minutes! A shilling a minute. McKenna doesn't even earn that, and he has to travel to the sick person's house. Quinn gets ten shillings for saying mass, and that takes at least a half an hour. The Ploverlegs is the highest-paid man in the Town and his wife does all the work. But all she does is lie there with her thin legs open and her dress up to her navel. She keeps a towel over her head. Just as well! Of course the Ploverlegs may make a shilling a minute, but that's only for a hundred and twenty minutes a week. I make far more than that. I make more than McKenna and Quinn and Sheehan combined. And I make it the easy way. I buy a piece of shite for a shilling, and then I put it in the window with four shillings marked on it. Eventually some eejit buys it. I can't believe the rubbish people buy!

Fuck! Here's Sheehan on the far footpath, coming home from the pictures with the money-bag. I'll just walk in and pretend I didn't see him. It's a real pain in my belly that I can't face up to Sheehan. I'm afraid of him now, the way I was once afraid of Doolin – that snivelling piece of misery, the cleanings of a bitch goat. Now it's Sheehan; has been Sheehan for a long time. I wish he'd die, the old bastard with his accusing eyes. 'It wasn't me,' I screamed at him. 'But you were there,' was all he said.

The fucker. He said that nearly twenty years ago and I can't look at him since. It was the other arses that let the whole thing out. It took about eight years, but it all came out – even though I made the fuckers swear that no one would tell. Worse than a crowd of old women, they were. I've never trusted anyone since. No one knows my business. No one, not even the wife. No one knows I'm in here doubling the price of everything for tomorrow's crowd. These pieces of shite! the black rosary beads in the little black leather purses! I bought them for ninepence and then stamped 1948 on the purses. Tomorrow I'll sell them for half a crown each, and everyone will think they're getting a souvenir of the opening of the Church wing. People are eejits. I was a fucking eejit to believe the others wouldn't tell.

I'll put a piece of sticky paper over that hole in the blind while I think of it.

It was Michael Butler, that short little man, who started it first, getting drunk and crying into his porter in little hints about what had happened. I took a terrible chance with him, but it just proved to me that if you don't tell anyone, you'll never get caught. McKenna – too drunk to know a live person from a dead one, too drunk to know a person from a pig – wrote on the certificate that Butler had died of a heart attack. Even though I knew I could count on McKenna being drunk, I had the scutters until he wrote down the cause of death.

But I had made a tactical mistake. I did not foresee that with Butler dead the dam would burst. Butler had pulled the trigger, because he thought I was a coward. They all thought I was a coward. I came so close to being the killer, so close! But it was Butler who had killed and, with him safely in the ground, Quinlan-the-Blacksmith let go the whole story like a shite out of a duck's arse. God almighty! Talk about fucking dense, dumb and stupid. Right at the graveside he said it, loud enough for twenty people to hear him. 'Michael Butler killed Willie Doolin.' It was like everyone turned into ice, like the birds stopped singing, like the wind stopped blowing, like everyone had elephant ears all of a sudden. Within one minute everyone in the Cemetery knew what Jack Quinlan had said. Within an hour everyone in the Town knew.

The big question was how did Jack Quinlan know that Michael Butler had killed Willie Doolin five years earlier?

It took three more years for the whole story to come out. I knew that my cowardice was going to be a big part of it. My fucking cowardice! As if I was afraid to kill someone. Me! I dropped Michael Butler in front of everyone in the Willow Bar; dropped him dead at my feet and nobody even suspected I did it, let alone how I did it; Butler still talking in Gaelic on his way to the floor. Fucking fanatic! I was no coward when I took old Joe Miller by the scruff of the neck and slammed him, face first, into the grating of his fireplace. He could have lived forever, and I'd still be driving that taxi.

When I had the gun to Willie Doolin's forehead I was no coward. I was thinking there were too many people – five of us altogether – too many to keep a secret. That's what I was afraid of and nothing else. And I was right. Even though I got the fuckers to swear to silence, even though I fed rat poison to Michael Butler, it still came out like I was afraid it would. That's why I hesitated and let Butler push me out of the way. Even though I was implicated, no one could ever say I killed the pauper. My caution paid off. When I sent old Joe Miller on his way to God I was cautious. Alone and cautious.

Holy Jesus! He's back at the window. That stupid fucking guard is going to be finished tomorrow, so it doesn't matter what I say to him. I'll sidle over to the door as if I was doing my business, then walk out before he has a chance to make an excuse. He's sniffling. What an arse of a thick man – spying on someone and giving himself away by sniffling.

I'll take that Blessed Virgin statue off the shelf, and go through the motions of dusting it. At the same time I can push back the sliding bolt near the top of the door without him hearing.

For a second McSwaine doesn't see me, he's bent over looking through the lower hole. Jesus, it's not him at all – it's that smelly little fucker Seanie Doolin, and when he sees me his face looks like he's seen a ghost. He starts to back away from me, but he falls on his arse on the footpath. He makes the same high-pitched sound a pig makes when it's in pain and knows the pain will only stop when it's dead.

SEANIE DOOLIN

When Mister Sheehan touches my arm I stop racing around looking for the word. It's as if all the heat inside my head drains off through his hand; like a sudden draining off when a dam breaks. Mister Sheehan is soft and strong and he has no sharp edges. Everyone else cuts me when they touch me and, only for Mister Sheehan, I would think every touch is a cut. Mrs Sheehan touched me that night, hugged me and Willie too, when we were leaving to steal the ale. She said it would be the last time we would ever have to leave when night came; that after tomorrow we could stay forever. Mrs Sheehan is dead. Daddy and Mammy are dead. Poor Willie. They are hurting Willie and the short one is shouting *Camarawn!* and Willie's wild eyes are frightened.

'*Camarawn! Camarawn! Camarawn! Camarawn!*' The word rips through my throat like a dry spiky seed.

But Mister Sheehan is looking at the knife in my hand, and the knife is pointed away from me and away from him. Maybe he'll tell the Priest about the knife. But he won't. Then he looks across the street. He says over to the Guard about the sloe missed her done for tea.

The Guard is like a big black beetle wheeling a bike on the footpath. He is going away, going away. The man who tied the rope is going away and Willie is lying on the grass on his back in front of me, lying and crying my name, Seanie Seanie Seanie, and I can't help him and he can see me not helping him. Willie Willie Willie Willie can't move with all the men lying on him. I can't move with my hands one side of the gate and me on the other. I am trying to make my hands small to slip them through the cutting rope. The short one is there shouting *Camarawn*, and that he will do it – 'Get out of my way!'

Oh Willie Willie! My hands are burning where the rope is sinking into the skin. I am wetting myself with helplessness, Willie Willie! Daddy Daddy they're killing Willie, and I can't help him. They are going to shoot him with a gun to his forehead on the ground. Daddy Daddy save him save him Daddy Daddy! I am blinded with the water in my eyes. Dead Daddy. Daddy is dead with Mammy.

There's someone squeezing my arm, squeezing softly, and when I look up from the men on top of Willie, Mister Sheehan is there. He is crying.

'I'm sorry, Seanie,' he says, 'I'm terribly sorry.'

He can't do anything. He isn't there and I don't know what he means about sorry. While I am looking at the street-light in the water at his eyes, the word *Camarawn* floats up my throat by itself and the sound of it sits there between us.

But he isn't there where Willie is, so he thinks someone called me *Camarawn*. But it was Willie who was called *Camarawn*.

'Who called you *Camarawn*, Seanie?' His hand on my arm is soft and strong. If only he was there. If Daddy was! If Mammy was there she would beat away the four men. The Priest said *Camarawn*.

'*Camarawn*,' I say to Mister Sheehan because I want to know what the Priest meant when he said *Camarawn* to the salmon.

The short man is sitting on Willie's legs shouting, roaring with crossness, '*Camarawn! Camarawn!*' Jumping up and '*Camarawn!*' he shouts. 'Give it to me and I'll do it.'

'*Camarawn*. Is that the word you are saying?' Mister Sheehan asks me. He must be getting deaf.

'Yes!' I say, real loud. My arm is warm where he is touching me, almost holding me. 'Hold his fucking head!' he shouts, and he pushes the other one away, grabbing at the gun. 'Hold his fucking head!' Daddy Willie Mammy. Daddy Daddy they're killing Willie. My arm is squeezed again.

'You want to know what *Camarawn* means?' he asks, and I think Mister Sheehan must be getting very deaf.

'Yes!' I say, and I nod so he can see as well as hear me.

'It means a weak person, Seanie,' Mister Sheehan says.

But Willie wasn't weak. Willie was. Willie was Lycidas. *and daffadillies fill their cups with tears to strew the laureate hearse where Lycid lies.* Willie was the chords of *the harp that once through Tara's halls its soul of music shed.* Why did they kill Willie!

Oh! Daddy they have murdered our Willie. They killed the sun. The sun went out when Willie died, shooting his legs out straight in the long green grass. The Priest said the fish was a weak person.

I lose my grip on the squeezing hand and fall away. I am part of the shadow in the Priest's gateway. I see Mister Sheehan changing the money-bag from one hand to the other. He turns to go, and the light from the pole glints off the water at his eyes.

'Good night, Seanie,' he says.

Good night, sweet prince, and flights of angels sing thee to thy rest.

I fold the blade of the knife into its handle and put it in my pocket. Daddy always said it, with his head back in through the almost-closed door on his way out. Only he said princes. Willie and me. We were the princes. Good night sweet princes and flights of angels sing thee to thy rest. If he wasn't home when we went to bed, he would come in and touch us, brush our cheeks with his fingers and we gone too far in sleep to talk to him. Even then, when he thought we were asleep, he would put his face back into the room and it was like a prayer, the way he said it. And flights of angels. I knew we were safe from everything in the night when Daddy said that. Mammy never said it because it was Daddy's to say. After putting the blankets up around our shoulders Mammy always said, 'John and William,' as if she was trying to hear herself, as if she was tasting the words. She only said that when we were alone. When Daddy was in the room she'd say: 'Good night, my babies.' She said that even when we were eleven. She said that the night she died, she and Daddy together.

I felt Willie crawling over me in the dark. When he was under the warm clothes he held my arm, and then his arms were around my neck.

The footsteps are coming closer. He is so frightened he cries.

When he started to cry he let go of my neck and put his arms around my belly. Sad, frightened crying came out of him, terrible deep crying, like a crying sound coming out of a deep down place.

'Da ha ha,' he said. 'Da ha ha. Shaw nee. Da ha ha Ma ha ha Shaw nee are de heh hed heh heh hed.' I turned to him and put my arm around his shoulder.

The footsteps stop and the bottle house is full of a soft 'Shush!' A footstep scrapes on the hard floor. Again I hear it. 'Shush!'

They're listening. *But only a host of phantom listeners that dwelt in the lone house then, stood listening in the quiet of the moonlight to that voice from the world of men.*

Willie was having a bad dream. I turned over on my back and pushed my left arm under his head. I rocked him gently. 'Willie, wake up,' I said. 'Wake up, Willie.'

But he was crying and crying and he talked again in that frightening sleep-talker voice.

'The heh heh are de heh hed de hed hed Shawnee.' Then it sounded like he breathed in all the air in the house, and real quick he said, 'Daddy and Mammy are dead.'

'Wake up, Willie,' I said crossly, and I shook him because he was frightening me. 'Wake up!'

In my ear he gasps in short breaths while I rub his forehead to keep him quiet. I breathe with my mouth open so no one will hear the air going in and out.

'What's wrong, doc?' a voice whispers.

'I heard someone.'

'This place is full of rats,' someone whispers. 'Drunk rats. Drunk Protestant rats, drunk on Protestant ale made in Dublin and Kilkenny.'

Then there is quiet laughing.

'Alright lads! The barrels are all over against this wall.

Start boring, and bore as near to the ground as you can so it all comes out.'

My hand was wet with Willie's tears and I could feel the sobs jerking his belly in and out.

'Wake up, Willie,' I said, while I shook him. 'Wake up.'

'Hi hi hime awake Shaw nee. Hi hi hime awake.'

'You only think you are. Come on Willie, wake up. You'll waken Daddy and Mammy and they're sick.'

'The heh he hare dead Shawnee.'

'Wake up, Willie,' I said. 'Wake up. Wake up. Wake up!' I shouted and shook, and I knew Willie was awake and I didn't want to hear what he was telling me. 'You never saw a dead person,' I shouted to keep Daddy and Mammy alive.

'They're dead, Seanie, I saw them dead.'

Doctor Kelly came with Father Waters. He poked at Daddy and Mammy and pulled their eyelids. He was rough.

'Spanish Lady,' he said.

The priest and the doctor were like people looking at two dead pigs. They didn't cry. They weren't sad. They spoke loud. Father Waters stayed when the doctor left. He told us to stop crying, for God's sake! We were men now. My lips and throat were dry all the time because I was breathing in and out through my open mouth. Father Waters told us not to hold hands anymore, 'That's what children do.' He said how could we be sad with Daddy and Mammy in heaven praying for us. Everyone in the parish had someone dead to cry about, and why did we think we were special. 'The Spanish Lady', he said, 'visits everyone's house.'

We went in to touch them before we left, with Father Waters hurrying us along. Willie touched Daddy's cheek and said in his wet voice, 'And flights of angels sing thee to thy rest'. The priest had to pull us out of the room. We were screaming and crying. We left Daddy and Mammy dead in their bed. Father Waters put us in a cart and that night we came to this town to the Workhouse.

It was a very grey house. I hate Father Waters. I could kill him with my knife in his neck. There is no one else in the world like Daddy and Mammy were. When they died all kindness and gentleness died with them, except for Mister Sheehan. Mrs Sheehan. Mrs Sheehan was dead after Willie was dead. The four of them. Four men against one boy, holding him down and shooting him in the forehead. They are boring holes in the barrels of ale and the ale is flowing across the floor to where we are sitting, only we don't know it yet. I am kneeling on the hard floor with my arms around Willie. He is still shaking and I am rubbing the back of his head to calm him down.

Since Daddy and Mammy died Willie is very nervous. He nearly went mad with fright when the Porter at the Work-house locked us in the Dead House for a night, because we wouldn't steal the ale for him. After a while we could see a body on the table in the weak light from the window. It had a piece of cloth around its face like a woman's headscarf, as if it was holding the dead face together. I sat on the cold floor and put Willie's head in my lap. He shook and whim-pered and I rubbed his head till he fell asleep. Poor Willie. They're doing it to him again, and he's crying Seanie Seanie, as if I am the only person in the world who can save him, and I'm tied up and he doesn't know that. If he can see at all he can see me standing at the gate looking in, looking in and doing nothing. WILLIE! I scream, WILLIE I'M TIED UP! I'M TIED UP, WILLIE! and the rising white light of the sun is in my face. One of the men throws a stone at me and hits me in the eye.

In the bottle house the yellow light of a flash-lamp is shining up, as if it is on the floor. Big shapeless shadows move across the ceiling when the men move from one barrel to the next. The men whisper things to make each other giggle. One of them says, 'Slip will write a song about us, how we freed the porter in Carther's Bottling House and struck a blow for freedom.'

I rub Willie's face even though the shaking has stopped. I hope he has fallen asleep, because then he can't be terrified with fear. Willie is the oldest by two minutes but, since Daddy and Mammy died, I have become his big brother. In the Workhouse when they shaved our heads, and left those little clumps of hair where the fringe should be, we cried clinging to each other – Willie crying for Daddy and Mammy; me crying for Willie and myself and for being in that place, full of dark and dank shadows dancing to the Workhouse Howl. I had never seen two women fighting and howling before; had never seen two big people fighting.

A shadow blocks out nearly all the yellow light on the ceiling and someone says, 'Where will you write eye or a, doc?' There is grunting and tittering. Then for a minute there's only the sound of the augers grinding through the wood of the barrels. Someone says, 'On the door and the barrels to make sure they see it, and in green paint too.' Then there's the sound of the augers again like the sound a rat makes when it's scooping an almost-hollow turnip.

When the flowing ale touches the calves of my legs on the ground I give a little yelp and jerk up my knees. It surprises me like a cold slithery thing would surprise you in the dark. When I jerk up my knees Willie makes a grunting noise and someone says, 'Shush!'

Willie's body goes as stiff as a board and I rub his face real quick. The shush seems to go on for a long time, and then someone whispers, there's someone in here.

'It's rats.'

Someone says that wasn't a rat, that was a person.

'Shush! Listen again.'

In the shadows of the gateway I hear the sound of the latch in the Priest's back door.

They listen and it's so quiet I can't even hear them breathing. I think if we can't hear them, they can't hear us. I can't even hear Willie, but he is still tense. I can feel the ale flowing under me and soaking into the seat of my trousers. And then the flowing ale must have touched Willie, because his body jerks and a noise comes out of him, the noise a sleeping dog makes when you accidentally step on his paw.

'Rats my arse! There's someone in here besides us.'

'There couldn't be doc; the door was locked.'

I hear almost-running footsteps on the packed gravel on the Priest's back yard.

There's another long silence, as if someone had given a silent signal. I feel Willie's tears. He is trembling again.

Willie.

When he was ten he could play all Chopin's 'Polonaises' from memory, and Mammy said he had a light touch. She taught him the piano, but only for a while because, she said, she had no more to teach him.

Willie is trembling still like a new calf, vibrating violently. We are waiting in silence for something to happen. A foot scrapes on the floor and someone says, 'We'd better look – maybe there is someone in here.' The flash-lamp is picked off the floor and then there is the crash of an empty bottle smashing.

Oh! God!

Oh! Jesus!

I jump out of the shadows of the Priest's gateway with the fright I get. My heart is pounding in my ears, sweat on my forehead. Even after I realize that the Priest's housekeeper has thrown another empty bottle into the little shed, my heart keeps going and I want to do number two. I am walking away from the Priest's as fast as I can before I even realize I am going. The Priest's housekeeper is all jagged edges and most times when she sees me she cuts.

When I used to come into the Town in the daytime I would sometimes meet her on the footpath, and she wouldn't notice me. But there were times when she would fly at me like a riled-up turkeycock, clawing at me and beating me with her wings, trying to peck at my eye. She is very bony and she has twenty elbows. She is long and thin. Her nose is like the humped-up beak of an exotic bird. Her mouth is shaped like the hole of a calf after it has squeezed out the last piece of dung, and her face is twisted like it's trying to keep out the pungent smell of the fresh scoury dung of a calf that's still sucking its mother. She once spat in my face and called me the devil's deserted bastard.

When I look back to make sure she is not coming out through the wicket door in the gate I hear a scraping sound, and the low powerful growl an animal makes to frighten you off when you corner it. The hairs on the back of my neck stand up. I hate the feeling; it's the feeling all over myself in the instant before he pulls the trigger of the gun that kills Willie. I turn around real quick with my hands out in front to keep the blow of a stick or a fist or a flying stone away from my face. And even after I see the two dogs in the street with the big bone, I make a fart that is wet. I can feel I have made a small number two. It's only when the dogs have gone past that I notice my breathing, the pain in my head. I am standing with my back against the wall of a house.

The growling dogs go on down the street without even noticing me, the big bone dragging. My heart slows down and I rub my itching forehead with my sleeve. There is no sign of the Housekeeper with the calf's hole for a mouth, no sign either of Mister Sheehan in the opposite direction. He must have gone around Robin's Corner already.

There is a light in a shop up the street. It's either Miss Lalor's or Mr Mahon's. Miss Lalor never cut me. Whenever she met me, before I stopped coming to the Town before dark, she always said, 'Shaw-nih!' and she'd keep walking as if she had to; as if she'd topple over if her feet stopped moving forward. 'Shaw-nih.' Miss Lalor used to give me hard sweets, but every time I ate them my teeth pained me. She sells women's clothes that you never see when a woman is dressed, 'Shaw-nih.' Her eyebrows look as if they are painted on, but too high up her forehead; little thin eyebrows as if she was going bald there instead of on top. Miss Lalor takes short steps and wears shoes with high heels. Her legs are so thin you'd think they'd snap like a twig in winter. 'Shaw-nih.' 'Seanie Seanie,' Willie whispered, 'they're going to find us and beat us. Oh! Seanie.' He is clinging to me the same way you'd cling to a pole if you were falling and falling out of the sky, knowing you were going to hit the hard earth in an explosion of pain, holding on tightly to keep the pain away. Willie.

It's Mr Mahon's shop window that's lit up. He must have gone to bed and left the light on. I never go into his shop, because he won't let me. He saw me looking in his window one time and he kicked me in the backside before I knew he was behind me. He called me a stinking little fucker. The kick of his hard boot got me when I was bent over, looking at a red fire engine at the bottom of the window. It seemed like I was paralysed for a while and I couldn't straighten up. The toe of his boot had got me right on the tail of my spine. I could hardly breathe. Miss Lalor came out and brought me into her shop, me all bent over; the pain like an expanding cold iron inside my backside.

Maybe I'll be able to see if the fire engine is still in his window. There are two holes in the blind; one high up and to the side; the other lower and in the middle. I bend over and put my eye to the hole. As I try to look down I have to scrunch up the side of my face with the bad eye. It hurts trying to bend my sight through the small hole. There's no fire engine down there, but there is a horse made out of delft, its mane and tail blowing in the frozen wind. My eye begins to water and a tear runs down my face, around the corner of my nose.

It's like a mare Daddy had once. We called her Ballyhoe, a big strong gentle mare who worked without being asked. We called her Ballyhoe because that's the town where Daddy bought her. Ballyhoe! She never had a foal.

There's a sound beside me and I turn sideways while still bent over. Mr Mahon is standing there with a doll in his hand. I feel the blood falling out of my face and I move backward, move away from him. My heel stubs against the uneven flagstone in the footpath and I sit down hard. A small frightened noise pushes my lips apart. Mr Mahon should have been in bed.

MISTER SHEEHAN

This money-bag! Pennies weigh a ton.

Peetie Mahon was there the night they killed Willie. When I think of who was there!

I have gone over it so many times that it is like a beaten track in my mind. There are no surprises left, just some useless questions standing there in the middle; questions that are not really questions, because they have no answers. Willie is dead, Seanie wild, Caithleen dead with sorrow. Perhaps she would be dead now, but she would not have died when she did. She would have had a taste of joy, even though Deirdre and Eileen were dead.

She loved them, the boys. Maybe for the wrong reasons. Maybe she wouldn't have loved them if the girls had lived. But it was difficult not to love them. It was as if they were reincarnations of what we had lost. It was like unexpectedly coming across a patch of pale snowdrops after a dreary winter. At worst it was symbiotic attraction. They were pauper orphans, we were bereft parents.

That first time I coaxed them into the house after school! Perhaps because the absence of the girls was still wringing my insides, those few hours with them were the most joyous I have ever lived, and I can say that without feeling I am betraying Deirdre and Eileen. Looking back it seems the house was full of bright light that afternoon, bright light and the sounds of joy resurrected.

Of course they were shy, like boys their ages are shy. Their heads had been freshly shaved and the fringes bobbed. Each had a hand flat on his bald head while I ushered them through the front door. Caithleen came into the hallway towelling her floury hands on the apron she had just untied.

'Now, let me see,' she said, 'there must be some way to

tell you apart.' She didn't look at their baldness. 'Dark blue and light blue eyes. That's it. Who are you?' she asked, and then she took Seanie's hand in both of hers and led him to the kitchen, Willie following. 'Come on, Willie,' she said over her shoulder. 'Guess what we're having for supper! Shepherd's pie, and after that we're having apple cake and custard.' What a show she was putting on!

It must have been like a home-coming for the boys. It was four months since their parents had died, four months since they had come to the Workhouse, and it was four months since they had been in a house, a warm house full of the smell of food cooking, of bread baking. They stood there in the kitchen in front of the open fire and, for the first time since I had seen them, they let go of each other. They held their hands out to the red warmth of the turf fire. As if afraid everything would disappear, they looked around, at first without moving their heads, swivelling their eyes as far as their sockets would allow.

Then Willie turned his head and said, 'We had one exactly like that.'

He was looking at a picture of the Sacred Heart with a small, red-globed, paraffin lamp burning in front of it. It was high up on the wall, from the time Deirdre and Eileen were small, so they wouldn't get burned.

'Ours was high up on the wall, too,' Willie said. 'Mammy was afraid we'd get burned when we were small.'

'She always took it outside to fill it,' Seanie said. 'She was afraid she'd spill the oil. She didn't like the smell of it.'

Caithleen and I were standing behind them and to the side. Afterwards she told me she was feeling something like I was feeling. She had wanted to take the boys in her arms and hug them. But she dared not. It was, she said, as if two nervous exotic birds had landed in our kitchen and the wrong move would frighten them away.

'Who are they?' Willie asked, and he pointed to a tintype of two girls in their confirmation dresses; the open inviting smile of Deirdre; the shy peeping of Eileen; white dresses foreshadowing marriage. I remember thinking on the day of their confirmation that when I'd see them dressed like that again they would be leaving home. Little did I think, little did I suspect.

The tintype was under the picture of the Sacred Heart, the little red lamp burning for both.

'That's Deirdre and Eileen,' Caithleen said. 'Our daughters. They died in January.' She said it without tears in her voice.

'On the same day? Did they die on the same day?' Seanie asked. Willie touched Seanie's arm and, without looking, sought out his hand.

'No,' Caithleen said. She went over to the tintype and pointed. 'That's Eileen. She died two days before Deirdre.'

In silence we all looked at the girls' picture. Then Seanie asked, 'Are they twins?' The boys looked at Caithleen, and they were holding hands.

'No. Deirdre was eleven and Eileen was twelve.'

Willie looked back to the tintype. 'They look like each other. Daddy and Mammy died at the same time. The doctor said a Spanish Lady made them sick.'

I saw Willie's misunderstanding as an opportunity to steer all of us away from our sadnesses. Maybe I should have let them talk about their dead parents, let them mourn. But I suspected they had had four months of unending sadness. I moved over near the fire and held my palms out to the heat.

'The Spanish Lady is the name people gave to the flu that killed all those people last year. It's just a name. Some people think the flu came from Spain.'

I was surprised to hear Seanie's laugh, a small laugh as if the sound of laughter might be inappropriate.

'That's funny,' he said. 'I've been thinking all the time that a dark-skinned woman with a lace shawl had made Daddy and Mammy sick.'

Willie tittered and he took his hand out of Seanie's. 'And it was the flu all the time,' he said. 'I thought she was fat and short and had a moustache and black eyes.'

They looked at each other and began to laugh.

There was an incongruity about what I was seeing, and it

took me a few moments to realize what was causing it. It was the laughter and the Workhouse appearance of the boys. There was nothing at all about The Workhouse that could be the source of laughter. It was present in the way the boys looked; the haircuts, the coarse cast-off and donated clothing – the trouser-legs ending above the knees; unmatched jackets too long, the sleeves too wide at the shoulders; no socks; the hobnailed boots.

It was the boots as much as the haircuts that advertised their pauperism. The hard, dry leather came above the ankles and the edge blistered a ring of flesh until a callus was formed, but even then the non-treated leather, as hard as iron on a frosty day, was a source of pain with every step taken. In the soles and heels was embedded a mass of close-fitting nails which saved the soles from ever wearing out. The boots were passed down from generation to generation of growing Workhouse feet. The hard noise of each footstep was a source of humiliation.' Here comes the Workhouse horse,' was a taunting childish cry I had often heard on the streets.

'How could a woman have a moustache?' Seanie asked.

As they spoke and looked at each other, I realized that Caithleen and I were looking in on an intimate relationship I had never before and have never since known. It was as if their words were superfluous, as if they communicated simply by seeing each other's eyes.

'Don't you remember Mrs Ramsbottom who taught us Roseen Dubh!' Willie said. 'She had a moustache and I saw it for the first time when she said, *Spanish ale shall give you hope, my Dark Rosaleen, my own Rosaleen.*' Then looking at each other's eyes they recited the remainder of the stanza in a stage-Irishwoman's voice.

'*Shall glad your heart, shall give you hope; shall give you health and help and hope, my Dark Rosaleen.*' They paused for a moment and leaned towards each other until their noses were almost touching. 'Beh heh heh, Ramsbottom!'

They laughed, not with gay abandon, but they did laugh.

Their Workhouse haircuts made it difficult to hone in on

their features. The perimeters were missing that give defini-
tion and scale to the parts of the face. Their ears stuck out;
their foreheads were all over the place; the eyebrows didn't
seem to be in the right places. As they laughed I tried to
imagine them with hair. I couldn't.

'Why did you think she had a lace shawl?' Seanie asked.

'The dictionary has a picture of a woman wearing a man-
tilla, and says Spanish ladies wear them. But I like the story
about Ramsbottom better. Beh beh. Ramsbottom's moustache!' and the two of them laughed again.

The moment Seanie saw the piano through the open parlour door he nudged his brother.

'Willie! A piano.'

It was Caithleen's. She had brought it to the house when
we were married. Its fretworked front was backed by red
cloth. The wood was a shining dark brown. When the top lid
was lifted a delicate frame could be swung out, and it hung
down to hold the music sheets. The ivory was yellow, probably more yellow than it should have been because of the
turf smoke.

'Can we go in there?' Willie asked. 'Where the piano is.'

'That's the parlour,' Caithleen said. 'Come on.'

It was peculiar how the boys affected us so positively that
day, even though the two things Caithleen and I had been
most sensitive about, the tintype and the piano, were
brought into focus by their presence. When Caithleen
moved the confirmation picture from the parlour mantel-
piece, and made it into a shrine in the light of the Sacred
Heart lamp, I had objected.

'Why?' Caithleen had asked angrily out of her grief.

'We can't keep looking back like Lot's wife,' I said.

'There's no place else to look,' she had replied with bitter-
ness. Now, by their innocent questions, the boys had turned
the shrine into a picture of two pretty girls; had spoken of
them in the present tense, had made them alive at the ages
they were when they died.

I followed them as far as the parlour door.

Caithleen declared, after the funerals, that she would

never play the piano again. With Eileen and Deirdre she had spent many hours teaching and laughing and playing and singing around the piano, the fire in the parlour grate warm on their backs in the winter, the lace curtains billowing over them in the flowered breeze of summer.

Now she was leading Seanie and Willie, two Workhouse boys smelling of Workhouse soap, into that sanctuary and, without her knowing it yet, they were leading her back to the piano.

'Do you play?' Willie asked her and, seemingly without being aware of it, he brushed the keys with the pad of his finger.

'I used to teach piano,' Caithleen said. She glanced over at me standing in the parlour doorway.

'Deirdre and Eileen must have played so,' Seanie said, and he too caressed the dull ivories.

I wasn't sure if Caithleen could handle all this, so I butted in to support her.

'Why do you think that, Seanie?' I asked. And Willie, standing at the far end of the keyboard, answered for his brother.

'Because our Mammy taught piano, too.

'Of course,' Caithleen said.

The quality of the afternoon sunlight changed. Looking back, it seemed the three of them had been positioned by an artist intent on geometrical balance. Willie at the far end, his left hand resting on the lid of the piano, looking down at his brother's fingers. Caithleen at this end, her hair circled on her head in a bun, her clothes dark on her tall, lissome frame. The back is still hunched with grief, the hands joined loosely behind her back. Her eyes are following fingers running unhurriedly up and down the keys. Seanie plays with the joy of someone who had believed he would never see a piano again. Caithleen is grinning. The eyes are drawn to the performer on the piano stool, but I can't see Seanie's bald head, or smell the sharp lye of the soap or his stale clothes. I cannot see the dirt under his nails, only his playing.

And suddenly the warm-up is over. The room is empty of sound and in my ringing ears I hear him asking, 'May I take off my boots?'

'The pedals,' Willie says by way of explanation.

Caithleen makes no audible reply but somehow, by crease of grin or nod, she tells him yes. Her mouth is open, her lips dry.

It would be nice to think that Seanie is aware of what he does to us as he plays, but I don't believe he is. What he is doing, what he hears, how he hears it, has nothing to do with us. He is a medium through which the past, as he knows it, flows into the present; all the practice, all the encouragement, the memories attached to every note, are being drawn together in him and emerging in Chopin.

But that's not what Caithleen and I are hearing. We are more than hearing. We are being infused with hope. We are faced, both of us know it together, with a second chance. It is a chance that makes us delight in the memory of Eileen and Deirdre. As Willie plays, the rest of the world is gone, except for Willie and Seanie and Caithleen and the sunshine on the green foliage of spring outside the window. As I look at Caithleen, the protective hunch is gone; the pillar of stone has come to life.

The slanting May sun filled our house with bright warm light. I don't know how many 'Nocturnes' they played; I don't know how often they changed places. I only know that if resurrection is possible then Caithleen and I were resurrected that afternoon, if transfiguration is possible then all four of us were transfigured. Without speaking about it, without even thinking about it, Willie and Seanie became our children, Eileen and Deirdre a source of happiness again.

Willie and Seanie had held their hands out to the fire, as if the fire was the first warm being they had encountered since their parents' death. In the end it seemed they were holding themselves out to Caithleen and myself in response to our love. Was it our loneliness that did it, or was it the obvious talents of the boys that made them so attractive? Was it just their desperate needs fulfilling our desperate needs? Do the reasons matter? I still love Seanie. I still love that crippled boy who cannot return my love. Is it out of pity that I love him – out of the memory of that afternoon when Caithleen and I rose from the grave?

Oh Seanie! There's only the two of us left: me an old man working late at night because there's nothing to go home to but a cold house; you wandering the streets and lanes till daybreak, then coming home to sleep in the shed. It took two and a half years after the killing of Willie, twenty-eight months after the death of Caithleen, to coax him that far. I have given up on the idea of ever getting him into the house.

Dear God! How many times have I come to the edge of despair where the next step would have been blasphemy? How difficult it has been to forgive, how difficult not to seek revenge. It was as if Caithleen and I were set up for a second time, and the second time Caithleen broke.

The money-bag is too heavy. I don't care how it will look or what people will say: this coming Friday will be my last day as manager of the Cinema.

And here I am already at Robin's Corner. Entering this street, a dark canyon called Monument Road, always moves my insides. It's a narrow street with drab terraced two-storeyed houses on each side. Dark slate roofs, grey plastered fronts, dull front doors; all with four grey steps up to the front doors, all with wrought-iron railings on each side. And there, up ahead on the other side, in the outer circle of the only street-lamp, is Enda at the grey door of his grey house. His back is to the street, his head bent to the key-hole. Is it coming or going he is? Drunk or sober?

Does he feel the same as I do every time he hears that wretched ballad? They still sing it in the pubs, whenever there's an occasion for the people to commemorate one of the country's innumerable risings or battles. 'The Ballad of the Protestant Bottling House' makes my blood boil. What does it do to Enda McKenna? When he hears about 'the five brave men' striking the blow for Ireland, 'the night they set the porter free in the Protestant Bottling House', what does he remember? Brave men! Five brave men!

He, the leader, hiding behind a headstone with his hands pressed to his ears, as his mutinous followers murdered a child, and would have murdered his twin brother were it not for Miss Bevan, out for her early morning gallop.

He has his little black bag with him. He's coming down the steps, holding onto the wrought-iron railing. I can hear the phone ringing in his house. Enda hesitates, but then he continues his careful descent.

I am five years older than Enda, so he's what? Sixty-three. He's been drunk since 21 January 1921. Twenty-seven years drunk – a few months longer than it has taken Father Quinn to collect the money to build the new wing. We were more than close friends once, Enda and I. Now there is a void between us – unbridgable. When we meet we throw greetings across to each other, but the words only cause pain, to me at least.

He couldn't stop the others. He didn't stop them; put his hands over his ears and hunkered down in terror behind a headstone. When it became known, at his own funeral, that Michael Butler had pulled the trigger, the others tried to keep their distance from the whole thing. They started betraying one another. Enda, the leader, the local IRA agent, the town doctor, washed up in the gossip as attractive as a rotting fish suspended in lapping water.

'Good night, Enda,' I say, my throat and face smarting from the stirrings of tears.

He's fumbling with keys at the door of his car now. Enda is a tall man, but there is a stoop which is almost a hunch, as if he has developed dowager's hump.

When I see the effect my voice has on him I know he has drink taken. The agitated keys become quiet and he twists his head to look up the street to his right. The head swivels back and looks up the street to his left. He puts his hand on the roof of the car and he shuffles around a quarter of a circle. The head comes up and there I am in his eyes with my left hand moving somewhere near my face.

'MJ!' He stands up straight and faces me. 'MJ!'

Enda McKenna was once a six-foot-four rugby player when rugby was for savages. Red hair. Handsome. He moved with grace and pride once.

'MJ! How's the hip?' He doesn't slur the words, but it sounds as if he has to consciously detach them from his vocal chords and fling them out through loose jowls, each syllable individually inflected. 'MJ! how IS the HIP?'

Twelve years ago I fell and jarred my hip. It was painful for a few months and it has been the subject of our conversation for the last twelve years. My answer is always the same to his same question.

Now that that subject has been dealt with, what will we say next? Enda holds the keys close to his eyes. His hips move forward and back again and a ripple goes up his body until finally the head comes forward and then back to its position. I notice the window of the car is open.

'Miss Dickingson is at it again. He just called me on the telephone. Noisy thing, the telephone.' He inelegantly picks out a key by grabbing at it, fearful he'll miss it.

'I don't imagine that's an easy call to make,' I say, and to myself I think, it's also one that doesn't pay. Professional courtesy probably extends to Father Quinn's housekeeper.

'Good seeing you again, MJ,' Enda says, and his swaying hips start another ripple up his body. He moves as if to turn back to the car, but he stops and faces me again, almost stumbles.

'I'll be seeing you at the big dinner tomorrow, MJ. Maybe we could sit together.'

'I wasn't invited, Enda,' I say.

'By Jakers!' he says. Then after a pause: 'That's a shame, MJ, a bloody shame. He's a peculiar man, Quinn.'

'But I'll be at the parade. Maybe we could walk together. Good night, Enda.'

'Good night, MJ.'

I shift the money-bag back to my free hand and walk out of the street-light. I wonder what degree of inebriation Miss Dickingson must reach before Father Quinn sends for help. Does she pass out; throw up; make speeches, like she does sometimes from the Cinema balcony? When I hear the doctor's car start into life behind me I wonder, unkindly, can one drunk person be good for another drunk person. The answer is yes, I suppose. There is that grating noise a car makes when the driver crashes the gears, a noise that sets the teeth on edge. I look around, and the car is pulling away from the footpath. Enda has forgotten to put on his lights, but he'll hardly run into anybody at this hour.

Enda knew that Caithleen and I were going to adopt Seanie and Willie the next day. He knew they were our children already. It was he who filled out the medical forms involved with the adoption proceedings; he who asked Caithleen and I if he could be the boys' uncle. Enda was there that last night when Seanie and Willie played five nocturnes in a row – Seanie the left hand, Willie the right.

Where is Seanie? What a strange word he picked up. *Camarán*. And I thought it was Guard McSwaine who called him that.

GUARD McSWAINE

Cowshite! The smell is not as bad as it was, or else I'm used to it.

The wife has my other uniform pressed and cleaned for tomorrow. I wonder should I chance putting it on. I couldn't go to the Ploverlegs smelling like this, and I couldn't go up not dressed in my uniform. She'll kill me if I put on the pressed uniform and get it dirty tonight.

There's Doctor McKenna's car parked two feet away from the footpath again, and the window left open. Drunk again! He pulled a tooth for me last month and I never felt a thing. Drunk or not he's a good doctor. They say he'd have been a surgeon if he'd stayed sober.

When I get home I'll examine myself for cowshite. I might be able to scrape it off. Maybe it's just on my boots. Only for Doolin none of this would have happened. And then Peetie Mahon with his remark about the smell of cowshite! Without them two dogs I would've been sunk for an excuse. Quick thinking! That's what they always said about me. That McSwaine, they'd say, he's a terrible quick thinker, he'd make a great detective.

The Monument. A place for dogs to piss against, and for the odd drunk to do the same. The names of the men who were hanged in '98 are in the stone, and a whole lot of nice things about how grand it is to die for your country. A hundred and fifty years! Two big events in the same year for the Town; the Church wing tomorrow and the Commemoration in September. Some of the lads were out this morning cleaning it up a bit, getting the grass out from between the stones and shovelling away the dogshites. They say they're going to put a railing around it before September, and each spike of the railing will be in the shape of a pike.

And there's the Garda Barracks! They were clever lads who came up with the idea of having the guard live in the Barracks. Always on the job, in or out of the uniform, is the result. Not even on your day off can you get away from it. I haven't had a full day off since I first put on the uniform. There's always something. I suppose they still call it the Barracks from the time of the English. Then there were twenty men in uniform, and a barracks was a barracks. Now it's just a house with one room made into an office; notices on the wall about noxious weeds, with pictures of thistles, ragwort and docks; dog, bull and stallion licences held up with a thumbtack; a calendar from Mick Dalton – why he bothers to drum up business I don't know, when he's the only undertaker in the Town; a different holy picture for every month.

The wife did a nice job on the curtains on account of Sergeant Keogh coming for the parade tomorrow. I dug up the grass around the low wall myself. Grass is a hure to get out once it gets its roots into cement. The neck of that young Padjoe Lennon charging me sixpence a load to cart away the pigshite, and then he selling it to Johnny Joyce for his greenhouses. We'll have to give Keogh and his lads tea tomorrow, and I wouldn't want to be hearing smart remarks about the pigshite, or the grass at the wall, for that matter. Apple cake and rhubarb cake is what's she's baked for them. That and custard. It's too good for them. A cut of bread and butter in the hand, is what I'd have given them. Then again the apples and the rhubarb were for nothing. Glanvil, down by the Canal! One of his sons had no light on his bike last Sunday night going home after serving at Benediction. The old lad was raging when he gave me the stuff out of his pony and cart. 'That it may scutter you from here to Queentown and back again,' says he, and he threw the bag on the ground at my feet. He'll be throwing more, the get!

Better be careful hopping off the bike so as not to spread the shite around. My hand feels like it's covered with drying plaster. The gate always makes a rusty squeak. How many times has she asked me to put a bit of grease on it!

'It drives me mad,' she says. 'It wakens me in the middle of the night when you come in.'

'That's the whole idea,' I say to her. 'No one can come near the Barracks without me knowing about it.'

'Anyone could jump over the wall and not use the gate at all,' she says.

That's when I give her the clincher.

'They wouldn't dare!' I say. 'They wouldn't dare!'

I won't lean the bike against the pebble-dashing on the gable tonight, there might be cowdung on the handlebars. I'll leave it on the ground. I can come back with the wife's flash-light to examine it carefully. Solid thinking! The gate has probably wakened her but I open the front door silently. No sooner have I stepped into the hall than she calls from above. I switch on the hall light.

'James!' She's cross. It's always James when she's cross.

'I'll be there in a minute,' I say. I start taking the boots off. It's Jim when she's not cross and Jimmy when she's going to let me have a hump.

'Come up here first!'

Whatever way she said that made me stir, even though she called me James a second ago. I can't see any shite on my trousers, even when I lift my leg up behind and squint down my side at it.

'I have to wash my hands,' I say, and I'm thinking of a quick one before I go up to the Ploverlegs to get the spuds. The water flowing over the dry cowshite at the kitchen sink brings the smell back to life and my face is all scrunched up, but the thoughts of the wife in the bed above and Hubey Sherlock's daughter's bubbies hanging out over her window sill make me hot.

'Jaa-mes!' she calls again, while I'm drying my hands on the towel. I look down through my arms at my trouser-legs again. No shite! It was all on the boots, thanks be to God.

Up the stairs I go softly, two steps at a time, loosening my tunic buttons at the same time, getting stronger all the time, the picture of her chest in my eyes, the two of them sticking out. Oh Jesus!

'I'm here.' I grope for the light switch.

'Don't turn on the light!' she says. 'I'm awake enough as it is, with that bloody rusty gate. Will you put a bit of butter or something on it. How many times do I have to tell you!'

'Only for that squeak...' I say. But she butts in. 'The phone went off a few minutes ago and I had to go all the way down to... What's that smell? Were you out in the pighouse? You must have stepped in something and now you're dragging it all over the place!'

'I took my boots off,' I say. 'Who rang on the phone?'

'Then you got it somewhere else besides your boots,' says she. 'I can smell it over here.'

'I got a bit on my hands,' I say, 'but I washed it off.'

'Then it must be on your ... Oh God! First it's the phone, then it's the gate and now it's dung!' The way she says dung!

My desire is dead in my trousers.

'Will you go down,' she says, 'and examine yourself. You smell like a farmer!'

'Who rang on the phone?' I ask her.

'Will you get out of the room with that smell! It was Father Quinn with a message for Butler-the-Butcher.'

'Father Quinn,' I say. 'For Joe Butler! By Jesus! And I was just talking to Father Quinn.'

'Get out of the room. He said you're to go and tell Butler-the-Butcher the minute you get in.'

'Tell him what?'

'Yes! Now get out of the room and look at yourself!' She is very cross. I can hear it in her voice.

'What am I to tell Butler?' I ask her.

'Tell him yes. That's all! Yes! Tell him yes!'

'I'll tell him yes in the morning,' I say, and I turn to go out.

'He said the minute you came in.' I hear the bedclothes and the springs in the bed. 'Now will you get out with that smell, dear Jesus!

Going out I can hear her plunking crossly down on the pillow and pulling the blankets up to her shoulders. I don't like it that Father Quinn is treating me this way. Nearly twelve o'clock at night, and I'm to deliver a message to the butcher! Yes! Yes what? It's as if I wasn't to be trusted with what the message is about. Yes!

I raise a leg onto one of the kitchen chairs, and Jesus, and fuck you Quinn, there's cowshite all up along the inside of the legs of the trousers. The spuds at the Ploverlegs is what I'm thinking about. Two bags are too much to lose. I can't go to Butler-the-Butcher like this. They'd never let me forget it. But I'm going to the Ploverlegs first, Quinn or no Quinn! So I'll change my trousers. If Joe Butler could smell the cowshite off me, then so could the humpers up at The Ploverlegs. And that wouldn't do.

So up the stairs I go again, and from the bedroom door I say I have to change my trousers. The bedsprings screech and the bedclothes make impatient noises.

'Why?' she asks.

'They're all cowdung,' I tell her.

'You can't,' she says. 'They're all pressed for tomorrow.'

'I'll be careful,' I say. 'I can't wear these up to Joe Butler's.'

'There's that smell again. Do you have them on still?'

'I do,' I say to the bed in the dark.

'Will you go out and take them off?'

'But the pressed ones is in here.'

'Well, take off the trousers downstairs and leave them there, and then come up and get the pressed pair.' The tones she uses tell me loud and clear that she thinks I'm stupid. 'When you're going bring the dirty trousers out to the shed. If you get the pressed ones dirty I'm not cleaning them again.'

Jesus! She's a terrible woman sometimes.

Ten minutes later I'm pedalling like a hure up Lord Edward Fitzgerald Street towards the Four Streets, going so fast I have to lean over to go around the corner into McDonagh Street. As well as everything else I wouldn't want these two to think they don't have to give me spuds every week. If I don't collect tonight they might think I won't collect next week. You have to keep the pressure on them lads.

There's Sheehan's house on the right. Two storeys, detached. There's more space up here. It's a lonely-looking house. I don't think I've ever seen a light in it since I came to this hole they call a town; hedges high inside the low wall all gone wild. They say he was married once. I can't imagine Sheehan between a woman's legs, going up and down, in and out. Jesus, Hubey Sherlock's daughter! Getting hard again. I'll have to be careful of that on the bike. It's a wonder Sheehan doesn't ride his bike down to the Cinema. He rides it to the school every day, but he always walks to the Cinema. I'm going to ask him about that some day; let him see I notice things. If he went on his bike he wouldn't have to carry that bag of money. He could put it in the handlebar basket or on the carrier. I wonder if he's home from the Cinema yet. How long was he talking to that hure Doolin? If he's not home I might meet him on my way back from the Ploverlegs. This has been one fucking awful night since Doolin came on the scene. If I hurry I might get the spuds and be back at Barracks before the Chief gets that far.

Here's the McDonagh Street railway bridge where Jack Quinlan's hure-of-a-son saw me in the bushes. I hope to God he didn't tell anyone. The Ploverlegs' house is around the next corner. I hope I'm not late for the spuds. If I am they know where to leave them, but I'd rather be there, so they have to hand them to me. That way I have more power, I'm stronger. I can do a little bit of digging at them, humiliate them a bit. 'Have a good hump tonight, lads?' 'Does your mother know you hump the Ploverlegs' wife, lads?' 'Does the Ploverlegs' wife stick it in for you, lads?' That keeps them in line; the hint about the mother frightens the hell out of them.

Shite! There's not a light in the house. Damn! Doolin and the bloody cowshite! Anyhow, the spuds will be in the bushes. I lean the bike against the gate, switch the flashlamp off and listen for a while. There's not a sound. Then I think that maybe they're waiting for me, so in a low voice I say, 'Hey, lads.'

Not a stir. The Ploverlegs doesn't even own a dog. He's

too poor to feed himself and the missus, never mind a dog.

'Hey lads!' After waiting another few minutes I switch on the flash-lamp and go over to the bushes.

The spuds aren't there. Shite.

'Is that you, Guard McSwaine?'

Oh! Jesus! Talk about a fright! Some hure is standing almost beside me and talking real loud. The hairs all over me are moving. Before I put the beam on him I know he saw me jumping with fright. Even if he didn't see me, he saw the flash-lamp jerking all over the place.

'Heh, heh!' he laughs, like he's very sure of himself. And when I shine the light on him, he says, 'Did I frighten you, Guard McSwaine?' like he was talking to an eejit.

It's the Ploverlegs. He talks very slow, as slow as a caterpillar slipping over the edge of a leaf. With the fright tightening up all my muscles I can hardly talk, but I'm determined to let this dirty fucker know he hasn't scared me.

'No, you – ' I'm like a chicken choking on dry oats. I clear my throat, but before I talk again the Ploverlegs laughs that easy laugh of his.

The Ploverlegs is as ugly as his wife. He hasn't shaved for about five days. He has one long yellow tooth hanging out of his top gum. He's about six foot two and as thin as a rake-handle. He's the only one in the Town who doesn't show me respect.

'What's so funny?' I ask him, and the beam of the flash-lamp shines off the greasy clothes that he mustn't have taken off since the first time he put them on.

'I frightened you, heh, heh,' he says slowly.

'You didn't frighten me,' I say.

'Then why did you jump? Heh, heh.'

'You gave me a bit of a start,' I say, because I know he knows he frightened the shite out of me.

'Heh, heh. I haven't frightened someone like that for a long time. Heh, heh.'

There's a smell off him like old turf smoke and boiled potatoes.

'Where's the two lads?'

'Heh, heh.' He scratches his balls, and then leaves his hand at his fork. 'Oh! they're gone. They're gone this ages. But they left a message for you. Aye!' He's scratching again, as if he wasn't thinking about it. He waits so long to tell me the message that I think of the wife not telling me what Father Quinn's message was.

'You must have ferocious itchy balls,' I say, casual like. And he says nothing for a while.

'Aye,' he says. 'Ferocious balls! They left a message for you with me. They said to tell you to go fuck yourself.'

For all the time I've been a guard no one has ever talked to me that way. And, by Jesus, if they did! But the way the Ploverlegs says it I have to stand there and tear my own insides apart. I'm standing here beside this smelly, dirty fucker who sells his own wife's arse and I'm shaking, I'm so cross.

'Aye! That's what they told me to tell you. Tell him to go fuck himself. Heh, heh.'

Mister Sheehan calls this scum *mister*! Say hello to Mister Dunne for me! I'd lay the mister out on his back, with that one long yellow tooth down his neck, only Sheehan knows I'm here. And the two humpers know as well. This long piece of dogshite thinks he has me in a bad place; thinks he'll be able to tell all the lads tomorrow how he told Guard McSwaine to go fuck himself. After running around in my brain trying to find a way to get him, I find the perfect way.

'You wouldn't want Father Quinn to read you out from the altar for running a hure house, would you now, Ploverlegs?' I say. I know the Ploverlegs part will shut him up entirely, if the part about Father Quinn doesn't. It's like a double-barrelled shotgun, my question is. Quick thinking! And I know I got him because he says nothing. Once you turn the tables on this kind of riff-raff they don't know where to hide. 'And now, Ploverlegs,' says I, 'if you don't mind I'll be on my way.'

I step around him and push the flash-lamp onto its holder on the bike. I'm out on the road with my left foot on the pedal when the Ploverlegs says, 'Hey, Baggy!'

I nearly strangle the bike. He says it again slowly. 'Hey, Baggy!'

I won't answer him, not when he calls me that. He says, 'I don't give a flying fuck what you tell Quinn about me. Quinn has other things on his mind. I hear Jack Quinlan's wife went to see him about a parsnip that the young lad saw in the bushes near the McDonagh Street railway bridge. Heh, heh. That's a good one. Heh, heh. Baggy's parsnip!'

With rage I am stuck to the road, glued to the bike. There is the sound of the Ploverlegs' yard gate opening and closing, and then in the distance there's that fucking laugh of his. I think I hear him saying Baggy's parsnip. I don't know how long I stand there, hands on the handlebars, left foot on the pedal, body ready to push off.

My two hands are squeezing the handlebars to death.

PEETIE MAHON

When I grab Doolin by the ear he jerks his head, trying to get free. He whimpers like a beaten dog.

'Get up, you little bastard,' I hiss, and I pull his ear. He scrambles around on the footpath, feet and hands trying to get the body balanced.

I'm getting hard.

'Up!' I pull the ear and he grabs on to the hem of my jacket to give himself leverage. I smack his hands away.

'Don't touch me, you filthy fucker. You smell like you did a shite in your trousers again!'

I let him lower his head so he can get his arse in the air and, when he finally gets his feet under him, I drag him into the shop. There is no one on the street. He holds his head sideways and pushes his face against my hand to keep his ear from being pulled out. I close the door with a touch of my heel. He smells like a dog that takes some kind of pleasure from rolling around in other dogs' shites. I push him away and give him a hefty kick in the arse. He cries out. When he grabs at the hurt I kick his hands.

God! I'm getting hard.

He's turning towards me when I kick again and his fingers fly to his hip. But he leaves himself wide open and I deliver a stinging open-handed slap to the side of his face, the side with the bad eye, the eye that Jack Quinlan blinded with a stone that night. Before his hands get to his face I kick him in the side again and, before his hands reach for the new pain, I slap him on the other side of the face.

For an instant Doolin stands there amazed, the good eye looking at me, water in both eyes. I smack his face on the bad side again and slam my boot into his hip. He starts to bellow like a cow when it knows it's going to be killed. I

78

grab his ear and twist it.

'Shut up!' He bends his body trying to untwist the ear. 'If you make another sound I'll cut your throat.' I drag him across to the sweet counter and push him up against it. 'Stand there!' I make a quick movement with my hand and his hands fly up to his face.

He is a pitiable excuse for a human being. The pale blue blind eye is horrible; the mark of Jack Quinlan's stone still there above and below; a red line at an angle, with the dead blue eye in the middle. His nostrils are big hairy holes, big from being poked at with fingers and thumbs. The black rotting teeth have gaps, and his breath smells like pigshite. The neck is long and scrawny. The body, small like the body of a twelve-year-old boy, is out of proportion with the big head. His clothes are filthy; the front of the jacket shiny, the area around the fork discoloured. It's seldom I've seen him without that great dirty horse blanket wrapped around him.

When I speak to him his whole body jerks as if avoiding a blow. One arm is in the air across his chest, the other dangling near where his balls should be.

'I thought I told you never to come near my shop,' I say. I feign another face-slap and his hands fly all over the place. He gapes at me. 'Well! Did I?' I ask sternly.

His whole face begins to work, and his chin moves up and down in short quick moves. No sound comes out.

'Did I or didn't I?' I ask him again, and the flesh on his face is running all over the place, trying to give shape to a word. I slap his face and his head falls over to the side from the force of the blow.

I'm harder.

'Did I?' I ask again.

As his face flesh struggles, the blood lunges up and the scar above and below the blind eye gets white. The mouth moves like he's chewing on a sound that won't come out. When I jerk my hands up he cowers away from me and whimpers.

'Shut the fuck up,' I say. 'Did I tell you never to come

near my shop again. Remember that kick in the arse I gave you when Miss Lalor saved you? Maybe you need another.'

He pushes up against the counter in remembrance of that kick. Only that dried-up bitch came out I'd have crippled him for good.

'Kneel down!' He gapes at me and I shout at him, 'Quick. Kneel down quick.'

He falls to his knees, looks up at me like a punished dog.

'Stand up,' I tell him. 'Up, up! Do it quick, you stupid little fucker.'

He has to put his hands on the floor to push himself up. As he's pushing, I kick his hands out from under him. He falls face first onto the floor.

'Get up!'

I grab a fistful of his dirty hair and pull his face off the floor. There's snots and blood around his mouth. I haul him up by the hair until he's kneeling.

'You scrawny little pauper. You and your scrawny little pauper brother. Get the fuck up!'

I let go of his hair. He draws his sleeve across his mouth and nose, trailing streaks of blood almost to his ear. He struggles to his feet.

'What do you remember?'

He draws his other sleeve across his face to his other ear. He looks like he has a moustache.

'What do you remember, fuckhead?'

He is looking at me fiercely with his one eye.

'Do you remember the bottling house and the fight about whether to kill you and your brother? Do you remember that?'

He just stares with the fierce eye. His hands are out in front, as if they could protect him from me. When I make a sudden move, his arms fly up around his face.

'Do you?' I shout. 'Do you remember McKenna wanting to let you go, that cowardly bastard? Did you see McKenna hiding behind the headstone crying, and I'm the one who's called the coward!'

I can feel all the old anger galloping back into my veins.

'Hah! Do you remember him crying like a girl to let you go, you and your fucking pauper brother? Like a girl he was crying!'

Doolin moves a step away from me along the counter. Then I notice he's shaking with fright, that a wet patch is spreading down the legs of his trousers.

I pull at the fork of my trousers to straighten myself up inside.

'You're all the same,' I say. 'McKenna was the same as you, off there behind the headstone. When he came out to fight the rest of us with Cashin, he was all wet in the front like you.'

I don't know I've unbuttoned the fork of my trousers until I'm reaching in to pull myself out, big and hard and long.

'Do you remember the fear, you weak little fucker? Do you remember your hands tied through the gate up at the Yewtree Cemetery?'

I can't talk any more because my hand is going up and down, up and down. Doolin is looking at my face with fear all over him. I'm drooling, but fuck it! Doolin can see me, what I'm doing. The muscles at the backs of my legs get ready for the great spurt. I have to squeeze my eyes shut because of the intensity of it, and I keep pumping and pumping, my breath coming and going in gasps, my shoulder against the showcase with the silverware in it.

When I begin to shrink I wipe my hand in the arse of my trousers. It slips back into place and I do up the buttons. There's a few wet spots near my feet and a few over closer to Doolin. I stand there filled with that odd feeling after sex has been done, sort of exhausted. I look at Doolin.

He stands there with that wild and fearful eye on my face, his hands in front of his body. A real gombeen he looks, the mouth half open, the blue blind eye, the wild staring good one. I go over and get the dusting rag, and throw it from his blind side. When it hits him he shouts and claws at his face, like someone attacked by a swarm of bees.

'Clean that up.' There is no reaction from him at all, just that eye on fire, staring at me. I grab him by the scruff of the neck and kick his feet from under him. He clomps onto his knees. 'Clean up my fuck, or I'll rub your face in it like I'd do to a pissing cat.' Still he does nothing and I do what I said I'd do. I rub his nose in my fuck. 'Dry it up, fuckhead!'

The hand with the rag moves, but he's not wiping anywhere near where the wet is.

'You stupid little bastard,' I squat down beside him, let go of his scruff and grab his ear. With my other hand I point to the glistening glob that is six inches from his nose. 'There,' I say. 'Mop it up!'

He mops it up. By the ear, I pull him on his knees across the floor. When I point out the other globs to him he mops them up.

'Get on your feet, fuckhead!' I yank him up and fling him back against the counter. I whip the rag out of his hand, throw it into a rubbish-box near the dolls' shelves.

'Do you remember the rope around your hands? You should, you dummy, because it cut into your skin and made you bleed. Hold out your hands,' I tell him, but he only gapes stupidly. 'Hold out your fucking hands,' I say to him with an edge on my voice, 'and pull up your sleeves. Pull them up!'

He draws the sleeves above his wrists and, sure enough, there are the marks.

'Do you remember how you got these?'

When I move towards him he pulls his hands back to himself.

'Put them out!' He puts them back out nervously, the wrists exposed.

'Only Miss Bevan came along on her horse you'd have been dead like that brother of yours. Then it would have been over and done with. But no! That Protestant bitch comes trotting along and we have to run. She saved you, you know. If I'd had another minute you'd have been dead.'

Doolin's arms begin to droop.

'Hold up your fucking arms,' I say, and I pretend to slap his face. To my great surprise his hands come up and grab the front of my jacket. 'Take your hands off me,' I say, and inside me I feel the rising blood, the rising pleasure of other people's pain. But he doesn't let go. That one eye is blazing in that stupid head, blazing like something evil. I shoot out my right hand. My fingers grasp the back of his neck and the thumb sinks into his windpipe. But he still holds on, that evil eye flaming away at me. I push in my thumb and, as his eyes begin to bulge out, I say, 'Let go or I'll fucking choke you!'

Instead of letting go it seems that his grip tightens on my coat, but then one of his hands comes up all of a sudden. I don't see it until it has come down on my face, the bitten nails scraping their way from my forehead to my chin across my left eye. I start choking the fucker in earnest.

Along the length of my arm I see that blindeye face turning purple. Through my thumb on his neck I feel the power beating into my body like a giant heartbeat. With one hand I do it. Water rolls out of his eyes and Jesus! I'm getting hard again. If only I'd waited till now. There's not even a sound coming out of his throat, but there's bubbles and suddenly he's gone. He has collapsed at my feet and one hand is still holding onto my jacket. I bend back the fingers and even then he tries to hold on. I kick him in the ribs. He grunts, and the clawing hand falls away from my coat.

When I look in the mirror near the door I see the marks of his fingers on my face. But there is no blood, no broken skin. The little fucker. While I'm looking at myself I hear him behind me. I whirl around, but he is on the floor where he fell, great lungs of breath moving his body. He seems to be unconscious still, his hands splayed out beside his head. I walk over to where he is and step on his fingers. When he makes no effort to pull away I put all my weight on the ball of my foot and rock back and forth. I can feel the skin of the fingers slipping every time my weight slips across the bones. Little fucker! He makes a noise of pain.

I know nobody will be in the street at this hour of the night, but I check to be sure. If you're careful enough you'll never get caught, that's my motto. And of course there is nobody, but I stand for a while listening. In the distance I hear the sound of metal on metal. Who could be making noise at this hour of the night? Maybe it's a gate banging shut up at Butler-the-Butcher's. He's hardly slaughtering this late. Him and his bloody bones.

I go back inside for Doolin.

He is not unconscious, but he hasn't moved. The eye stays on me as I approach him, the fierceness gone out of it. When I get near he pulls his two hands over his head.

'Get up, pauper,' I say. With the toe of my shoe I poke his ribs. He doesn't move. 'Get up, fuckhead!' I push my shoe below his ribs and dig my toe into his soft belly. He grunts. 'Get up, you fucking eejit!' Grasping the dirty head hair I pull him up off the floor. The bloody moustache is still in place and drying snots are on his cheeks. His neck is red where my thumb squeezed him.

'Get the fuck out of my shop!' I say, 'And don't ever come back! If you do I'll shoot you in the forehead like your brother was shot. Get out! Get the fuck out, you stinking bastard!' I pull him out through the door and fling him by the hair over to the edge of the footpath. And holy fucking Jesus Christ! there's a car coming along the street not thirty yards away with no lights on. What can I do but hold my ground and, if any questions are asked, say Doolin was trying to break into the shop.

Fuck! It's McKenna's car. Jesus! Talk about luck! If anyone had to see me roughing up Doolin I would have picked McKenna. No one with half a brain would believe what he saw at midnight. It looks like McKenna didn't see anything, and he's going to drive right on. But just as he's passing, Doolin stumbles off the footpath and falls into the gutter. McKenna never drives very fast and he quickly comes to a stop a few yards down the street past my place. It's a long time before the car door opens. Doolin is back on his feet before McKenna gets out, and just as he does, the car bucks forward and the engine dies suddenly.

DOCTOR McKENNA

I used to sleep with the bedroom door open to make sure I'd hear the phone in the office, but the clanging suddenness of the ringing always terrorized me.

The only one who ever calls me is Father Quinn, and the only reason Father Quinn calls me is because his termagant of a housekeeper is drunk again. Drunk and in heat!

I push my bony, red-haired toes into the slippers. The heels of the slippers are collapsed and it hurts to stand in them. They have been like this for several years. I must get a new pair at Seerey's. I say that every time I put these on.

Using the bounce in the bedsprings to boost myself up, I stand at the door with the knob in my hand. It's like those few seconds before you force yourself to jump into a cold swimming hole.

He never asks me to come to attend to that bawling bitch; he tells me, orders me as if he was my commanding officer.

I nod my head with each ring till I get the rhythm down. Then, pulling the door open, I take long steps, trying to get to the phone before it screeches again. Sometimes I make it. Tonight I don't, and the ragged jangle stabs at my earholes. I yank the phone out of the cradle in mid ring.

'Hello.'

'McKenna! Is that you?'

Who the hell else could it be! There's only four other phones in the Town besides his and mine.

'Yes.'

'Miss Dickingson is ill. Take care of her.' He hangs up before I can respond. He always does. Rudeness marches in step with power. I put down the phone.

Back in the bedroom I kick the slippers off and pull my

85

clothes on over my pyjamas. The sleeves run up over my elbows when I stuff my arms into the jacket. Shoes! Where's the shoes? Gone! They're not in the office either. Back to the bedroom and I pull the slippers back on, fix the heels with my index finger. Tomorrow I'll go to Seerey's for another pair. These are three or four years old. A Christmas present from the nuns. It's hard to examine a nun. I'd rather examine a nervous beluga whale. Bag! I don't need the bag. All I do is get her to bed, and wait for her to fall asleep. But a doctor can't go on a sick call without his bag.

Before I go down the stairs I look in the mirror, bending down to see myself. Ever since I hung that mirror, over thirty years ago, I've been threatening to raise it. The mirror and the slippers! Big red face looking back at me in surprise. I've never got used to looking at myself in the mirror. I get embarrassed. The hair is still in place, going grey the way red hair goes grey; takes its time. Hairs at the nostrils still bright red, but the ones at the ears are silver. Curious. With a spit on each hand I divide my hair and flatten it down along an ill-defined split. I tug at the collar of the pyjamas, making it vaguely symmetrical with the collar of the coat. Ready! Ready for Miss Dickingson.

My head throbs with every step taken down the stairs, the slippers not helping matters. The bag is on one of the kitchen chairs and the overcoat, hanging like a shroud with a hump, is on the nail in the back of the door. If I'd ever married, the first thing my wife would have done is take that nail out of the door. Of course I should have put on the overcoat before I picked up the bag, but I didn't. After struggling for a few minutes, like the one-armed paper hanger, I put the coat on the table, put the bag on the table, pick up the coat, put it on, do the buttons and pick up the bag. There's two buttons missing off the overcoat. Before the big parade tomorrow I'll have to go into Seerey's and get a few matching buttons; get the slippers as well. Why haven't the nuns given me a new pair?

Tomorrow? It's almost tomorrow already. Twenty to twelve. The day of the big opening. Twenty-seven years of gathering pennies and threepenny-bits.

The keys! Miss Dickingson's going to be out of action for the big dinner tomorrow. Quinn will have to ... Where's the keys? There's the shoes under the table, but I'm not going to change now; not for Dickingson. She won't notice. The keys! They must be in the jacket pocket. Damn! Bag back on table. Open overcoat buttons. Hand into left pocket. Hand into right pocket. Where are they? Quinn will call me again if I don't get to hell out of here. I must have left them in the door when I came in. Button up overcoat.

Bag!

Sure enough the keys are hanging from the latchkey on the outside of the door. I could have been murdered in my bed. Everything seems to be a two-handed job tonight. I have to put the bag down on the step to get the key out of the door; damn thing gets stuck. Quinn will have to call in the nuns tomorrow to serve the dinner; they will have to cook too! Usually if I pull the key out a little bit and then turn it ... But no. It's not going to budge. With the nail of my thumb I spread the key-ring and turn it around till it comes off the key in the door. If someone breaks in they can steal my shoes. And the phone, if they like. It was Quinn who insisted I get it. Before Post and Telegraph would bring the wires to the Town, they wanted a guarantee of six customers. I was the last. I haven't used it yet, only to receive messages. The only message I've got so far on it is that Miss Dickingson is ill. Drunk and in heat.

Half-way down the steps I hear the phone ringing inside the house. I hesitate and think. No, I'll go on. Let him ring! Maybe she's lepping on him, as the farmers around here say when they talk of a bull mounting a cow. He's lepping on her!

I'm trying to get the key into the car door when I realize I didn't lock it before. A voice behind me raises the hairs on the backs of my hands. But once I hear the voice I know who it is, and uncontrollable things begin to happen inside my body.

'Good night, Enda.'

It's MJ – only I have to look around a bit before I can see him on the far side of the street. There he is with The Cinema money-bag in his hand, the other waving to me.

'MJ!' I say in a greeting tone of voice, and compress my lips involuntarily. I wish, like I always wish when I see him, that I could go up to MJ and put my arms around him; tell him I'm sorry. But I can't do that. I never will do that. We are painfully polite to each other and we should be more than friends. We have a child in common and we have a dead child in common.

'MJ!' I say, 'How's the hip?' I always say that. Before he fell and hurt his hip it used to be, 'How's the teaching going, MJ?' Before that it was trust, respect and love for each other.

'The hip is fine, Enda,' he says. He is the only one in the Town who calls me by my first name. That, at least, is something we didn't lose. I'm probably the only one who calls him MJ – Michael John. He is a true Israelite.

For the want of something – anything – to say, I say, 'Miss Dickingson is at it again.'

MJ says something with sounds of empathy in it, something polite. I don't know what the words are. We are like two people split by a catastrophe, sending painful signals to each other from a distance, but unable to help, unable to touch.

'Good seeing you again, MJ.' It seems like we are going to be parted again for a long time. We gaze across, neither of us knowing how to take leave of the other.

'It's good seeing you, too, Enda.' That's what I think he says. That's what I hope he said. Did he say anything at all? He changes the money-bag to the other hand. He's old and tired, I think. It's sad. We were brothers once.

He turns to go.

'I'll be seeing you at the big dinner tomorrow, MJ. Maybe we could sit together,' I call.

He looks down at his feet for a moment before he answers. 'I wasn't invited, Enda,' he says.

I am so taken aback I blurt out, 'By Jakers! That's a shame, MJ, a bloody shame. Quinn is a peculiar man.'

'But I'll be at the parade,' he says. 'Maybe we could walk together.'

'I'd like that, MJ,' I call back to him, and inside me I have a distant feeling that maybe we are talking about something more profound than walking together in a parade. I know I'm a little drunk. I know my tear-ducts are swelling.

'Good night, MJ,' I say.

'Good night, Enda.' He shifts the money-bag again and turns towards home. Michael John Sheehan. The Chief. He has the respect from the people that Quinn wishes he had.

I've had this car for six years now, and I still can't find the place for the key in the dark. Two hands again – one to feel the keyhole, the other to guide the key. There it goes. Turn key. Press starter. Jakers! I hate when that happens, when I clash the gears. The shock goes up my arm to my teeth and makes them jangle. The noise announces to the world that McKenna is locked again. MJ! Well, MJ probably knew I was locked before he heard the gears. He knows how long I've been plastered. Twenty-seven years ago it was; the constable standing there about to knock again and me drunk, with Peetie Mahon over the constable's shoulder, sitting at the wheel of his taxi at the kerb. 'A body,' he was saying, 'up at the Yewtree Cemetery,' and I didn't want to get into that car that I had been in twice already that night, once on the way up there with the two boys and then coming back fast so Miss Bevan ...

Fuck! I'm at it again; that fucking night and that morning!

I shake my head and slap my own face as I head into Bridget Street. Bridget Street. O'Neill Street. Clark Terrace. Dwyer Street. Lord Edward Fitzgerald Street. Saint Fintan's Terrace. More patriots than saints. Patriot names for every street in the Town. There's no difference between a saint and a patriot in this bloody country. Patriot names and patriot games. That's what it was, a big game, a big bloody game; grown men playing at little boys' games and a child had to be killed. MJ. Fuck! MJ and Caithleen and Seanie and Willie.

Shut up! Shut up!

Think of Dickingson. There's something to think of. Dickingson. Dick. Ing. Son. Chopin's 'Nocturnes'. Five of them one after the other. Uncle Enda. Dickingson. Dickingson is the tallest, boniest, skinniest woman I ever came across. Her elbows are razor-blades, her knees chisels. No breasts. She has no female softness about her. She doesn't even strike you as a female; but give her booze and she becomes a nymphomaniac. Of course the first time Quinn called me to treat his ill housekeeper I wasn't prepared. I thought she was in a state of collapse, that she was clinging to the newel post for support. The instant I touched her she sprang at me, her legs around my thigh, her groin grinding. Quinn discreetly withdrew while ... What's that?

Someone. Someone wobbling across the footpath and Peetie Mahon's shop all lit up. What's going on? At the edge of the footpath the wobbler is trying to keep his balance, teetering on the edge of the ... It's Seanie! Aw fuck! He's fallen on his face in the gutter. That poor child. Jakers!

It takes forever for the car to stop, like in a nightmare pushing your foot to the floor and the car keeps going and going. I can't see the key to turn off the engine, so I leave it running and find neutral. But I didn't find neutral, and I have the door open and my head half-way out when I take my foot off the clutch.

It's a real bugger getting hit on the head when you haven't the foggiest notion where the hit could have come from. I didn't hit the car. It hit me, squashed my ear against my head. While running back to Seanie I'm holding my hand against the sharp pain. Seanie is on his feet. Peetie Mahon is in the door of his shop, the light behind him, but the light from the window beside him gives shape to his features. It's as if Seanie suddenly realizes I'm there. When he spins around at the sound of my approach a shriek comes out of him. To calm him down I say, 'Seanie! It's Enda.'

And, God, my heart is ripped again in my chest. On his face is that same expression he had each time I tried to get near him those two years after Willie was killed, the years he spent in the wild, as the people of the Town used to say.

Seanie Doolin is living in the wild.

There's the terror in his eye, around his mouth.

'Seanie,' I say again, and I reach out to him with my free hand. 'Seanie, it's Enda, Uncle Enda.'

But I know he is gone again, back to the wild place in his mind.

'Seanie.' I know it's useless. I'm almost touching him. There is blood smeared across his face, away from his nose as if he wiped his bloody nose with both sleeves. There's drool flowing over his lip. There's terror in him, and his body is trembling. The shriek comes again and again. He's backing away and it takes a while for me to hear the sound he is making. He's screaming 'Illy, illy!' in that squeaky pent-up voice of his.

'Seanie, it's alright,' I say, but he's gone. He has turned and is running away into the darkness like a lame turkey, wings flapping to maintain balance.

'Seanie,' I call, like I called a hundred times, a thousand times, when I was trying to get to him while he was living in the wild.

I turn from the darkness. There's a rage in me when I look at Peetie Mahon in his doorway and I lunge across the footpath towards him.

'What did you do to him?'

With hands in trouser pockets Peetie Mahon smiles up at me.

'Well, look what the wind blew out from behind the headstone,' he says. 'If it's not Uncle Enda!'

'What did you do to him, Mahon?' I demand through clenched teeth.

'I didn't do anything to anyone, Uncle Enda,' he jeers. All I can think of doing is ripping his testicles out and stuffing them down his throat. Then above me I hear a voice that has been insistent since I got out of the car.

'What's going on down there?'

While Peetie Mahon's grimacing head hangs there in front of me, the voice above me keeps saying, 'What's going on down there?'

I have to close my eyes and shake my head. Too many things are happening. Dickingson, Quinn, Seanie, Mahon and this voice. I'll have to get new slippers in Seerey's tomorrow. My feet are cold.

In a loud voice Peetie Mahon says, 'It's alright, Miss Lalor. Doctor McKenna is making a sick call and he lost his way.' Then he lowers his voice and jeers at me again. 'Did you lose your shoes, doctor, or is it that you can't find them? Maybe if you look where you left them you'd find them. Maybe they're in a bottle like a little ship.'

What I want to do to Peetie Mahon I can't do because I'd go to jail. What I want to say to him I don't say because he'll only turn the words back on me, slap me with them like a nun slapping a child's face with the child's own hand.

'Is anyone hurt?' the voice in the sky asks.

'Nobody is hurt,' Peetie Mahon says loudly, the sly smirk at his mouth, his eyes boring into me. 'Anyhow, if there was, the doctor is here. Everything's alright, Miss Lalor,' and he drops his voice, 'except that Uncle Enda is drunk. What do the Church Building Fund and drunk Doctor McKenna have in common? Twenty-seven years. Good night, Uncle Enda. Go away and heal yourself.' He steps back and closes the door in my face.

I would march into hell if I could drag him with me.

My ear is throbbing. In my rage I go back to the car and try to start it while it's in gear. Down toward Dwyer Street I drive, my ear like an overcooked rasher, my brain spitting like a fry on a hot pan.

Seanie's gone again into the wilds of his own mind, and I know that bastard Mahon ... God! God fucking God! If there is a God he is a cruel bastard. I should be going after Seanie instead of taking care of Dickingson; taking care of Dickingson because if I don't I'll have to deal with Quinn. It's the same all over again; a choice between the boy and the Cause. God DAMMIT! A choice between the boy now and Quinn. Fuck!

Outside the priest's house I step on the brake so hard that my forehead hits the windscreen. Fuck the bag! I step out of

the car and the right slipper gets caught under the seat. In
the dark I fumble around, feeling for the thing, the cold of
the footpath hot on the sole of my foot.

For two years he ran away from anyone who came near
him; two years living like an animal, the eye festering from
him picking at it, long cracked nails, hair down his back,
the smell. Seanie. MJ and myself were like competing
hunters; Cashin up there praying like an idiot.

Where's that fucking slipper? Fuck it. Fuck me. Afraid!
So fucking afraid.

I stride across the footpath to the wicket door in Quinn's
big iron gate. When I step through it there's sharp pebbles
underfoot. Fuck them! I deserve them. Along the side of the
house I go, then a right turn toward the back door, my siz-
zling ear enough to override the pains in the sole of my foot.
The back-door latch is familiar to me, only because of Dickingson's drunken bouts; no invitations to me to sit at the
priest's table. The drunken doctor! Tomorrow's the first
time.

My thumb is on the latch and the ear is frying on the side
of my head. He's flapping away in the dark somewhere, flapping away into a shadow, hiding again from all the fuckers
in this town, including me. My thumb pushes down.

Goddam!

Fuck you Dickingson.

I turn back, run with a sore-soled limp, the sharp pebbles
cutting deliciously into my foot.

Where would Seanie have headed for? Where? He could
be anywhere. He knows all the hiding-places in the Town.

SEANIE DOOLIN

When I hear the shot that shoots Willie in the head every-thing changes. All the colours leave the world, float up and away and leave everything black and white. The sun isn't warm anymore and I am cold. The number two running down the backs of my legs is cold. The number one all over my front is cold. Something has happened inside me as well. It's like a big piece, the size of an apple, has been cut out of my heart. It's like my heart is leaking. Leaking.

Oh holy God! Holy God! Willie's dead. Let me be with Willie. Let me die, too, to be with Willie. Oh! Daddy Mammy! I want to be with you and Willie.

Willie's poor legs are twitching in the long green grass. Oh Willie! I couldn't help you. My hands were tied. I would have died for you. Died for you a million times. Willie, Willie.

Then the sun goes out because someone is standing be-tween me and the white sun. His face is up against mine on the other side of the up-and-down bars. It's the one was sit-ting across Willie's feet, the one who had the gun first.

'Shut your fucking mouth,' he snarls like a dog.

I close my mouth but I can't breathe through my nose because it's stuffed with tears. I open my lips a little bit to breathe through them. My lips keep touching each other real fast like my teeth when I'm shivering.

'If you shout once more I'll rip your fucking tongue out.'

I wasn't shouting at all, I think. The man goes away. Then all of a sudden there is shouting and the men are moving around, going away and coming back. One of them falls backwards over Willie and, for a second, he sits on the grass with his feet one side of Willie and his backside on the other. His knees are like a bridge over Willie's chest. Then

94

he jumps up like he has sat down on the point of a pencil.

Oh Willie. What can I do without you? The world is over, Willie. I couldn't get loose. I couldn't get my hands free. I tried, Willie. Willie, I tried.

Don't sit on Willie. Don't fall over him.

Someone is running towards me and the men are shouting. I think he is going to hit me but, when he gets to the gate, he falls down like he fainted. The one who lay on Willie's feet is standing there right in front of me. He has a big stone in his hand. The one who fainted starts to get up, but the one with the stone hits him on the head hard. Then he turns back to the others who are around Willie and he shouts. He drops the stone and goes to the side of the gate where the high stone stile is. Stone stile.

The sun goes out again and a man is opening the ropes on my wrists. But the one who had the gun first is suddenly beside me on my side of the gate. He says, 'Christ almighty! This one made a shite in his trousers, too. You stinking little fucker of a pauper.' Across the back of my head he slaps me with his open hand. My forehead bumps into the iron bars. He kicks me on the side of the knee and I fall to my knees in the stones of the lane.

'You stinking fucker!' he says again, and he hits me on the back of the head again. When my forehead hits the iron bars I realize that I'm not feeling pain. Where he kicked me on the knee is not hurting. The sharp stones under my knees are not hurting.

'Hurry up with that rope,' he says. The man on the other side of the gate, who is kneeling on one knee, says, 'It's a black knot.'

'Cut the rope, you eejit,' the one who had the gun first says crossly.

'I might cut him,' the one who is kneeling says.

'Fuck that! He's going to be dead in a minute so what's the difference! Here!'

Through the bars of the gate he hands an open knife to the other man. The other man takes it and starts cutting the rope carefully. I wonder who they are going to kill.

The one who had the gun first, and who then sat on Willie's legs, catches me by the ear. He growls through the bars at the kneeling one, 'Cut the fucking rope!' The bottom of my stomach is gone on the inside, or else it is full of rusted barbed wire. Willie's feet are not moving anymore. There's a man kneeling beside him and he's doing something to his head. I'm not afraid all of a sudden. Nothing matters anymore. I can't feel anything. I can't see any colours. I'm cold to the bone. The world is over.

The man kneeling in front of me cuts through the rope and my hands fall apart. The one who had been hit on the head moves and puts his hand to the back of his head. The one who had the gun first is pulling my ear, trying to lift me off the ground by the ear. But I am too heavy. He catches me by the other ear with his other hand.

'Get up, you little fucker,' he hisses.

I'm too heavy for him to lift me that way. I catch onto his jacket to pull myself up. But he jumps away as if I had touched him with a hot iron. He slaps my hand away.

'Don't touch me, you filthy little shite,' he says.

He lets go of one of my ears and, now, I can get my feet under me. He drags me after him. It is all bright again, all white. He flings me forward. As I'm stumbling he kicks me hard in the backside and I can feel the pain again. I clutch at the pain and he kicks the backs of my fingers. They are hurting me so badly that I stick them in my mouth. I get a sharp pain in my hip. I rush one of my hands to my hip, and then the side of my face that I can't see out of goes on fire. Then my hip explodes again and my hands don't know where to go to rub away the pain. Daddy! The other side of my face bursts into flames.

There's water in my eye but I can see Mr Mahon standing in front of me all of a sudden. He's lifting his foot to kick me in my hurt hip. When I put my hand down to protect the bone, my face on the bad side crackles again. He has slapped me but I didn't see him doing it. My hip! It feels like someone hit me a sharp blow with an iron hammer. But it's alright. The pain is alright. It's for Willie. It's for you, Willie.

I couldn't help you when you called me. My pain is for you, my brother. I put my arms around you and hug you. The men are all gone and there is something sticking out of the hole in your forehead. My pain is to make it easier for you, Willie. It's to let you know that I wanted to help you. They can cut me up in little pieces with a saw and it's for you, even if I cry at the pain it's for you. They're gone, Willie. They've run away, my poor dead brother.

Oh Willie! I love you I love you. My arms are around you in the long green grass, trampled as if an ass had rolled in it after a day's work. How pale! Willie. Good night sweet prince and flights of angels. Oh Willie! I can't think of it. Flights of angels. And flights of angels. It's a piece of wire that's in the hole in your forehead. Willie! Willie! My baby Willie.

'Shut up!' Mr Mahon says, and he twists my ear for you, the pain going out to you, like a white line in the air, my pain taking away from Willie's pain, in the long green grass. Mr Mahon tells me if I make another sound he'll cut my throat, like I'm a pig that Daddy and Mr Boyle used to kill each winter, the two of us hiding under the bed with Rover because of the pain in the squeals, Rover whining.

Mr Mahon pushes me up against the counter in his shop. He tells me to stand there. All the others are gone. They were all fighting when, suddenly, they all looked in one direction and then ran away. Mr Mahon says, 'I thought I told you never to come near my shop.' He is going to slap my good side, but I protect myself with my hands.

'Well! Did I?' Mr Mahon asks crossly.

I can't get the words out. I am trying to say I wanted to look at the red fire engine in the window but my throat is dry all the way down. The little wells of saliva under my tongue are dry and I smack my lips together trying to rise them, like Daddy used to rise the pump in the yard in the long dry summertime, pouring a cup of water down the hole before the water came, the pump making noises like a big animal trying to catch its breath. Sometimes you'd think it would never come. But it always came, Daddy going up and down fast with the pump-handle.

Mr Mahon is going to kick my sore hip and, by themselves, my hands fall down to save it. But the bad side of my
face blows up for you, Willie. Take it, my brother, and put it
where they hurt you. Then Mr Mahon moves really quickly
as if he's going to hit me again for you, to make you better. I
fall back against the thing at my back and, while I'm falling,
he says something that reminds me of you lying in the grass
on your back with that piece of wire sticking out of your
forehead, your poor eyes opened, frightened. When the man
who had the gun first pulls me over by the ear to where you
are, I have no pain at all, even with my foot twisted. It
twisted when he pushed me off the top of the high stone
stile. The stone stile. The stone stile. Stone. Stile. Stop.
Story. Strong. Sting. Stink. Step. Stab. Stone stile. Stone
stile. Off the top I fell like a crow with clipped wings and
my foot twisted under me at the stone stile.

Before I am up he has me by the ear, pulling. Then it
looks like a man pops up out of a grave from behind a headstone. He runs to us shouting. He is huge. He was the one in
the bottle house who kept saying 'no, no we can't, no no'.
He runs towards me and the man who had the gun first. He
is huge. It looks as if his arms are folded across his chest.
When he gets to us he pushes his folded arms into the face
of the one holding my ear.

And then I'm free! Willie, I'm free. I'm coming, Willie
Willie. Then there is terrible roaring near my ear.

'RUN SEANIE, RUN SEANIE!'

There seems to be men all around me pushing and hitting
and shouting. I hobble off to where you are lying in the long
green grass. I hop along on my left foot because I think I'll
fall over if my right one touches the ground.

'RUN SEANIE, RUN SEANIE!' someone is shouting, and
then my feet are kicked out from under me. With that kick I
feel my twisted ankle. It is a bad pain for you, Willie, and I
crawl to you on my hands and knees. I'm crawling on the
gravel just inside the cemetery gate. I'm going toward that
long green grass, where the ass rolled to get the feeling of
the tacklings out of herself after a hard day's work. There's

big boots in the gravel around me. Sometimes the boots kick up the sand and stones, they come down so hard.

'GET UP AND RUN SEANIE! RUN SEANIE!'

Two hard boots come running backwards across the gravel at me. When I know they are going to hit me I lie down on my belly, my hands over my head. There is a big grunt and someone says fuck. On all fours, I am almost at the grass when someone kicks my hands from under me. I smack, face first, into the gravel. There are hard boots standing on my fingers. I am a butterfly stuck to a wall with a pin through it.

Someone yells out, look.

'Look. Look. Look.'

All the shouting and the fighting stops, and there is only the sound of the hard boots in the gravel. I crawl off onto the grass and just as I reach Willie's feet there's a lot of talk. It's all very urgent; quick short words. Then someone says run.

'Run. Run to the motor. Run.'

The boots make running noises on the gravel. Then they're gone. Willie, they're gone. No sooner have I thought they're gone than I hear quick boots in the gravel. I am grabbed by the shoulder and pulled over onto my back, like I was a sack of straw. It's the one who had the gun first. He flops down on my belly and the wind gushes out of me. I think I'm going to die, because I can't get air into me. His knees are on each side of me and his thumbs go to my throat, the fingers around my neck. His face is close to me. The drool from his mouth comes down and falls into mine.

It's the motor driver, Mr Mahon, who's choking me. I know it's him even though his face is peculiar. His eyes look as if they are going to come out of his head. His teeth are together like the teeth of a dog with his lips pulled back before he bites you. It's the drool coming down into my open mouth that I see shining like a spider's web in the bright sun. As his thumbs go in, Mr Mahon is moving on my belly, snarling, squashing me down into the ground.

I'm not frightened. There is even a gladness about the

way I feel; so relaxed, I am floating on the soft earth. Floating away, I reach out for you, Willie, feel around in the bent green grass for your hand, Chopin in your fingers. I find your hand. Illy Illy oi uv yooo. Oi uv yooo uv yooo uv yooo.

Everything goes red. Mr Mahon is gone, and in his place is Miss Bevan, dressed in her funny horse clothes, but she's not on her horse. She is down on one knee beside me. I have never been this near her before. She is always nice to Willie and me. She gives us a bag of broken biscuits sometimes. Miss Bevan is touching the side of my face. I try to answer her when she asks me am I alright, but I feel as if I have a bad sore throat. There is a nice smell from her hand. Like flowers. Like primroses.

I start to tell her about what they did to Willie, but tears start choking me. Miss Bevan puts her hand behind my neck and she tells me to sit up. She even knows my name. When I sit up I twist over onto all fours. I move over to where Willie is lying looking up at the sky with fearful eyes, and that piece of wire sticking out of his forehead, blood all over his face as if it was painted on.

Oh Willie! My arm is around his poor neck. Willie Willie my baby baby baby Willie. I'm pulling him into me, pulling me into him. Miss Bevan is kneeling there trying to put her arm between Willie and me. She's saying things, but I am crying for my dead brother, Willie, for Daddy Mammy. It's as if Miss Bevan is trying to take Willie away from me, to take Willie away. When I say 'no no' to her, the sound that comes out is like the sound a dying cow makes, only not as loud. I hold tighter to Willie, one arm under his head, the other across his throat and my fingers all tied together. I'll never let go.

Miss Bevan goes away, Willie. We are alone, my little brother, Oh Willie Willie! My hands were tied, and I was tied through the gate. Oh Willie. I wish they had killed me instead of you. It was Father Waters first, pulling us away from Daddy Mammy dead. And then the porter locking us up in the ... And I couldn't save you then either. And now, Willie. Oh God! You are dead dead dead oh! my Willie. How glad we used to be before Daddy and Mammy died. If Daddy and Mammy saw you like this they would be terribly sad. Poor Willie.

Gently I take the wire out of the hole in his forehead. I have to hold it over to one side to see it, because I still can't see out of that eye where the stone hit me. There is shiny stuff on the wire shining in the sun. And now with the wire out I am going to bring him back. I rock him until I get him on his side. My left arm is under his head and my right one around his shoulder. I press him to me. On my elbow, I lift myself up and put the side of my face on his face. My chest is to his chest. Our bellies are touching. I throw my right leg over his legs. With all my body I squeeze us together. Into his ear I whisper little things I only whispered to him. Little baby things I say, and sounds I make.

'Illy Illy oi uv yooo. Yooo am i aby. Yooo am i illie buddah. I illie buddah. Oi uv yooo. Oi uv i illie buddah. Come bas ee. Oi illie buddah.'

I rock him in my arms in the long green grass, and rock him, and rock him. And Daddy Mammy, his face is cold and there are no moves out of him at all. And Illy illy oi uv yooo. I uv yooo. And I cry from the bottom of my soul, my body going in little jerks with the sobs, and Illy Illy lying there in my arms, only moving when I move. Oh Illy Illy oi uv yooo uv yooo uv yooo! Come ba oo ee. Come ba oo ee. Illy Illy. Oi Illy Illy.

I don't know if I have fallen asleep, but it seems like only a few minutes since Miss Bevan left when I hear boots on the gravel at the far side of the cemetery gate. Gently I take my arm out from under Willie's head. Gently I lay his head in the green grass, the eyes looking at nothing. When I sit up I see the constable, with the funny hat, coming down my side of the stone stile. There are others with him.

A fierce anger springs up in me, because I know why they have come. They're going to take Willie. It's only when I stand that I remember the pain in my ankle. The minute that foot touches the ground it screams at me, but I hobble over to where the grass and the gravel meet. There's loose stones, as big as hen-eggs, all over the place. When I start throwing them the constable bellows, as if his voice alone could arrest me. His sounds have no shapes, just dread in them, but I keep throwing the stones. I have to keep moving my head because of the hurt eye. There's three of them altogether. The constable has his back to me. He's waving his arms at the others at the bottom of the stile, shouting at them. The other two start running and I throw at them. But I have to keep turning my back on some of them, because they are coming at me from three directions. When I stoop down for more stones the constable shouts, 'Now!'

They all start running towards me at the same time. I hobble back as fast as I can to Willie. When they get to me I have my arms around his neck, my fingers knitted. I press my face into Willie's neck, put my leg across his legs, my ankle screaming.

I know they are standing around looking down at us. I can feel feet against me when they move. They are talking, some of them talking the way people talk in the presence of the dead, others letting their hard voices fall all over the place – as loud and rough as metal buckets blowing along a yard in a storm. Someone touches my paining ankle and, before I can stop it, a cry of pain has jumped out of me. Someone says Jesus Christ. Someone kneels on the grass behind me, his knees touching my back. He says Seanie.

'Seanie, it's Uncle Enda, Seanie.' His mouth is close to my face. He smells the same way the Workhouse porter smells when we bring him the ale from the bottle house. It's Uncle Enda,' he says almost in a whisper. 'Uncle Enda, Seanie.'

Uncle Enda, I think. Uncle Enda was with us last night in Mister and Mrs Sheehan's house when we played the piano, when we laughed at the way Daddy tried to make his face fit the music. Uncle Enda was in the Bottling House last night and there was a fight against him. Uncle Enda jumped out of a grave a few minutes ago. That's who the giant was. Uncle Enda.

'It's Uncle Enda,' he says and his hands are getting firmer

on my shoulder. 'Seanie, we're here to take Willie home.'

When he says that I squeeze my fingers tighter and press my face deeper into Willie's neck. There's noise, voices, coming through my crying, loudness and anger. Suddenly it feels as if my knitted fingers have been crushed under a rock. A hand grabs me by the clothes at the back of my neck. I am pulled to my feet, my crushed fingers slipping apart of their own accord. I am flung aside. I stumble through the long green grass and fall on my face. Someone speaks.

'Stinking fucker.'

MISTER SHEEHAN

Camarán!

Where on earth could he have picked up that word? It hardly slipped to the surface from his memory because it couldn't have been there. But then I keep forgetting how capable Seanie was, he and Willie. After twenty-seven years it's easy to forget; seeing him hobbling around the Town – dirty, stinking, blind in one eye, unable to talk. Maybe the first thirteen years of knowledge and light, are in there, buried under the last twenty-seven of darkness. I don't know. I don't know what I'm trying to ...

This blessed money! I have to put it down again.

At least I'm as far as the Monument! Not only is the money-bag getting heavier, but the walk home is getting longer. I could bring the bike of course, but then my chances of meeting up with Seanie on the streets are lessened, and that's the only place I see him. It took many years of communal cruelty to turn him into a creature of the night. What does he think about as he steals around the Town, lurking in shadows, disappearing when he hears someone coming? In the summertime he leaves the shed when it's still bright, but it's off to the River he'll go, or to the Paupers' Cemetery, away from the people, limping behind high hedges, peeping through gaps before he climbs into new fields.

All this has happened to him because five idiots thought they were striking a blow for Ireland's freedom by boring holes in porter barrels. Patriots, they called themselves. Perhaps some time a monument will be erected to them, or maybe their names will be inscribed on the Monument there. I wonder what did those men really do in 1798 that brought them to the gallows. Did they do anything more imaginative than break a few porter barrels? Throw rocks from behind a hedge? Kill a child? And it's from their monument that the entire town will march tomorrow to the Church. When we have our '98 commemoration later in the year we'll march from the Church to the Monument.

Not to lose heart is the whole thing. I did lose heart once, I know, and I know the precise moment it happened. But I will not admit it to myself. I want to believe in God. I want to believe in the goodness of us people.

Tying my shoe-laces I was, with one foot up on the seat of a kitchen chair. The fresh shoe-polish on the laces was coming onto my fingers and I knew I'd have to be careful not to touch my new suit until I got to the sink. I was all dressed up in my best clothes. There wouldn't be time to come home after school to change. Peetie Mahon would come and get Caithleen in his taxi, and then meet the boys and myself outside the school at three o'clock. At half past three we would be in Queentown for the judge to legalize the adoption. Two Workhouse guardians would be there on behalf of the state.

The winter's sun was spilling into the early morning kitchen, filling it with brightness. Caithleen and I were as excited as children about to make their first communion. We hadn't slept much. I was impatient to get out of the house for the long walk to school. If I brought the bike I'd have to leave it there.

'You should eat something, MJ,' Caithleen said from the range.

'Put a few extra cuts of bread in the bag and I'll eat them in school,' I said. 'I can't eat now.'

With my hands stretched out from the white cuffs of my shirt I went to the sink. Over the sound of the running water Caithleen said in a raised voice, 'I heard a knock.'

I glanced up at the clock. Twenty past eight. 'It's your imagination,' I said. 'We're the only ones up for miles around.' I pressed the nail-brush into the soap and scrubbed my hands.

'There *is* someone!' Caithleen said, and she left the

kitchen.

When someone knocks at your door early in the morning there's something wrong. I rinsed off my hands, took the towel off its hook and went after Caithleen. When I came into the hall Enda was there. Caithleen had already closed the door behind him

'Enda!' I said. It looked as if he'd been in a fight, even though his shirt and suit were neat and fresh. One eye was swollen and his bottom lip was broken and swollen. His hair was combed.

'Are you alright?' I asked him, and I knew he wasn't . His eyes weren't focusing; there was fear in him. In those days Enda had a habit of brushing his fringe off his forehead with his fingers. It was a nervous habit, because most of the time his fringe was not on his forehead. In the hallway Enda indulged his tic and Caithleen gasped.

'Enda! Your hand! What on earth happened to you?'

Both of his hands were damaged, skinned knuckles, scratches on the backs. I smelled his breath.

'Enda,' I said, and I reached out to touch him. He withdrew so suddenly that Caithleen was startled and edged her way over to me. He held out his right hand as if indicating to us that he needed a minute to collect himself, to catch his breath, as it were. He looked at our feet or else his eyes were closed. His chest lifted suddenly and he straightened his shoulders. He looked at me first, then at Caithleen. It seemed to take an effort to focus his eyes.

'I have to tell you something terrible,' he said. He was drunk. He had lost his focus, his shoulders had slipped back into their slump. He raised his head and his focus went past us. A tremor shook all his face flesh.

'Say it, Enda!' I reached out to grasp his arm; to bring his eyes back to us.

But Enda stepped back and as he moved he said, 'Willie's dead.'

'You're drunk, Enda,' I said. Caithleen's hands tightened on my arm.

'He's dead, MJ, Caithleen, he's dead. Miss Bevan found

him dead this morning.'

'What are you saying, Enda?' Caithleen said sharply, the way she'd speak to an insistent child.

But Enda had his hand to his face, his thumb and finger squeezing the top of his nose between the eyes.

'Enda,' I said severely. 'Enda!'

When I stepped forward to grasp him, to shake him, Caithleen remained clutched to my arm. I hit him on the shoulder with the heel of my hand, hard. His head jerked up.

'What are you talking about, Enda?' I hit him again and he moved back, as if he wanted to put distance, more than physical distance, between us. He took in a deep breath.

'Willie fell last night and hit his head,' he said.

'Is he alright?' Caithleen asked. 'Say he's alright, Enda,' she pleaded. Enda seemed to be losing his focus again.

I shouted at him. 'Enda, why are you drunk? It's only eight o'clock in the morning.' I had never seen Enda drunk before. I have never seen him sober since.

Caithleen fled to where Enda was, his back to the front door. She grasped his forearm with her hands. 'Enda,' she said quietly. 'Enda, how is he? Where is he? Enda!' She shook his arm and suddenly she was hysterical. 'Enda! Tell me he's not dead! Tell me he's not dead!' Her hands flew up to his jacket lapels. She shook him, and then she saw the water flowing out of Enda's face. His voice sounded out into the hall through stringy saliva and uncontrolled muscles.

'He's dead, Caithleen. He's dead.' He put his arms around her and pulled her head into his shoulder. His face was all misshapen, his big body jerked like a dying fish.

I was bristling with numbness. Grief and anger welled up out of me and I roared in anguish. Slumping forward I pounded the wall above my head with clenched fists.

'NO!' I bellowed. 'NO, NO, NO, NO, NO!' Then I was sobbing. I went over to Caithleen to take her from Enda's arms, to put her arms around me. The moment I touched her she jerked her face out of Enda's shoulder.

'You're lying, Enda,' she screamed. 'You're drunk, Enda.

Willie's not dead.' She started to beat him on the chest. 'Why are you doing this? Why, Enda? Stop doing this. Say he's not dead. Willie's not dead, Enda. Stop it.'

I put my hands on her shoulders to turn her towards me. She spun around at the pressure. Caithleen! She was like a wild thing that had never known tameness.

'Get away from me,' she screamed. She put her back to the wall and stretched her arms tightly around her chest. She glared at me like a wounded cat at a farmer coming with a shovel to finish it off.

'Ask him how. What happened?'

Enda had his two hands to his face, his head bent down.

'TELL US!'

The screech shook Enda. When he lowered his hands he was changed. He seemed to have sobered. He spoke carefully.

'They were up at the Yewtree Cemetery. He fell off the pillar with the stile in it. He fell onto the gate. One of the spikes went into his forehead.'

'God!' Caithleen gasped, and she buried her face in her hands. 'God God God,' she said, the words muffled.

Enda fell back into his alcoholic haze. He swayed forward and, for a moment, I thought he would totter. Caithleen's crying stopped suddenly. She drew her hands down her face and the red of her lower eyelids glistened. She spoke almost normally.

'You've made a mistake, Enda. Oh God! Enda, you made a terrible mistake. It can't be Willie. Willie and Seanie were here last night until twenty to seven. You were, too. It always takes them twenty minutes to get back to the Workhouse along the river bank. Enda, you're wrong. It's not Willie. How could they even be near the cemetery? It's a mile beyond the Workhouse.'

My heart clanged with hope when I heard Caithleen. The boys were never late for the Workhouse curfew.

Enda was searching for a handkerchief by the time Caithleen had finished speaking, and as he searched he shook his head. In the hallway the sound of his nose-blowing was magnified. Before he removed the handkerchief from his face he said something that was too muffled for either Caithleen or myself to understand.

'What?' we said at the same time.

In his drunkenness and grief Enda was maddening. He cleared the emotion from his throat on the third attempt. As he fumbled the handkerchief back into his pocket he said, while not looking at either of us, 'They were drunk.'

Caithleen stared at him. 'Who was drunk?'

Enda looked from Caithleen to me, his eyes squinting.

'The constable came at half six this morning and brought me up to the Yewtree Cemetery in Peetie Mahon's taxi. When we got there Willie and Seanie were on the ground inside the gate. Seanie had his arms around Willie's neck, hugging him. Willie had a hole in his forehead. He was dead. There was a smell of ale on them.'

'Did you see Willie yourself, Enda?' I asked. Caithleen's hands went to her mouth. My knees were weak. I put a hand on the wall to steady myself. Enda's focus was gone out through the window at the end of the hall, and I shocked everyone when I shouted, 'Enda! Did you see Willie dead?'

'I did, MJ,' he said. 'Willie is dead.'

'Oh God!' Caithleen said. She fell or knelt down in the hallway, her face in her hands, her body bending forward until her forehead touched the floor. She began to rock, saying over and over, 'Oh God! Oh God!'

The next thing I remember was being face to face with Enda, him trying to look sideways, me with a bunch of his shirt in my fist. I shook him till he looked at my eyes. 'Are you sure you saw Willie? Are you absolutely certain?' I know I was spitting. I know there was despair in my voice, in my eyes. Enda's head fell over to one side. I shook him again. 'Look at me, Enda. Look at me. Was it Willie?'

When he spoke he was looking at my chin, my nose. He wasn't looking in my eyes.

'It was Willie, MJ,' he said, almost whispering. 'It was Willie. There is no mistake.' He raised his eyes to mine. 'I'm terribly sorry, MJ.'

I kept my hold on the shirt. I said, 'Were you drunk when you saw him, Enda?' I had to shake the answer out of him.

'No. Afterwards I got drunk to come to tell you.'

'Where's Seanie, Enda?'

His head fell over. I shook him again, drove my fisted knuckles into his chest. 'Where's Seanie?'

'He ran away.'

'Where? Where, Enda?'

'I don't know.'

'Enda, you must do something. Do you hear me! How did you get here?'

'Pettie Mahon's taxi. He's outside.' Enda's head rolled on his neck.

'Go to Nurse Molloy, Enda, and be back here with her in less than five minutes.' I opened the front door and I steered him on his way. Leaving the door ajar for the nurse, I went back to Caithleen on the floor. All the way up the stairs she said names.

'Oh! MJ, MJ, Willie is dead. Willie's dead. Deirdre and Eileen and now Willie. Willie Willie.'

Half-way up the stairs she gave a loud cry and stopped.

'MJ. Where's Seanie? Seanie will need ... Oh MJ! Get Seanie and bring him. Willie. Oh God! Deirdre and Eileen.' She moved upward again, calling to them, calling them to her. 'Deirdre, Eileen. Willie's dead, Deirdre.' Then she stopped again and, God have mercy on her, she said quietly: 'MJ. There is no God. There is no God at all. It was silly of me to believe again after the girls. There is no God, MJ.' She stroked the length of my face, felt and saw my tears. 'You, too, MJ. You feel it like I do. I'm terribly sorry, MJ.'

She moved again and I had her lying on the bed when Nurse Molloy walked into the room. 'Dr McKenna told me what happened. I'll take care of her.' She knew we were about to adopt the boys. As the representative of the Workhouse she had inspected our fitness to adopt.

I said, 'I have to ...' But she interjected, 'Wherever you go, be back here by eleven o'clock.'

Caithleen was staring into the distance. She held her

hand out, turned her head towards me and asked, 'Where are you going, MJ?'

I took her hand. 'I'm going to find Seanie.'

'Poor Seanie,' she said. 'Poor Willie!' and she started crying, not covering the ugliness in the face that crying makes. Nurse Molloy steered me out of the room.

'Eleven o'clock, Mister Sheehan,' she said.

In those days the RIC Barracks was just the far side of where Peetie Mahon's shop is now. It was there I was heading on my bike. I had a fierce sadness in me, and a fierce anger and the only thing giving it purpose was the need to find out about Willie and to find Seanie. It was for Seanie I was afraid, afraid that he would not be able to bear this last blow.

The constable's name was McSherry, a big simpleton of a man from Kilkenny; rotund, red-faced, as soft-looking as a baby. He was a young man. When he came to the door he was chewing with his mouth open, and there was egg-yolk at the middle of his top lip.

Without the usual courtesies I asked him if Willie Doolin was dead.

'Who?' he asked.

'Willie Doolin,' I said, realizing this man's stupidity was going to be as bothersome as Enda's drunkenness had been. 'The boy from the Workhouse. Up at the Yewtree Cemetery.'

'Oh him. The pauper. That's his name! I was trying to remember it. Miss Bevan mentioned his name.'

'Is he dead?' I asked him.

'Dead as a doornail,' he said. 'I knew it myself, but the law says the doctor has to say it, drunk or sober.' I only heard his last remark when I was looking down at Willie's pauper coffin in the pauper grave, in the Paupers' Cemetery, myself and Miss Bevan.

'Where is he?'

'Who? The doctor?'

'No, the boy, the dead boy. Where is he?'

'We took him to The Workhouse. He's theirs.'

'Did you see his brother, his twin brother, Seanie?' At this point I wanted to strangle the man, God forgive me.

'He's up in the cemetery. Mahon had to crack his hands between two stones to make him let go of the dead one. The stink on the two of them! Porter and shite.'

I glared at him. 'Mahon didn't have to do that,' I said loudly, and before I could stop myself I shouted, 'And Willie Doolin was not a pauper, you big halfwit! He was a boy.' I know I did not educate the constable, knew I wasn't even trying. He was just someone to shout at.

I turned and left him to finish his egg. Even he, isolated as he was from the people, shared the people's rejoicing in their superiority to the pauper boy. As I mounted the bike I felt I had to vomit, to cry. A clammy sweat oozed through me as I pedalled madly through the nightmare that had already trapped Caithleen. 'Stop doing this,' I heard her cry again. 'Say he's not dead. Willie's not dead, Enda. Stop it. I can't wake up!'

I cried all the way to the Yewtree Cemetery; past the Church, over Madden's Bridge, around the corner onto Red Hugh O'Donnell Road. Some children were already at the school, calling my name as I sped by.

It was an uphill climb all the way from the school, and when my muscles screamed for relief I ignored them to the point where I had to stop, get off the bike. But off the bike I ran, until a different set of muscles cried. On the bike again, but off the saddle, I sawed from side to side. Finally, my chest on fire with so much cool air, I came to the head of the short lane that leads up to the gate of the Cemetery. I flung the bike into the bushes at the side of the road.

The lane off the road is narrow, a low earthen embankment on each side, covered with bushes. The short journey along that overgrown path is burned into me. I thought I would never reach the iron gate at the end, nausea sweeping through me, legs like rubber. I was calling for Seanie, but I knew no one could hear me, only myself. I also knew that this lonely place, eerie in its silence, in its distance from living people, was not a place Seanie and Willie would have come to by themselves at night-time, or in the daytime. Willie was too nervous for that kind of adventure.

When I reached the iron gate I grasped the upright bars. My legs trembled, but the nausea had passed.

'Seanie,' I cried through the bars. 'Seanie,' I cried and the tears started again, started again and interfered with my voice. My hands slipped down the bars and I knelt in the gravel on the lane. 'Seanie,' I cried and I could only hear myself in my head.

Again the tears are on my face. What's wrong with me tonight? Why all this remembering, all this sadness? Caithleen and Deirdre and Eileen and Willie. Was it meeting Seanie that brought it all on?

Camarán. The poor boy. Oh dear God! here they come again, running down my face, tickling my lips. Down with the money-bag again and out with the handkerchief. They wouldn't let me bury Willie in our family plot. He was a pauper, a guest of the nation, and the nation would bury him; the final indignity. More tears. I'll have to stop this. If you don't wipe the wet tears off the bottom of your glasses they dry of their own accord and leave a streaky deposit behind them. That's one way you can tell a person has been crying. This is the second time tonight I've had to stop and dry my glasses. At least it's dark here. There's just one street-light on the far corner, over on Clarke Street, and there are lights on up in Joe Butler's; shouting too, like someone shouting at an animal.

I put the glasses on, and there are two lanterns bobbing around in the dark. Then I hear the hoofs of a running animal on the tarred road.

'Stop the bullock, stop the bullock!' someone shouts.

There's an animal on the loose! As fast as I can, I go over and stand at the end of Clark Street where it runs into the Four Streets. Stretching out my arms, I make noise with my shuffling feet and shout, 'Whoa boy! Whoa boy!' The running hoofs slow down. In the dimness of the street-light I see the head of the big bullock, puffs of wet breath shunting out of flared nostrils.

One of the lanterns moves cautiously along the hedge until it's on my side of the animal. It's Joe Butler. He's panting.

'Hello Joe,' I say.

'Mister Sheehan! Thank you. This lad got away on us. Only you were here he could have gone anywhere. I'm sorry for shouting, sir. I didn't know it was you.'

Joe Butler moves off with his animal.

I'm glad I was there, glad something happened to distract me from my thoughts.

I'll go back for the money-bag and head home.

DOCTOR McKENNA

If I close the car door quietly Quinn and Dickingson won't hear me. There's the other slipper, snagged on a spring under the seat. But it's like trying to get the hook out of a fish's gullet. My forehead is on the steering-wheel, my hands between my legs, and I'm red in the face from pulling the slipper. Finally an almighty yank tears it free. Of course when I put it on I can feel it's loose, because I've ripped the heel. Seerey's! I wonder why the nuns didn't give me a new pair last Christmas. What did they give me? It could have been a scarf or gloves. I have enough scarves and gloves to outfit a whole tribe of Eskimos, and I never wear scarves or gloves. Buttons too. Two buttons for my overcoat while I'm getting the slippers.

I should get away from here. But the key! Where in God's name did I put it? It's not in my overcoat. Trying to get at my other pockets, without getting out of the car, is like wrestling with half a dozen blankets in the dark. I can't find the damn thing, and Quinn will be sticking his head out, looking for me. Jakers! It's in the ignition all the time. Damn! Let me get to hell out of here.

The engine sounds like a volcano on the empty street. I take off like a bat out of hell and head for the Cinema yard to turn.

A Spiritual Bouquet! That's what they gave me, the nuns last Christmas. A Spiritual Bouquet! So many Rosaries, so many Holy Hours, so many Ejaculations, so many First Fridays – all offered up for my intentions. For my intentions! They really mean *their* intentions, and their intention is that I stop drinking. I can see it on their faces when I turn up half plastered to examine a sick nun. Beluga. Their faces

115

reflect how I smell, how drunk I am. It's not a Spiritual Bouquet I need. It's a magic wand to change the past I need, and a pair of slippers and two buttons.

I miss the place in the footpath that is sloped to the street and the two right wheels bounce over the kerb when I drive into the Cinema yard. I make a big circle and wheel back out onto the street. Nothing coming, of course, at this hour of the night. It must be after twelve. About a hundred yards past Peetie Mahon's shop I stop the car and get out. It's no use driving around the streets looking for Seanie. He'll be in a gateway or a laneway. He'll be in a shadow someplace. My ripped slipper scrapes the footpath with every step I take away from the car. Then I think of the flash-lamp I keep under the seat for when I go out into the country at night. You'd fall into ditches and step in cow dungs. It's easy to find because I always keep it in the same place.

I poke the darkness of doorways and gateways with the beam as I walk along. At the same time I lilt his name softly.

'Shaw-nee. Shaw-nee.'

Shaw-nee Shaw-nee. That's what Willie kept crying out when they, when we ...

Every now and then I stop and shine the light at the shadows across the street. He could be anywhere. I'm tempted to go home, to leave him alone. He has survived a lot worse than being slapped around by Peetie Mahon.

'Shaw-nee. Shaw-nee.'

That bastard is sick in the head. He loves to kill. I'd swear he killed that old uncle of his, who happened to fall head first into the grate of his fireplace. If you happen to hit your head into something you only hit it once; you don't keep bouncing into it like a rubber ball.

'Shaw-nee. Shaw-nee.'

He inherited enough to buy that shop of his. It was Mahon who started the whole thing about killing Seanie and Willie. And then the cute bastard! When it came to pulling the trigger the bold Peetie stepped aside and let Butler do it.

'Shaw-nee.'

Here's Plumtree Lane. If he's anywhere he's down there.

116

No street-lights, all shadows. The lane goes down between the back yards to the Playing Field, high wall each side. But he could be anywhere. I'm wasting my bloody time. All the time I spent out looking for him after they, we, killed Willie. Goddam! Say it, say it! I killed Willie. I killed Willie. And I'm to blame for Seanie. I'm to blame for Caithleen Sheehan. I did it.

'I did it.'

Damn! I said it out loud and frightened myself. I did it by not stopping the others. John Cashin put up a better fight than I did. Cashin was the only one who took my side. If only he had sided with me in the Bottling House! We only started fighting the others after they killed Willie.

The beam of the flash-lamp, and the darkness of this lane, are dragging me back to the Bottling House. God, no! I can't go back there.

My slippers! That's what I'll think about. The right slipper makes that scratchy sound on the laneway every time I take a step. My feet are cold. Tomorrow I'll go to Seerey's before the parade. Why do I have to go before the parade? There's something else too. The buttons for the overcoat! Slippers and buttons.

'Shaw-nee. Shaw-nee.'

That's what Willie kept crying. It's the darkness and the silence and the beam of the light. I think I'll go home. But jakers! If I do Quinn will call me again to take care of her ladyship.

It was Miss Dickingson, An Tarav's favourite runner, who brought the orders to raid the Bottling House. Stupid bloody orders they were: raid the Bottling House, break the barrels and let all the porter run off. I told her it was stupid when she came to tell me. 'Stupid or not,' says she, 'they're the orders from An Tarav.'

An Tarav! The Bull. A *nom de guerre*. IRA commandant for this part of the county; giving orders for burnings and killings. The whole thing goes back to him. He was never told that Willie was killed, that Seanie went mad, because of him. He never even knew them.

'Shaw-nee. Shaw-nee.'

I say it a bit louder, now that I'm away from the houses. I'm almost at the Playing Field. I can smell the hawthorns. It's chilly out here. I'll have a good drink when I go home, to keep away the ague, to keep away what happened. It's always there waiting to burst in and display itself to me, a whole mess of maggots, waiting to burst into my brain.

Stop!

'Shaw-nee. Shaw-nee.' I sound the word out into the darkness of the lane. There's the Playing Field now. The beam of the flash-lamp gleams on the goal-posts at the near end.

'It's Uncle Enda,' I call. 'Shaw-nee. Shaw-nee.'

That's what Willie kept calling out in the Bottling House. Shawnee. Shawnee. Goddam! Stop it! Stop! Stop! Stop! It's the beam of the flash-lamp and the dark and the silence. Shawnee, Shawnee. No! Stop it. It was as if I'd stepped into another world when I lit up the two boys with the beam of my lamp. There was total silence in the Bottling House.

Three hours earlier the twins had left the Sheehans to go back to the Workhouse. The five of us had spent a grand afternoon together, the boys splashing wonderful music out of Caithleen's piano. MJ and Caithleen were about to get two new children. The boys were not only getting a father and mother; they were about to leave the horror of the Workhouse behind them. They wouldn't be paupers anymore. They wouldn't be orphans. Since the two girls had died Caithleen hadn't looked so well, so happy. The air was thick with joy.

The boys, who had made us laugh at their memories of their dead parents, were now two terrified animals lying in filth. Oh God! Oh God! They were sitting on the floor with the porter flowing under them, terrified in the beam of light, the smell of the porter rising like the smell of a primeval swamp.

Oh God!

Their arms are around each other, Willie whimpering 'Shawnee Shawnee,' his face buried in Seanie's shoulder as if he's trying to keep a horror away by not looking at it.

Stop looking at it. Stop it.

'Stop it. Stop it.'

The others are behind me in the dark, silent at first, looking down at the boys in the beam of my flash-lamp. Then there's words. Horrible sounds, frightening, floating on the stink of the porter.

'Shaw-nee Shaw-nee,' I shout out into the field, desperation, fear in the sound. My feet are wet from the dew on the grass.

Seanie pushes himself back against the wall with his heels, one hand on the back of Willie's head, the other arm across his front. In the stinking mist the horrible words float again.

'It's them or us.'

And I hear my own angry words filling up the Bottling House, my anger feeding on my fear.

'It's not going to be them.'

It's as if there's a pack of wolves baying behind me in the dark, in front their cornered prey. My anger consumes my fear, as if I know that anger is the only thing that will get the boys safely out of here.

'It's not a question of them or us,' I say. 'They haven't seen anyone.' Then I shout at the boys, 'Get up! Get out of here! Get out and don't come back!'

The boys don't move. They're too frightened to move.

A heavy hand falls on my shoulder. 'Nobody's leaving here yet, Doc,' Peetie Mahon says. That bastard. 'They heard us, Doc. They heard us using each other's names. And maybe they did see us.'

Seanie is crying now. Maybe Willie is too, only I can't see his face. If only MJ were here. Seanie turns his face away from the light, twists his head until his cheek is resting in Willie's hair. Tiny waves of porter flow under the boys.

'They're only paupers from the Workhouse. No one will miss them.'

On my neck I can feel the breath of the wolves.

'We're not going to touch them,' I say. 'We'll find out what they're doing here and let them go.'

'Shaw-nee Shaw-nee.' To my knees I fall in the wet grass at the goal-posts in The Playing Field.

Behind me in the dark I sense an impatient movement running through the pack; it's in the harsh words, the grunts of support, in the shuffling feet. I know a challenge to my leadership is going to be made and I know who that bastard challenger is going to be.

'We can go to jail for what we've done here, Doc,' Peetie Mahon says. 'There's no question of letting them go. The Black and Tans could shoot us for this.'

Sarcastically, over my shoulder I say, 'And what are we going to do with them, Peetie? Kill them so we won't go to jail?'

'It's them or us,' he says.

It's obvious that the boys are hearing what we're saying. Seanie tries to push himself into the wall, and he tightens his grip on Willie. I turn to the four men behind me.

'We'll go outside and talk about this,' I say, and start walking towards the door.

'There's nothing to talk about, Doc,' Peetie Mahon calls after me.

'That's right,' Michael Butler says. 'It's them or us.'

I stop and turn around. For a long time there is only the sounds of the boys in the Bottling House.

'Shaw-nee Shaw-nee,' I roar into the darkness of The Playing Field. 'Shaw-nee Shaw-nee, I'll help you.'

The hairs on the back of my neck are moving, my stomach is floating of its own accord when I come back to where the men are standing, the beam of light at their feet shining in the flowing porter. My whisper is so fierce it comes out like a hiss.

'We are not going to kill anyone. Now, come on out and we'll talk about this outside.'

John Cashin and Jack Quinlan-the-Blacksmith begin to move towards me, and, before I know what he's doing, Peetie Mahon is going towards the boys. He switches on his flash-lamp, shines the beam in Seanie's face and grabs him by his Workhouse fringe.

'Stand up!' he snarls.

'Let him go, Peetie!' I say.

Seanie cries out in pain and Willie cries out in fear at the same time. Mahon pulls Seanie to his feet, Seanie's hands grasping at the pain in his head.

'Let him go, Peetie!' I say again. I stride over and put my hand on Mahon's shoulder. 'Let him go!'

Peetie Mahon ignores me.

'What are you doing here?' Mahon asks Seanie, violence in his voice. Seanie's mouth is wide open, his eyes bulging.

'Let him go!' I shake Peetie Mahon again. 'Let him go, Peetie. That's an order!' and behind me I hear Michael Butler mutter, 'Fuck the orders. It's them or us.'

Willie has scrambled to his feet and he grabs at Peetie Mahon's fingers in Seanie's hair. Willie is making crying sounds that come to a sudden stop when Mahon smashes him in the mouth with his flash-lamp.

'Willie Willie. Oh God! Caithleen. MJ. I couldn't stop them. I tried I tried. I did try. I did. I did.'

The dreadful feeling that I am losing control falls over me like an icy shroud. Weakness flashes in and out of my knees. Willie is bent in two, hands to his face. Seanie tries to hit Peetie Mahon in the face and has his head slammed into the concrete again. For an instant Seanie loses control of his eyes. From behind him I swing my right arm around Peetie Mahon's neck. I don't squeeze hard, just enough pressure to let him know I can hurt him.

'Let him go, Peetie!' I say. 'We're going to stop all this nonsense now.'

There is silence in the Bottling House that seems to last a long time. Maybe it does. I can see Seanie's face, unbelieving, a mask of terror.

When I hear shuffling feet behind me I turn, move the front of my body away from Peetie Mahon. With a short movement of his left arm, Mahon jams his flash-lamp into my testicles.

The leadership of the local IRA cell is snatched from me before my knees plop onto the concrete floor. The fate of the two boys is determined before I keel over into the flowing porter, hands in my crotch.

'Forgive me, MJ. Forgive me Willie. It was all so stupid. So goddam stupid. SHAW-NEE!'

God God God. How long ago is it since I've cried for Willie? The poor little bastard. It was me that should have been killed trying to save him. I could have saved him. John Cashin would have been on my side, only then I didn't know it, not until the Cemetery. Jack Quinlan would have been neutral because he couldn't have made up his mind whether to be faithful to his IRA oath, and obey me, or to be afraid of Michael Butler and Peetie Mahon. We could have beaten them in the Bottling House if I had handled it differently. We should have attacked them in the Cemetery before they killed Willie. We attacked too late to save Seanie – he had already been destroyed.

I curse God and I curse myself and I curse Ireland and her weak rebellions. For God's sake! We struck against the might of the British Empire by breaking open barrels of porter! And Willie died because he was unfortunate enough to see us – five big fucking eejits playing at being revolutionaries. I wish it had been me they shot. Living with this mess of maggots for how long? Twenty-seven drunken years.

I can't forgive myself for what I did to the Sheehans. I can't abandon Seanie, leave him here in this town to be beaten by the likes of Mahon. Why does he still beat him? Is it for the same reason that I try to protect him? Why does everyone treat him the way they do? Don't they know what's inside him, that trapped mad thirteen-year-old who saw his twin brother being murdered by four, five, big men using a humane killer – a thing that's used to kill cows and bullocks – the six-inch spike of metal shooting through the skull. No wonder Seanie went mad, no wonder he went mad. Who wouldn't! Oh God!

'SHAW-NEE SHAW-NEE!'

Oh Jesus. How sad. How terribly fucking sad.

I wish I had the balls to kill myself. I use Seanie as an excuse. I live to take care of Seanie, I tell myself. I stay drunkenly alive to take care of Willie's brother. But I don't take care of him. I only imagine I do, like I imagine I tried to save them in the Bottling House, a half-hearted effort, grateful that I got smacked in the balls so I wouldn't have to be killed. It was a good show, McKenna.

I haven't done anything for Seanie since That Night in the Cemetery. And what did I do for him! Fight for him when it was too late, when Willie was dead, when Seanie was mad. Then we all ran away because someone was coming.

In the Playing Field I drag myself to my feet, the trousers wet to the knees, the slippers soaked.

I'll look for him. I'll go and get John Cashin out of bed. We'll look for Seanie together. I'll go home and get a quick drink first.

It takes me a few minutes to figure out how to get back to Plumtree Lane. Finally it's the silhouette of the houses in the Town against the night sky that helps me to find it.

In the distance I hear the bawling of an animal.

SEANIE DOOLIN

I was lying there for a long time, my head resting in the grass, my knees pulled up, my hands in my fork. They were warm there.

I was staring down the hill forever. Forever staring. It was nice to stare, the stalky grass of winter a forest in my eye; the dried stalks moving in the wind like distant and bare trees; all moving so gently in the wind that shakes the barley in the summer. I didn't feel the wind because there was a thick hedge against my back. They were all moving, waving silently from side to side; moving together, sometimes out of harmony bumping into each other; dancing dancing *fluttering and dancing in the breeze*.

Far away there were things moving, four round things rolling on the tree-tops, like balls floating. Then there were six all in a row, going up and down as the trees beneath them moved in the wind. Up and down they went and down, but they never dropped below the tree-tops, *below the kirk, below the quay below the lighthouse top*. They came closer all the time, getting bigger until they were heads on shoulders, all moving closer to me silently. Then there were heads and shoulders and swinging arms, and there were sounds too. Words and pieces of words floating over me.

Boys.

Featureless they stood there looking down, looking.

'The stink!'

'Is he dead or what?'

'His eyes are open.'

'The stink of him!'

'Look at his other eye, it's all bleeding.'

'He's one of the twins out of the Workhouse.'

'We know that, you eejit. All you have to do is look at his fringe.'

There was silence. Then:

'Give him a poke with the stick, Billy.'

I was poked in the belly, the way you would poke a dead badger in the belly to see its liquid guts moving around inside its stretched skin,

'He's alive alright.'

'He's alive alright. He's just pretending so we won't touch him.'

'He's so stinking he could be dead!'

'Poke him in the balls. That will make him move whether he's pretending or not.'

The stick tried to get past my warm hands in my fork.

'His hands are in the way.'

'Pull them out of the way.'

'You pull them out of the way.'

'The stink!'

There was silence. Someone walked behind me, caught the sleeve and tried to pull my arm up. He grunted. He let go of the sleeve.

'I think he's dead and stiff.'

The ones in front of me moved back.

'You're all cowards. He's not dead at all.'

'Pull his fringe.'

'You pull it.'

'He might bite me.'

'He's dead.'

'He's not.'

'He could be, he's so stinky!'

'How could he be dead, you eejits! Look at his chest going up and down.'

'Pull his fringe and we'll soon see if he's dead or not.'

'You're all so brave.'

There was silence. There was no movement. Between the legs of one of the boys I saw a strange thing – a horse with a rider moving across the hill of stalky grass and up the hill too. It was a nice picture, the rider going up and down without effort in perfect harmony with the trot of the horse.

Someone behind me moved my head. There were fingers in my hair. The hair was tugged back and forth. I felt the grass under the side of my face scraping, not hurting. My head was pulled up and then let go. The grass came against my face. The horse and rider were gone from between the boy's legs.

'He's pretending.'

'We'll see if he can pretend this away.'

The swish a thin stick makes, when it's quickly swung, was in the air. A painless numbness fell into my thigh. One of the boys almost shouted.

'Jesus! It's Miss-Bevan-the-Protestant.'

There was silence. Someone behind me said, 'There's a gap down here.'

The boys went away. The horse came into my eye again. It had no legs because of the long stalks of grass. As it came closer I saw the legs appearing, easily moving silently along, the rider moving so well with the horse they were one animal.

Centaur.

I could see where the blacksmith had twisted off the nails that came through the hoofs when he shod the horse. Then the legs of the rider came down, high shiny boots. The knees bent and there were white trousers stuffed into the boot-tops.

'Seanie!' It was a woman. She sat on her hunkers, her knees stretching the white trousers tight. A soft hand was on my cheek. 'You poor child.' The hand was on my forehead. 'Your eye, Seanie. What happened to your eye, you poor child?'

A hand went under my face, a hand on the top; like a farmer's wife holding a shape of butter between two paddles, getting the butter ready to sell to a shop. There was a smell of primroses.

'Can you talk, Seanie?' One hand stayed beneath my face. The other ran down my body, followed my left leg to the ankle that was hurt. She touched it kindly and the pain flared like an angry rat, little sharp teeth showing. 'You poor boy. Can you get up?' She was looking at me, even though all I could see was the tight white cloth at her bent knees. She stroked the top side of my face. 'You poor boy.'

Gently she pulled her soft warm hand out from under my face. 'I'm going to leave you for a while, Seanie. I'm going to get Mister Sheehan. But I'll be back.' Her knees creaked when she stood up. 'I'll give you the mare's blanket to keep you warm.'

For a while the booted legs stood there, the toes pointing down the hill. The horse's feet never moved in the grass. The woman grunted and bent over quickly. She laid the saddle on the ground. Her toes turned back to me. I heard the noise a blanket makes when you shake it out. Suddenly I was covered with warmth, my head left out. The knees bent again and her hand was on my shoulder. 'I'll be back in a little while, Seanie.'

There was a grunt and the horse's saddle went off the ground. In a while she went away, getting smaller down the hill, the horse's legs disappearing, then its belly, and then only the woman floating on top of the moving tree-tops. And then she was gone. I looked at the spot where she disappeared, the grass tree-tops moving and bending.

I was so warm, so comfortable I could have fallen asleep. But if she knew where I was, and if the boys knew where I was, I wouldn't be left alone under the snug blanket. So, painfully I stood on that ankle. I would go away, keep walking until I was so far away from where I was that she'd never think I had gone away that far; nor the boys.

Before I had gone a hundred yards there was a badger's burrow in the leafless hedge. I stood to look at it; one of those old burrows that had been there for years, sand falling away from the gaping hole, the sand there for so long that little trees were growing in it, and grass in clumps.

Feet first I eased down into the sloping hole. I couldn't put the blanket over me. The hole was too narrow. Out I came, a badger, I was, with a sore ankle, and it was lucky I did. The marks of my boots were in the sand. All the time, while backing down into the burrow again, I scratched at the boot-marks until they were only damp patches. Feet first I went down, the blanket caught between my boots, my ankle crying. Down I went until I couldn't see out. If I can't see out, they can't see in, I thought.

So snug, it was. So quiet. I wasn't afraid. My own smell, and the smell of the horse on the blanket, would keep any animal away. For years I slept there. I'd waken sometimes and feel the cosiness. Then I'd go back to sleep for more years; sleep and sleep in a great deep place. It was so nice, deep and dark, no breeze, no cold, no noise, no dreams; just sleep and sleep and cosiness. It was like how nice it is to sleep when you are so tired you will either sleep or die.

Years later I woke up. The tiredness was gone. I could get up again. But I lay there for a long time thinking about getting out, about leaving the cosiness. As the cosiness decreased it got easier. My body was stiff. I had to turn over. I had to scratch and make number one and maybe number two. I had to run for a while. Run and jump and roll around in the grass to get the cramps out.

When I put my right foot on the ground I made a noise, it was so stiff, my ankle. I folded the blanket away and hopped out through the bushes.

Boys were less than twenty yards away, standing like statues, standing as if they had heard a wild animal in the bushes, waiting for it to run out and tear them apart. I turned away from them and started to hobble along the side of the hedge. I knew there would be shouting.

'It's him!'

They were running, their boots making swishes in the grass.

'His trousers!'

'They're covered with dry shite!'

I got a kick in the bad ankle. When I fell someone plopped down across my shoulders and lay there. I was as helpless as a Christmas turkey waiting for the knife across its throat. Rough hands pulled my trousers off without opening the buttons that were looped into my braces. I was turned over and caught by the feet, pulled away from the hedge on my bare bottom. They danced around me like children playing ring-a-ring-a-rosie. But they chanted hard words at me and pointed at my fork. The one with my trousers twirled them over his head. I waited for them to finish. They would go away.

'Follow me, lads.'

The others fell in behind the one with the trousers. He stopped at the hedge. When he let go they cheered. The trousers went into a whitethorn bush. With the toes of their boots they kicked clods out of the ground. The way they shouted was worse than the clods that hit me. The sound of the shouting was worse than the words they shouted. The sounds made me feel like I was a curse, like a disease, like the leper with the bell.

They went away.

I lay in the grass. Like icy feathers the chill wind played around my legs and belly. The wet cold of the earth seeped into my bottom. I was hungry. I had to do number one.

It wasn't difficult to get the trousers with a stick. The wind blew up my front and back when I stretched upwards. I peed before I put the trousers on.

I didn't know where there was food. I knew I'd have to go somewhere; find a house. I followed the hedge to the gap where the boys had gone. There, higher up the hill, was a house. When I got close it was only a shed for the cattle to keep warm in winter and get away from the flies in the summer. There was a loft, with nothing but hay in it. I was hoping there might be a few turnips.

I sat in the hay. The nice musty smell and the shelter from the breeze dulled the hunger. This would be a nice place to live. Soft warm hay. A roof. I would bring my blanket up here.

It was down the hill, I decided, I should be going to look for a place to sleep, for food. I stopped and peeped, this time, before I stepped out through the gap. There was a man on the other side. He was near the bush where my trousers had been. His back was to the hedge. Quietly I crept along my side of the hedge until I was almost opposite him. I knelt down behind a clump of briars to watch him. A brown paper bag was grasped in his fingers behind his back.

The man turned towards where I was kneeling. I thought he had seen me. When he suddenly called out he startled me.

'Seanie. Seanie.'

His voice rolled, it was so big. Slowly it rolled up the hill, passing through every nook and cranny in its way.

'Seanie. Seanie.'

He stepped closer to the hedge, peered through. He was ten feet from where I was hiding. He had glasses. For a long time he looked through the hedge. I didn't move.

'Seanie. Seanie. I have food for you. Come here and get it.' Bo boom bo boom bo booooom.

For another long time he stood silent, watching. I looked at the ground to rest my eye. At my knees there were snow-drop shoots, the same as daffodil shoots, but shorter.

The noise the big man made startled me again. It was a gulping sob that jumped out of him, twisting his mouth out of shape. The big man didn't cover his face. He just looked straight ahead. Tears fell off his chin to the ground.

'Seanie, Seanie,' he whispered. 'I love you.' He covered his face with his hands and bent forward. Sobs shook him. I was embarrassed. I looked back at the snowdrop shoots.

'Seanie, Seanie,' his voice rolled out. 'I'm leaving a bag of food for you at this whitethorn bush. Seanie, we love you.'

The man went away. He went down the hill, getting shorter and smaller. I pulled my eye back to rest it, but I saw where he disappeared into the hedge at the bottom of the field. I waited for a long time. It was almost dark when I went around to look at the bag.

Every day there was food at the whitethorn bush.

The boys caught me one more time. I wasn't used to not seeing a whole space that I had been able to see. This time they took off all my clothes, except for my boots. They tied my hands around a thin tree with my back to the trunk.

They piled clothes and wet them with water from a bottle. When the bottle was empty all except one backed away from the pile. He struck a match and threw it. There was a shoosh and red flames jumped out of the ground. The boys cheered. When the flames got low they poked the ashes with sticks. I was very cold. They called me Blindeye.

When they started throwing clods at me, one of the boys shouted, 'See who can hit Blindeye's mickey first.'

I pulled my hands, tried to get them out of the twine they had used on my wrists. I kept my face down, my chin on my chest, so I wouldn't get hit in my good eye. I pulled.

There were no more stones or clods, no more shouting. Someone said softly, 'It's the fucking Chief.'

I looked up, moved my head all around, but they were gone. The man with the big voice was coming. I pulled my hands.

'Seanie! Don't hurt your hands. I'll get you out,' he shouted.

I pulled, and the twine came off one of my hands. I ran along the hedge to the gap, a big piece of skin flapping against the back of my hand. When I went through the gap I stopped and came back to peep.

The Big Man was standing. He was looking at where I had disappeared. He stood there for a long time, me peeping through the bushes until my eye got tired from looking so far. I looked away, looked at the ground near my boots to rest my eye. He had taken off his coat when I looked back.

'Seanie! listen to me,' his voice rolled out. 'Listen to me, Seanie! I'm leaving my short coat here for you.' He stopped and he looked at his short coat on the ground at his feet. He picked it up. 'Listen Seanie! I'm going to leave it at the Tree you were tied to. Put it on. I'll come back after a while with more clothes for you.'

Like a dog listening for a rabbit to move again, he stood there. He had a red jumper on, one with long sleeves. After putting down the short coat again he swung his hands up and grasped the jumper behind his neck. It was like magic, the way it came off. One minute it had his shape, the next minute it was hanging in front of him like an empty skin. He picked up the short coat and went to the tree.

When he started down the hill I ran along the other side of the hedge until I saw the top of the Tree above the bushes. He went down the hill in a jerky walk because of the steepness. Down he went without looking back. When he went through the hedge at the end of the field I knew he hadn't set a trap. I could run and get the clothes before he could run back up the hill.

I was cold, all goose-pimples. The red jumper was grand. The short coat came down to my knees but the wind was blowing up my legs. I needed a piece of twine and I knew where there was some, besides the piece still in my wrist. The Shed.

The loft in the Shed was where I slept in the hay, in a corner. The loft was a triangle; no sides, just floor and roof. A man came every morning, with the cattle trotting after him across the field, pucking at each other; prancing at the prospect of the hay; trying to sing, but sounding the way they always do; bucking their hindquarters into the air, their legs kicking out sideways.

The first time he came I burrowed under the hay. I thought he had come to beat me. But he just threw the fodder down into the manger. Below, the cattle jumped around in six inches of their own dung. They made happy sounds. After that first time I stayed in the loft every day until the man had come and gone. That way he never saw my footprints in the dungy mud. Every time the man found the twine in the hay he wound it around his fist and hung it on a nail in the rafters. The twine was used to tie down the cocks in the fields.

I never went to the Shed in the daytime. There was only one way out. But I wanted twine to tie the Big Man's jumper between my legs to keep the wind out. It took a long time to cut off a short piece of twine. In the end I went outside and beat it between two stones. It was difficult to keep a firm grasp on the stone because of my fingers. They felt as if I had banged their backs hard against something. Maybe one of the boys stepped on me. Back in the loft I tied the jumper between my legs. The twine scratched my legs. It was better than having the wind blowing up my chest and back.

Empty nail-holes in some of the slates were my peep-holes. There was no one in sight. I was hungry and I knew there might be food in a brown bag at the Tree.

The wind was colder. The sun was going to set soon; the weak wintery sun, a silver button near the edge of the earth. When I peeped through the gap near the Tree, two people were coming up the big field. They moved slowly, arms linked, as if they were helping each other to climb the hilly field.

It was a man and a woman. The man had a bag in his hand. They would stop and the woman would look up the hill, as if she thought she would never get to the top. Then she would put her head down and start walking again. Slowly they came up, stopping and looking and starting. It looked as if the man was helping her, keeping her going. One time when they stopped the man left the bag down and put his arms around the woman. They stood like that for a long time. Sometimes, on the wind, I could hear the noise a dog makes when her pups have been taken away and drowned; a keening kind of whimper, soft and sad.

On they came, as if every step they took was hard to make. I wished they would go back. They were in my way. The place on the back of my hand where the skin was torn was on fire. I blew on it the way you blow on hot porridge. I looked at my feet to rest my eye from looking far away.

If they came and stood opposite me on the other side of the hedge the man and woman wouldn't see me. I was screened from them by furze and briars and alders.

When I looked up the two people were at the Tree. The woman had her hand on the trunk, her arm straight out as if she was pushing it over, only she was holding herself up. She was looking at the ground. It was the Big Man who was with her. The bag was at his feet. He was looking around as if expecting to see someone. I heard them plainly when they spoke.

133

'Was it here they tied him?'

'Yes.' He put his arm around her. 'Do you think you'll be able?' He stroked her back.

'I will.' She started crying, saying words through her crying. 'Oh! em jay em jay. It's too terrible. It's all too terrible.'

He rubbed her back, rubbed her black overcoat on her back.

'We'll have to try, Caithleen. Try to call his name. Say it with me a few times.'

She took a hand out of the overcoat pocket. There was a handkerchief in it. She blew windily and bubbly.

'Now, as loud as you can.' The Big Man started rolling his voice all over the place.

'SEANIE. SEANIE. SEANIE.'

As he called he put fingers under the woman's chin, tilted her face up.

'SEANIE. SEANIE. SEANIE.'

I could hear her, too, but only when she went before or after him. Her voice was weak, exhausted. When he stopped calling I could barely hear her. She sounded as if she was in a deep hole full of despair. Four times she said the word. Then her face exploded. It looked as if the water burst from every pore in her face.

The Big Man put her head on his chest. She kept saying words over and over, her sounds chopped up with sobs.

'Will he will he.' Then she cried. 'Deer dre. I lean. Poor Shaw nee. Poor Shaw nee.' She was quiet then for a while.

The Big Man rubbed her head through her headscarf.

The sun was gone. The breeze was cold. It felt like wet sandpaper on my legs.

Softly the woman spoke to the man. He started rolling his voice again.

'Seanie! Can you hear me, Seanie. Seanie! Listen to where my voice is. Mrs Sheehan wants to tell you something. Listen, Seanie.'

She took her head off his chest. She held onto his arm. When she spoke she wasn't loud.

134

'Seanie. We love you Seanie. Come back ... ' Her face erupted. The man's arms went around her again.

'That was good, Caithleen. I'm sure he ... ' The Big Man cried then, his head hanging over her shoulder. Drops of water fell from his face into the back of her coat.

I looked back at my feet, my boots. My eye was watering from the breeze, from peeping through the bushes. Even though I was shivering I couldn't move. They would have seen me. After a while the big voice rolled again.

'Seanie! Seanie! I'm leaving a bag at the Tree. There's clothes and food in it. We're leaving now, Seanie. Mrs Sheehan and myself love ... ' When he said that his voice collapsed: an armful of dry sticks falling on a floor.

They went away.

The cold stars were out before I went down to the gap in the hedge. When I came back to the Tree the bag was there.

I went home to the loft in the Shed. My ankle was paining from all the running and walking. After wrapping myself in the blanket I snuggled down into my nest in the sweet-smelling hay. The next morning when I woke I had the bag pressed against my belly, my arms around it the way a child would go to sleep hugging a doll.

After they burned my clothes the boys never caught me again. At times it seemed someone was always trying to catch me. The boys were the easiest to lose. When I'd disappear they'd get frightened. One minute they were chasing me through fields, through hedges and bushes, throwing stones and whooping. Then I'd slip into one of my places. When they couldn't see me they'd get silent. They'd get together in a bunch and whisper, look around with hooded eyes. After a while they'd sneak away. When they'd reach an open field they'd run as if a wild animal was after them.

For years it was only the Big Man who came to the Tree. He came every afternoon; even in rain or snow he'd come with the brown bag. Sometimes he called out. He always stayed for a while at the Tree, as if he was thinking or remembering. The woman never came with him again.

One day another man came. He was as tall as the Big

Man. When he first came he stood at the Tree and talked as if someone was listening to him. 'I'm sorry, Seanie,' is what he mostly said. Sometimes he would look around, making sure no one could hear him. Then he'd call in a loud voice: 'Seanie. Seanie! It's Uncle Enda. It's Uncle Enda, Seanie.' A few times he sat at the bottom of the Tree and drank from a small bottle until it was empty. He always took the bottle with him when he left. He had red hair.

The food that Red left was different. You knew it was a man who cut the slices off the loaf and buttered them. They weren't like a woman's slices, even and not too thick, with the butter spread evenly. He put in more meat than a woman would.

By the time Red started coming I had found another hill two miles away. Whenever I saw too many boys coming up Shed Hill I'd disappear. About an hour later I'd turn up in one of my hiding-places on Snowdrop Hill. They never came looking for me on Snowdrop. Maybe it was because they knew about the cemetery there. The other cemetery, the one on Shed Hill, had a wall around it. There were white headstones and flowers on the graves, the pebbled paths were free of weeds, the grass was cut. It was like a garden.

The cemetery on Snowdrop Hill was wild. A wide over-grown hedge surrounded it. Long briars snaked through the tangled grass; docks, gone to seed, stood like rusted minia-ture pylons. The graves had sunk down the way a cow's grave sinks when the cow in it rots. I didn't know I was stumbling across sunken graves until I saw a fresh one with flowers on it. Then I was afraid I'd sink into a grave, afraid I'd find myself knee-deep in a rotting body.

The clay on the fresh grave was still in a mound, no weeds or grass growing on it yet. A jam-jar was pushed into the clay and a bunch of snowdrops hung their heads over its rim. When I saw that pile of fresh earth, almost hidden in the tall brown grass of winter, saw those sad snowdrops, tears fell out of me. It was the loneliness of it all, the beauty of it all, that saddened me; someone coming through this field of forgotteness to find one particular grave; to put a bunch of fresh flowers in a jam-jar. How they must have loved the person in the grave; picking the snowdrops one by one, heads trembling on delicate necks; how they must have cried with each flower picked for the one they loved.

As the springs got warmer it was primroses that were in the jam-jar, and then daffodils; then lilacs; cowslips; long daisies; a rose; purple violets and, at the end of each summer, a begonia, with leaves the size of rhubarb leaves, was planted in the freshened mound. When the winters came the begonia died, cold rainwater collected in the jam-jar. The vague track from the grave to the unhinged, rusty gate disappeared. But then again, one day in the spring, the snowdrops were back in the jar again. The love was still there. Maybe that's why I went to the grave every time I went to Snowdrop Hill. I felt warm in the embers of some-one else's love.

People came to stroll on Shed Hill every seventh day – Sundays, I supposed. In my hiding-places I heard their words as they passed, the men and women with their arms linked, the men with ash-plants cutting the heads off weeds as they strolled along. They peered into the hedges, and girls said, 'I don't want to see him.'

'He could jump out at us.'

'He's only got one eye.'

The men made brave-sounding noises and said, 'He's afraid of people.'

'I'd flatten him with one box in the mouth.'

'I'd love to be the one to capture him.'

The couples met other couples. They spoke excitedly.

'He was running around for weeks with no clothes on, only boots, in the middle of winter.'

'He has a mark across his eye like the mark of Cain for killing his brother.'

'They found a badger burrow where he'd been sleeping for weeks.'

'He eats turnips and hasn't washed himself since it hap-pened.'

'They say he's dressed in a woman's clothes. Daddy says

he stole them.'

I listened from my secret places.

As the couples strolled and peered and talked, I knew I knew something, that it kept slipping away from me whenever I tried to look at it. But one day! When I least expected it, in a heaven-sent moment, I would know what I knew.

Then the Centaur appeared on the hill, a ghost in the silent distance cantering across the dreamscreen. But there was a purpose to the direction it took. Every strolling couple was visited by the Centaur; every couple was spoken to. After each encounter the strolling couple walked smartly down the hill. One hurrying couple passed my secret place and the man said, 'Protestant bitch.' The Centaur appeared, too, when boys came with sling-shots and old twine. Silently they skulked down the hill when they were spoken to.

Before the lilac faded the hill was as empty on Sundays as it was on Mondays, except for the cattle.

One day the Big Man's bread-slices were thick and hacked like Red's. The food was clumsily wrapped. I thought he had brought Red's bag by mistake. But the slices stayed thick and hacked. Shortly after this change a new man began to come. I called him Bare Face because he always looked lately shaved, his face shining. The first time he came, Bare Face left hot potatoes and butter. By the time I found a pointed stick the food was cold and I used my fingers.

Some days, when I thought it was a certain time, I walked around Shed Hill. In a field of yellow-flowered furze which overlooked the garden cemetery, I'd wait for a funeral. Seeing all the people was like looking through thick glass at something that happened long ago. In the place I sat there was no sound. The people moved slowly, as if rushing feet would disturb the people under the ground. When the grave was full, filled by furious men in their shirt-sleeves, the silent shovels were laid across each other on the grave. For a long time the people stood with lowered heads; looked at the cross the shovels made, rosary beads hanging from fingers, hands joined at their forks, men and women. When the priest waved holy water at the grave the crowd came apart slowly. Individuals and couples drifted off to different parts of the cemetery with bowed heads. They knelt or stood at graves where people they loved were buried. Most days there were no funerals.

Sometimes when it was empty I went down to the cemetery, climbed over the wall because the gate was on the far side. It was nice in there; as if I was with people who wouldn't hurt me, who didn't want to hurt me. But all the time I was there I had the urge to make number two. Even before I'd get there, when I'd decide to go, I'd get the urge. It was this that made my cemetery visits short.

One day in a springtime, when the bushes were still bare, I was hurrying to leave the cemetery. And there I saw a jamjar stuck down in a grave with snowdrops hanging their delicate flowers over the rim. So pale. Even though I was bursting I knelt on one knee and touched their beauty with my fingertips. The loneliness of that other grave on Snowdrop Hill squeezed my heart. Sadness slipped out of my eyes and fell in big drops on the grave.

Up in the Furze Field, the furze wearing their springtime flowers, I edged my way between the bushes, careful of thorns. I came to the small clearing I used whenever I was in this area. There I undid my buttons and sat on my hunkers. I remained squatted for a while after I was finished, half in the daze you sometimes get into while doing number two. I saw, close by, a cluster of snowdrops, their heads quivering in the same breeze that chilled my bare backside. I stared at them for a long time until my legs began to cramp. I reached out to pull a handful of grass and I heard a piano note, as delicate as a snowdrop in a January breeze. When I stood up to do my buttons I heard the sound again.

a man and a woman and a boy and a piano and sunshine

It was the clink of the cemetery's iron gate closing; the hasp that goes up and down. A woman and two children had come to visit.

After covering my number two with kicked-up clay I knelt and pulled the snowdrops; laid them across a long piece of grass and tied them. I set off for Snowdrop Hill along a path where I knew no one would meet me. Down the slopes of Shed Hill I went, clutching the flowers, the first flowers of spring. And then up again along a track, a fox's or a badger's.

Like an animal I had learned never to walk boldly out into an open space. There was a gap a man could go through in the hedge and, before I stepped into the graveyard, I stopped and looked.

Because I was not expecting to see anyone, and because I was in a graveyard, the sight of the kneeling black figure at the grave shocked me. Until he moved I was attached to the ground with fright. He was on his knees with his back to me, but he wasn't praying. He was stirring up the mound of the grave with a small tool, stretching from his kneeling position to reach the far side.

I stood invisible in the bushes watching him, wanting to see the face of the man who loved so much. I had to rest my eye. When I looked up he was standing at the end of the grave, his joined hands at his crotch.

It was the Big Man.

The shock of seeing him made me gasp. I had only seen him in one place before; in the place where I lived on Shed Hill. And here he was on Snowdrop Hill, too. It was as if there were two of him. Maybe there *were* two of them, brothers, twin brothers. My heart leaped at the thought of walking into that quiet overgrown cemetery. As I worked up the courage to step out of hiding, the urge to make number two gave me a pain. I looked down to be sure of my footing and I stepped forward, my breath held in, a fart escaping.

When I looked up the Big Man had his back to me. He was walking to the gate, and he left the cemetery without looking back.

I felt as though I'd had a meeting with a ghost. My breath rushed out.

There were fresh snowdrops in the jam-jar. I made a hole in the mound with a stick, put in my flowers and patted the clay till they stood up. I kept looking at the cemetery gate.

After a long time I sat beside the grave, my legs under me, my arm slung across the mound.

There were many changes in the flowers in the jam-jars, but I never saw the Big Man again on Snowdrop Hill. Every time I went there, now, I brought flowers of the season with me. In my head I spoke to the person in the grave, spoke to him about the seasons, about the flowers, about the Big Man who loved him. I told him about the Tree and the three people who came there. Sometimes there were clothes at the Tree. It was Bare Face who left the first pair of long trousers. They were warm, so warm and cosy, especially in the bushes with rain on them. Sometimes there were new things in the brown bags: an orange, a chocolate bar, a piece of sweet cake. Once, when the Big Man came, he spoke without rolling his voice around the fields.

'Seanie! I think you can hear me. You have to trust me, Seanie. I won't hurt you. I love you, Seanie.' Then he raised his voice and spoke so loudly he frightened me. 'Seanie, Seanie! You must come to me. Come to me, Seanie. I need you. I need you, Seanie.' He cried then for a long time. He would stop shaking for a few minutes, then all of a sudden a sob would shake him, as if he'd been hit in the back with a fist. I was invisible in the bushes not ten yards away. But I coughed. The sound I made was the sound of a calf with the hoose coughing. The next day there was a bottle in the brown bag. A piece of paper was stuck to it. 'Drink two cap-fuls in the morning, at dinner time, at supper time and when you go to bed.' 'Drink me,' was on Alice's bottle. She got small. My cough went away before the bottle was fin-ished.

I always waited for the visitors, watched them climbing up the hilly field, looked forward to what would be said. Red nearly always said he was sorry, and he'd say Uncle Enda.

'It's Uncle Enda.'

Bare Face said very little. After his first few visits he knelt at the Tree, bowed his head, joined his hands at his chest. Most of the time when he stood up the knees of his trousers were wet.

The Big Man spoke the most. There was always a plea in the sound of his words, even if his words had no plea in them.

Sometimes in the warm snug hay, in my blanket like a growing butterfly, I slept for weeks when the weather was rainy and miserable, the fields muddy, the bushes and grass wet. I peed over the edge of the loft onto the cattle below. If I had to do number two I'd do it on a piece of hay near the edge. Then I'd push it over. I was a young swallow.

The man who fed the cattle was thin, his face-skin the colour of faded white paper. If the small boy came with him the cattle-feeder told him not to play in the hay on the loft.

'Miss Bevan doesn't like the cattle to eat dirty hay,' he said one time, as he climbed the straight ladder. Sometimes the man would tell the boy not to get too close to the edge.

'If you fell down there you'd be covered with cow dung!'

The boy giggled at that.

Back into sleep I would fall.

the blackbird, picking food, sees thee, nor stops his meal, nor fears at all; so often has he known thee past him stray, rapt, twirling in thy hand a withered spray, and waiting for the spark from heaven to fall.

Every year when the spring grass came back, and when the cattle hadn't to be fed anymore, there was hay left over in the loft. On summer evenings the boy came with the man to inspect the cattle. The man would tell the boy how to look after animals.

'If they're lying down make them get up. Watch to see if they all dung. Look at the bullocks' bellies when they're peeing.'

'Blood murraine!' the little boy would say to show he knew.

'That's right. If the pee is red they have blood murraine.'

'Remember which bullock it is,' the boy anticipated.

'That's right. You're learning, Willie.'

'The cud,' Willie would say.

'That's right. Make sure they're all chewing the cud.'

'Loners.'

'Yes. If one is off by itself it might be sick.'

Every evening I saw them coming from the other side of the hill. A little dog, black and white, ran around the boy, jumped up as he passed, red tongue out to lick the boy's face. If the dog ran after the cattle the boy shouted angrily, 'Spot! Spot!' and the dog came back ashamed, ears back, head down, tail pulled in.

Then one evening the man would say to the boy, 'We're putting the hay in the shed tomorrow. You can bring Spot with you in case there's rats in the old hay.'

The meadows on Shed Hill came alive when the hay was ready for cutting. The horses pulling the mower lashed their tails and jerked their heads at the flies. The men on the seats hupped incessantly at the horses until they didn't know they were hupping. Their shirt-sleeves were rolled up on white winter arms, handkerchiefs tied around wet necks keeping the hay seeds from going down their backs. The machines made loud clacking noises at sharp corners, or when the horses were made to back up.

When the hay had dried on one side men and boys came with pitchforks to turn the swaths, the hay rolling over at the touch of the forks as if it were a wave breaking on a strand; little whirlwinds, *'fairy blasts' Daddy called them*, touching down and spinning strands of hay into the air the height of a man and higher.

Women and girls came with apple cake and custard. The sweet tea was in shining gallon-cans that once held sweets. When the hay was ready to be cocked, horses with wheel-rakes and tumbler-rakes came; the boys built the lower half and the men finished the cocks. There was loud happy talk. I watched and listened from my secret places and I was happy.

The night before the hay was put in the Shed I gathered my hidden things, piled them up for my early departure the next morning; scissors, pencil, jumper, trousers, socks, knitted cap, a book I'd never read. All these had come in the brown bags. In the morning I bundled everything in the blanket. Before I set off for the Furze Field I fixed the hay so no one would know I'd been sleeping there.

Among the furze was the best hiding-place. The first year of the hay I hid the blanket in the hedge near the Tree. When I returned the cattle had walked on everything with their dungy hoofs. With the bundle over my shoulder I sidled into a dense stand of flowered thorns. There I hid it, the smell of the horse still on the blanket.

When I stood up I looked down on the garden cemetery. The early sun had turned every dewdrop into a bead of glass. The silent headstones stood like unbending sentries defying death to wipe out the memory of the dead. I felt the urge to do number two the moment I decided to go down there, to feel the presence of the people. Even with living people I had a need to get as close as possible. The dead couldn't see or hear, but getting close to them was more perilously exciting than approaching a living person unseen.

Down the hill I went from bush to bush, hesitating each time before I showed myself again. I moved to a whitethorn, the tiny leaves making a solid wall between myself and the cemetery only twenty feet away. Just as I was about to step out I heard E-flat.

a man a woman a boy a piano empty boots beside the pedals sunshine

Confusion blew around me like a fairy blast in a meadow, gone as quick as it came. I took the step out from behind the bush and I heard it again, the E-flat.

may I take off my boots
the pedals

The fairy blast touched me again, unplayful, chilly. I stepped back behind the wall of leaves. It's the gate, I thought. Someone has come in through the cemetery gate.

The blood galloped around inside my head. I was almost light-headed; my eyesight darkened around the edges and for a moment it seemed I was looking through a small hole. It's only the latch of the cemetery gate, I told myself. But I couldn't make myself look for a long time. Something had frightened me when I heard the gate latch.

But I looked, and I made the sound you make when you

pull in a lot of air quickly through opened mouth. The Big Man was kneeling on the concrete kerb at the foot of a grave. I stood there shaking, my good eye at the edge of the leaves, my heart racing. He knelt as motionless as the headstone at the other end of the grave.

My eye grew tired, and I looked down at my boots. When I looked back the Big Man was getting up. He stood for a moment looking at the headstone, as if he was reading it. Then he bent to a bag on the ground beside him. He took out two bunches of flowers and laid them carefully on the grass. He took out a hand-rake and went to the top of the grave. Before he knelt on the side kerb he pulled up the legs of his trousers. He freshened the soil, bent across the grave, resting his left hand on the opposite kerb. Without getting up he moved his knees until the rectangle of earth was black, was a different colour to the surrounding graves, still glistening under their coatings of beaded glass. My eye was tired.

When I looked out again he was picking up one of the bunches of flowers he had brought. He pulled a string off their stems and put them in a jam-jar. He used the same string to tie up the bunch of dying flowers he had removed.

Using the toe of his boot he banged the damp clay off the rake. It looked as if he had done this many times. One little task followed on the other without hesitation. He put the old flowers in the bottom of the bag, then the rake went in. When he picked up the second bunch of fresh flowers he touched it back into shape. He put that in the bag, too.

The Big Man stood there at the foot of the grave looking down, the early morning birds calling. It was a ghostly scene. Even when he moved away the Big Man moved in silence, the bag hanging at the end of his straight arm. He didn't use the gate. Instead, he climbed up the stone stile. As I watched him sinking down out of sight my ankle pained me and I moved my foot.

Out in the lane he took his leaning bike by the handlebar and walked away. I stood there staring at the spot where he had disappeared, the heightening sun moving out of the dew, the birds warming and raising their voices. The urge to do number two came on again as I went down.

The Big Man's tracks were plain to see where he had stepped in the short dewy grass at the grave. It was a bunch of big-faced daisies he had put in the clay. Dog daisies.

Daddy called them dog daisies a man with laughing eyes and dog daisies stuck in his hair behind his ears

There were so many flowers it was hard to see the jam-jar. I touched the daisies, my fingertips familiar with the texture of the long white petals. They are my favourite flower, so simple, two colours, so perfect. I love the season of the daisies; faces held above the breezy meadow grass, a million suns dancing and looking straight into the face of God. I would want dog daisies on my grave, waving and swaying forever over me. The person on this grave must have loved daisies, too.

But there were three people buried here. The white head-stone had letters carved in black, a heart at the top surrounded with thorns; the thorns of sadness, of grief. That's what sadness is like – thorns in the heart. The name Shee-han was below the heart.

SHEEHAN
In loving memory of
Eileen and Deirdre
11 and 12 years old
Died January 1919
And their dear mother
Caithleen
Died March 1921, aged 37

two girls in white a red-globed lamp a bunch of daisies

I knew that something was happening inside me, but I couldn't get hold of it. I knew the spark was falling, giving light. What it was shining on did not make me feel good. A wave of panic washed over me and left me goose-pimpled in the warm sun. I sat on my hunkers and touched the white petals again.

faces smiling above white dresses

I leaned over, touched my cheek to the daisies, turned my

face into the flowers. The earthy smell was the same as daffodils, the same as snowdrops, the same as dandelions, a smell that had to be smelled many times before it is liked; it is not a fragrance.

The cemetery on Snowdrop Hill had been floating around in my head, and now my mind fell on the grave there. I had once seen the Big Man on Snowdrop Hill, and that day the flowers on both graves had been the same – snowdrops. Now, today, he had left a bunch of daisies and taken another away with him. If I went the quickest way to Snowdrop Hill I knew I would see him at the other grave. The urge to do number two was painful.

I lifted my face and laid my palms on the flowers, gently touching them, letting them feel me. I stood up.

The first thing I had to do was do number two. As I scrambled up the hill to the Furze Field, I knew the cemetery was not the only reason for the pain in my belly.

In the furze I squatted and it came out of me like a squart from a duck,

as Mammy used to say a woman with flour on her hands curl of hair annoying her eye bottom lip out directing her blow bending down smiling saying move my curl baby

Spears of darkness quivered in the air nearby.

I shook the stare out of my eye and pulled a handful of grass.

the stone stile

It was too early for anyone to be in the fields. I took short cuts I had never taken before. Running down Shed Hill, the morning air rushed in around my body through clothes openings, through holes, as I sped towards the knowledge that held no goodness, only evil. Blindly I reached the bottom, lumbered across the narrow valley. I don't want to know, I shouted inside, as headlong I flew to find out.

that's right Willie you're learning Willie

Across the foot of Snowdrop Hill to the badger track I plunged, through alders and hazels and ferns. The slope of the hill did not slow me down at all. I knew I was going to know. I had had flashes of the knowing and I knew the

147

knowing was going to be terrible. I would never undo my corded bales of knowledge. My knowledge had been there all the time. I knew that now, and I knew the cover was being pulled back. Dreadful black knowledge would be unbared, and onward I rushed.

I plunged through the gap in the cemetery hedge and stopped and looked. He was there. Across the grass, across the rusted miniature pylons, across the sunken graves, across Willie's tended grave we looked at each other. There was a bunch of dog daisies in his hand.

MISTER SHEEHAN

Standing at the Four Streets I can hear the shouting fading as the bullock is driven back to Joe Butler's place along Clark Street. I can smell the May bushes.

The lateness, the stillness, the darkness; they all magnify the voices and the noise. I wonder how long the animal has to live. Imagine being forced into a slaughterhouse. The smell of blood, the smell of death, the smell of the animal's own death making it bug-eyed with terror; the ash-plants swishing through the air before laying down thin lines of pain along its back. The cruelty of it; tying an animal into helplessness, then shooting it. It's the struggling and the tying and the helplessness that make it monstrous.

I don't like the word slaughter. It excludes all trace of kindness, of thoughtfulness.

The slaughterhouse images shudder themselves out of my head as I walk away from the Four Streets, the money-bag a dead weight. At the juncture of the Four Streets I hesitated on my way to Father Quinn's house that Sunday eight years ago. I got off my bike here and had a talk with myself: my sensible self telling me to go home; my responsible self telling me to go on. Reluctantly I threw my leg over the saddle and headed into the Town, my mind full of the man I was about to face.

When Father Quinn came to the Town in 1921 he was not shy about letting his feelings about the English be known. God was a Catholic God, an Irish God who would bring the Protestants to their heretical knees. He screeched his opposition to the 1921 Treaty which partitioned the country, and during the brief civil war he condemned the Free Staters to a special place in hell. There was only one political truth, and Eamon de Valera was its incarnation.

149

The people sat and listened. There was fear in those days hanging like a grey, cold cloud over the country. The people were not just afraid of Father Quinn: they were afraid to declare for either side. Anyone could come after you with a gun, or a hammer, or a piece of two-by-four.

I wasn't on either side. Caithleen was dying; Willie had just been killed and Seanie was living like an animal up on Miss Bevan's estate. All so long ago!

Father Quinn's ambition to build the new Church wing and the reality of the political situation diluted his zeal. The anti-English tirades dwindled to a couple a year. But the whole thing flared up again in 1938, when de Valera was named President of the League of Nations and Father Quinn accompanied him to Geneva as his German interpreter. On the way they had stayed in Nuremberg and heard Hitler's foreign-policy speech about Czechoslovakia, and the three million Germans who were living in the Sudeten. Father Quinn made parts of that speech his own. The Sudeten became the north of Ireland. The Czechs were the Protestants. The Sudeten Germans were the Catholic nationalists and southern Ireland was Germany. The partition imposed by Versailles was the partition imposed by 10 Downing Street.

He came back to the Town as if he'd been in Jerusalem on the first Pentecost. He spoke in tongues, in his excitement running from Gaelic to English to German in meaningless sentences. He pounded the pulpit; he salivated, sending his venomous spittle down on the congregation. Over and over he quoted Hitler, paraphrasing him so often that the people knew the words by heart.

It was on the Sunday after Dunkirk, June 1940, that I hesitated at the Four Streets on my way to see Father Quinn. Maybe I should have gone home. All that I achieved was the priest's everlasting hatred and the contempt of his housekeeper, whose stinging words followed me down the steep steps outside the house.

Father Quinn had danced in the pulpit that morning; danced and screamed like a fundamentalist preacher who has worked himself into a state of ecstasy over other people's sins. It was humiliating to be subjected to such evil gloating. The people sat and looked up at him, speechless every one of us.

And then in the afternoon the schoolteacher stood before the priest: the clergyman positioned on the second step of his stairs so he could look me in the eye; Miss Dickingson in the kitchen doorway, arms folded across her chest, her black stockings like jackboots in the corner of my vision.

'You'll be standing up in the church, next thing, to challenge me! Is that it? Is that what you'll do next?'

I didn't attempt to answer this question that he roared at me, spittle in the air.

'Well, will you? – you Free Stater!'

Miss Dickingson straightened her back. I didn't answer the question because I thought it was a question to humiliate me – a small boy being reprimanded. The priest glared at me in the unlit hallway.

'Go ahead!' he shouted. 'Go ahead! Stand up in the Church and defy me! You'll be out of this town in two shakes! And you won't get a job in this country again. You can go up to the North and join the Protestants! You Free Stater!'

There was no point in trying to reason with him, in trying even to speak to him. There seemed to be more than anger in the priest's eyes.

'I'll be going now,' I said.

'And don't come back,' the priest shouted. 'Show him out, Miss Dickingson!'

As I turned toward the front door the housekeeper clacked past me. She yanked the door open and, when I descended the steps, she cried out, 'Bloody traitor! You should be shot like the rest of them, you bloody Free Stater. We all know about you hob-nobbing with Miss Bevan and her Protestant gang!'

On the bottom step I stopped and put my hand on the cast-iron railing. Now, I believed, I had a new duty – to defend Miss Bevan. But I didn't even turn around. Miss

Dickingson's flood of abuse rushed down the steps and washed me out onto the footpath.

'That Protestant hure on her high and mighty horse! The two of you should be tarred and feathered. Was it she sent you to threaten Father Quinn, your own priest! Go on out of here, you Protestant sympathizer. Go and sit in the back seat of Peetie Mahon's taxi and hold hands with her. Get out of here, you bloody Free Stater!'

As fast as I could, I went away from that house. Before I got on the bicycle I looked up and down the street, but it was Sunday afternoon and the Town was empty; no one had heard her. Even though I felt like a kicked dog I tried to ease my feelings by making excuses for the two attackers. I should have laughed. It had been nineteen years since I'd sat with Miss Bevan in Peetie Mahon's taxi on the way to Willie's funeral. It was nineteen years since the Free State had become an issue. But I was too humiliated to laugh. As I rode away, her tirade followed me up O'Neill Street; she on the top step outside the front door grasping the iron railing, a demented Ahab on the bridge of *The Pequod*.

This burden of pennies! I have a pain in my shoulder. Switching the bag to my other hand I hear the fading sounds of Joe Butler directing his hungry bullock through a gate.

Miss Bevan!

The natives of the Town call the woman they see on horseback Miss Bevan. She was called Miss Bevan when Willie was killed. She was called Miss Bevan in 1940. The present Miss Bevan is the granddaughter of the Miss Bevan who found Seanie and Willie in the Cemetery in 1921. None of their names was Bevan. None of them was Protestant.

They all lived in the big house called Summerhill on the edge of the Town. Summerhill was built in the 1600s by a Quaker family named Bevan, and for a long time it was Bevans who lived there. But men from other Quaker families married into the estate and the Bevan family name died out more than a hundred years ago. The lady who found Seanie was Mrs Shillitoes; her daughter's married name was Bell, and the present Miss Bevan is Mrs Fry.

I had never spoken to Miss Bevan before Willie's murder, except to nod at her as she cantered by on one of her horses. It was outside the Cemetery gate, when I went looking for Seanie, that I first spoke to her.

At the Cemetery gate!

I can see myself still, kneeling at the gate, my hands grasping the bars, chest heaving after the desperate bicycle ride from the Barracks, after the frantic run up the short lane to the gates. And then all I could do was whisper.

'Seanie. Seanie.'

I was crying out of sheer desperation. If Seanie had been standing beside me he wouldn't have heard his own name. The sound was only in my head; it wasn't even getting to my lips.

Two imperatives had immobilized me. I heard one time that, if all the conditions are perfect, a monocular animal will starve to death if it can see two sources of food at equal distances. At the Cemetery gate I was rendered helpless. Seanie had to be found. Caithleen had to be comforted. *Delenda est.* And Willie's death was there, shrouding my brain.

I called Seanie's name again, and the sound in my head was like a sound made in an empty house; an empty house with every door open, the sound going into every dusty, cobwebbed corner.

'Seanie. Seanie.'

I wished I were holding his hand; hugging him; telling him ... telling him ... What?

Between the two iron bars my face was pressed, saliva stretching down off my chin; mouth open and breath rasping, making sounds like those of a broken-winded horse.

'Where are you, child? I have to get back to Caithleen.'

Then I heard my name.

'Mr Sheehan.'

But I thought it was in my head in the empty house with all the doors open, floors and floors of them.

'Seanie!' I cried.

'Mr Sheehan.'

'Come to me, Seanie. Come to me. Where are you, Seanie?'
My own name came back at me through all the doors.
'Mr Sheehan. Mr Sheehan.'
I felt a hand on my shoulder.
'Mr Sheehan.'
I let go of the iron bars. In one motion I turned and fell back against the gate. There were two white things aiming at my face for a while, and then they became bent knees. It was Miss Bevan in her riding outfit. I was surprised to see holes in the black velvet of her cap, the underlying brown material like blots of splashed dirty water.

'Give me your hand,' she said. She pulled and I pushed. I stood up with my back to the gate.

'I'm sorry, I'm sorry,' I said. 'I couldn't stand up before.' Then I said: 'Seanie is lost.'

The money-bag! This blessed money-bag! I'll tell Father Quinn tomorrow that I'm finished with the Cinema. It's over and done with. I don't care what people will say. I don't care anymore. I'd like to leave this bag in the gutter and walk away from it. That would be symbolic! To leave it there and walk away. But I won't do that. There's only another half-mile.

Miss Bevan told me to go home to Caithleen, that she herself would look for Seanie; that she would get some of her men out to look for him.

I asked her questions. Miss Bevan told me how she had seen a man running out of the Cemetery.

'He went out through the gate,' she said. 'From where I was, up the hill near that field of furze, I could see the two boys lying on the grass over there.' She pointed through the gate.

When I looked back at her she was crying. She moved over to the gate and grasped one of the bars. In a ladylike way she used the flat of her index finger to brush away the tears.

'I was going to be in Queentown today on behalf of the Workhouse. When I learned about the adoption I was very happy for you and Mrs Sheehan. After the girls ...' She hesitated. 'For the boys too. And now this.' She stared out into the Cemetery, grasping the iron bars of the gate as if wrestling with something.

I said: 'You will have to tell me about the boys; how they were when you found them.'

'Let me tell you later,' she said.

'Later for my sake or yours?' I asked. 'If it's only for my sake I'd prefer you'd tell me now.'

'Later, Mr Sheehan,' Miss Bevan said. 'Now it is too much to know that Willie is dead.' Then she gasped, put her hand to her mouth. 'You do know about Willie?' she asked.

'Yes. Enda, Dr McKenna! He told Caithleen and myself. Poor Willie. He was a nervous child.'

We stood there together, each of us with a hand on the gate, each gazing out at the headstones. Miss Bevan said: 'Seanie will have to be dealt with very carefully.'

I looked at her. Although we had met in passing many times before, I had not seen her face until now. She did not have the face of a beautiful woman. Her features were sharp, her lips thin.

'How was Seanie when you saw him?'

'Distressed beyond...' Miss Bevan hesitated. She looked at the ground, at the scuffed toes of her riding boots. Lifting her head she continued: 'I have seen many poor souls in the Workhouse; people suffering from great losses, especially during the Spanish Lady. Some of the worst ones were gone into themselves. There was no touching them.' She paused again.

'Please tell me,' I said. I was so drained of emotion that I thought nothing could touch me now. Miss Bevan put her hand on my arm.

'Seanie may be insane,' she said.

We looked at each other. I was aware of the pressure of her hand.

'I only think that, Mr Sheehan. I don't know. Maybe when the shock wears off he'll be alright. But you know better than I how close they were, Willie and Seanie. Seanie saw something dreadful last night, saw something dreadful happening to his brother. When I saw him this morning ... he ...' Miss Bevan put her hands over her face. I put my hand on her arm. She made a sniffling noise and drew in a deep breath. Her hands went back to the gate.

'Seanie was unconscious at first. When he came around he looked at me as if he knew me. He had a cut on his right eye. I thought he was going to talk to me, but he turned away and ...' Miss Bevan took off her riding cap and leaned her head against one of the brown bars, one hand holding the bar beside it. 'I think he was trying to make Willie better. He was ... It looked as if he was making ... It looked as if Seanie was making love to Willie, whispering things in his ear that I couldn't understand. He was rocking him in his arms, muttering all the time. Oh! Mr Sheehan. It's too hard to tell.'

She cried, her shoulders shaking, the riding cap on the ground at her feet. I touched her. Then, as if she were talking about something completely different, she said, 'Seanie seemed to fall asleep. I left and went for the constable.'

Her changed voice, her reclaimed self-possession, encouraged me to question her.

'Was there a smell of porter on Seanie?'

It was a while before Miss Bevan answered. In her head she put the proper words together, weeding out what she thought I couldn't bear, weeding out what she couldn't tell.

'There was a smell of stale porter.'

'Enda said they were drunk. I can't believe that.'

'Nor I, Mr Sheehan. I smelled porter, but it was on their clothes.'

My shoulders sagged. It was as if the details didn't matter. All that mattered was that Willie was dead. Seanie was lost. I shuddered. I turned and leaned my back against the gate, looked down the narrow lane that led back to the main road. Miss Bevan's horse was pulling at a clump of dry winter grass in the hedge.

'Enda said Willie fell off the stile and hit his forehead on one of the spikes,' I said.

'I thought you ... ' Miss Bevan said, in a startled voice. I looked at her.

She was looking at me, anxiety all over her face.

'You thought what, Mrs Shillitoes?'

'Fell off the stile!' she said incredulously. 'Off this stile here?' She went over to the stone steps.

'What is it, Mrs Shillitoes?' I felt as if I were looking at a dream from a distance.

'I was wondering how he had been hurt. Maybe that's what happened. Maybe he fell.'

I knew she was not telling me something, but I hadn't the energy to pursue it. I said, 'The man who ran away – was he trying to help them?'

'I don't know what he was doing, Mr Sheehan. I don't know. It's all confusing.' Miss Bevan came back from the steps. She looked at the spikes on the top of the gate, touched some of them and looked at her hand.

'I'm going to call for Seanie,' I said. 'Maybe he'll hear me.'

Miss Bevan came over to me. She put her hand on my arm. 'Go home to Mrs Sheehan,' she said. 'I'll find Seanie for you. You can't be in two places at once. Go home and take care of Mrs Sheehan.'

'I'll call once,' I said. 'I couldn't call when I got here.' As I turned around to the gate Miss Bevan's hand fell off my arm. I called the boy's name twice. We listened and looked. There was no response, no movement, no sign at all.

'Seanie,' I called.

Miss Bevan touched me again. I looked at her and I was crying, uselessly crying.

'You're very kind, Mrs Shillitoes,' I said. 'Very kind.'

The trace of a smile moved her face. She said, 'You're the only Catholic from the Town who has ever called me by my proper name.'

'Mrs Shillitoes!' I said, and I pulled the back of my hand across my wet face. 'Yes. But I think of you as Miss Bevan.'

She squeezed my arm. 'I saw a bike down there at the head of the lane. Is it yours?'

'I threw it down when I got to the bottom of the lane. I ran the rest of the way and I couldn't even call his name when I got here.'

Miss Bevan said, 'That's why I came back – to find him. But I think it's Seanie who is going to find us. I think the best thing for us to do is make ourselves available to him.'

I wasn't sure what she was talking about. I didn't question her.

'When you find him bring him home, to our house, please.'

'I will. Don't worry. Will you be alright on the bike or would you rather I walked home with you?'

'I'll be alright,' I said. 'It's all downhill to Madden's Bridge.'

We walked down the lane to her horse. As she untied the reins I said, 'Did you know they played the piano?' And then I wondered why I had said that. Was I trying to tell her how much I loved the boys?

'No, I didn't know that,' Miss Bevan said. 'I'm afraid I knew very little about them.'

'Poor children,' I said.

When I got on the bike I glided down to Madden's Bridge without pedalling once.

I don't remember what was in my head as I wheeled down the hill towards Caithleen. But now that I think of her ...

I don't like the thoughts that I know are working their way into my consciousness. I have dealt with them before, have buried them many times because I know there are things better left alone, forgotten, whether in the ground or in the head.

And here it is, floating again in my head – my remembrance of dragging Caithleen up that hill the day the boys burned Seanie's clothes. Before we reached the spot where I had seen Seanie earlier in the day, naked except for his boots, I knew the mental battering was crippling her.

'We'll go back, Caithleen,' I said, when I realized what was going on.

But she wouldn't go back. Once she got it into her head – once I had put the idea into her head – that she could make contact with Seanie, there was no way to stop her.

It wasn't for her own sake, nor for her love for Seanie, that Caithleen got out of her deathbed. She was going to steal something back from the God she had come to hate.

May God have mercy on her. Have mercy on her, Father. She was damaged.

She was determined to beat the God who had taken her children; to snatch back at least one of them from his grasping, sadistic clutch. She knew she might fail. Even before she arose from her bed, she said she would be like Christ calling to Lazarus, except that Christ knew his own power.

When she did fail to make contact with Seanie, she went home and died. God had beaten her, mocked her; Seanie, so close on the other side of the hedge looking at us, not knowing us; Caithleen seeing him through the bare winter branches as clearly as I could see him; Seanie gaping, dishevelled, drooling, blood and dirt caked on his face; the red wound above and below his eye like an arrow piercing a dead heart in a picture.

Picking up the money-bag, I can see myself kneeling beside her bed telling her how Seanie would come back with her. I even told her how the boys had burned his clothes; used that incident shamelessly to make her get up. I convinced myself that, if only I could get Seanie to come to her, each would give to the other the will to live. Oh Caithleen! Every day after school when I climbed that hill there was desperate hope in me that, maybe today, Seanie would come to me; that once together Caithleen and Seanie would save each other.

Poor Caithleen!

Poor child! Seanie! Just staying alive was a triumph; out there in the fields and hedges without getting an infection in his dead eye, without permanently damaging that twisted ankle. For two and a half years he was out there, clever and sly; terrified of anyone who tried to get near him. Even now, I'm not sure if Seanie knows me, beyond my name. He has never given any sign that he remembers Caithleen or myself; that he remembers the house where he and Willie came back to life and lifted us out of our grief.

What was in his mind all that time when he avoided everyone for two and a half years?

Caithleen went down that hill knowing she would never see Seanie again; knowing he could see us fading out of his life; that he was watching us disappear through the hedge at the bottom of the hill. She sobbed herself into a state of unconsciousness before we reached Peetie Mahon's taxi. It took the two of us to get her into the back seat, Peetie as solicitous as Florence Nightingale.

How Peetie laughed up his sleeve at us all. He must have seen the whole thing as a great joke – me hiring his taxi to go rescue Seanie. As the years went by, and the truth oozed out, Peetie Mahon's taxi ran through the story like a refrain. It was in the taxi that the boys and the killers went to the Yewtree Cemetery. Mahon must have billed the IRA for that trip. When Miss Bevan showed up during the killing it was in the taxi they escaped. The constable hired the taxi to bring himself and Enda up to the Cemetery after Miss Bevan's report to the Barracks. Willie was brought to the Workhouse morgue in the boot of the taxi. Enda came in the taxi to tell us what had happened. I hired the taxi to take me to the Paupers' Cemetery behind the hearse, Miss Bevan sitting into the back seat with me after she had dismissed her own chauffeur and car.

Dear God!

The sad funeral for Willie. The final humiliation for the pauper boy: a grave in a field far away, lest somehow in death he would contaminate the parish cemetery. Miss Bevan and myself sat in the back seat of the taxi, and Peetie Mahon smiled to himself as he got paid to drive the players from scene to scene of a tragedy he had helped to create.

And then! As we walked away from Willie's grave, walked through the long grass to the fallen gate, Miss Bevan told me that Willie had been murdered. She told me about the piece of wire in his forehead. The terror the poor child had to endure. The cruelty Seanie had to witness!

Change the money-bag to the other hand yet again, I see the familiar silhouette of my house.

It's not home anymore. It's only a place to get old in.

Just as I step off the road onto the loose gravel, the light of a bicycle comes around the bend in the road ahead. When I close the garden gate behind me I wait for the cyclist to pass. I can now hear the noise of the approaching bike; hear, too, angry mutterings.

The lamp sways from side to side with the downward push of each pedal. The mutterings grow louder. As the bicycle passes my gate I call out, 'Good night!' and am immediately frightened by the reaction of the cyclist.

'Oh Jesus!' The light veers sharply. The bicycle sways into the loose gravel in front of the garden wall. As the tyres plough through the gravel the cyclist shouts in terror, 'Oh fuck!' Then the noise in the gravel is suddenly gone.

I'm sure that was Guard McSwaine.

'Are you alright, Guard?' I shout after him.

But there is no response. He's gone.

It was McSwaine. He must have had a long chat with someone when he went to collect his little bribe outside Dunnes. He's never out this late.

My heart is still racing from the fright as I walk up the short garden path to my front door.

JOHN CASHIN

The dark is black. There's not even the hint of light at the windows. If the light can't come in then it can't go out. That's the one thing that worried me at the start. They would have suspected something if the light got out. Some one would see it, someone going home late from a wake or going for the doctor or the priest or the vet in the middle of the night. That's how the stories get started: I hear John Cashin is up all night praying at the side of his bed. The next thing you'd know they'd be saying I fast every day and lash myself with a whip and wear a hair shirt. But I do nothing like that at all. Every day I examine myself to make sure I'm not doing anything odd. That takes up the first quarter of my Holy Hour at six. It's only when I wake up like this and have to wait for the alarm clock, *vox Dei*, that I examine myself so I'll have more time during the Holy Hour to praise Jesus in the tabernacle.

Even though it is only God who can see me, praise to you, Lord God, I examine my behaviour inside the house too. Little peculiarities can creep into my way of doing things unless I am always on my guard, like that time I found myself using gloves to avoid touching my private parts when I washed. Looking up into the darkness above my face, I can see nothing. This is a more perfect time and place for going through my check-list – not that the Church is imperfect in any way; it's just that there are no distractions here in the house, and I know God wants Brother Dismas to do the examination here if He wakens me up in the night.

I am almost all Brother Dismas. John Cashin is almost gone. Shaving twice a day does something to my skin that makes people say things which could be a source of pride to me. Paddy Lennon tells John Cashin what other people say, which helps me to oversee myself; he is another expression of *vox Dei*. Paddy is not like everyone else. He thinks something happened to John Cashin's voice after Mr Sheehan's wife was buried. Everyone else thinks his voice went away in the Yewtree Cemetery the night Willie Doolin was killed.

My face is so clean and so shaved that it looks as if light is shining out of my chin and cheeks. Some say the light of God is shining through me from the inside. I must beware the sin of pride. Some people think I have a skin disease. Others think I never grow old and that my youthfulness shines through my skin. I'm forty-eight. My age is always easy, because I was born in the year the century began. Paddy Lennon says it is the constant shaving that makes my skin glow. Sometimes *vox Dei* gets lost in Paddy's cynicism.

My fingers, too, are spoken about. They are as brown as my bald head, both weathered, but for a farmer, the hands are in good condition. Paddy says some people think I have the fingers of a pianist. Others say I have a priest's fingers. I like that one the best. The fingers of a priest!

John Cashin was twenty-one when Willie Doolin was murdered.

Of course people are always remarking on my sanctity, and here's where I have to be very careful. Trying to be holy is one thing, but thinking you are holy is another thing altogether. It's because of the things I do which I can't do in secret that people think I'm holy. If they only knew what I do in the house, they'd try to have me canonized. But I do the things I do for the salvation of John Cashin's soul.

Every morning I attend the Half Seven Mass. Every evening there's the Holy Hour at six, when I kneel in the gloom near the back on the Mens' Side. Kneeling erect, I rest my elbows on the pew, hands pointing towards the altar, my long brown fingers, with their quarter-moons near the quick, joined so perfectly they could be one hand lying on a mirror. When I close my eyes at the beginning of the Holy

Hour they stay closed till the Church bell strikes seven, till the seventh ring of the bell.

People ask me to pray for their intentions. I have to be wary of pride here, too, because this puts me on the level of a priest. Lay people usually ask each other to say a prayer for the missus or for the cow that is sick, or for the rain to stop. Only a priest is asked to pray for one's intentions.

John Cashin held Willie Doolin's arms when Michael Butler shot him in the forehead with the humane killer, the boy's head locked between Jack Quinlan's knees.

After shaving, using cold water winter and summer, I take off all my clothes and step into the enamel basin my mother washed me in when I was a child. The basin is always surrounded with towels to catch the splashes.

The feet is where I start, and I work my way up, using a soaped face-cloth to clean out all my nooks and crannies. When it's time to rinse off the soap, I fill a sponge in the nearby pail of clean water, and squeeze it over my head. Down my body I go with loaded sponges until I am glistening. Goose-pimples come up all over me. I stay in the basin until I have dried myself from head to knees. Then I spread the towel on the floor and step onto it. After my feet are dried I stay naked until the wash-water is poured into two galvanized pails, the basin is dried with the towel I have used on myself, the basin has been put under the bed, and the splash towels have been picked up and folded neatly. Then I dress.

I can't see any kinks in all that, although some people might think the part about doing things with nothing on is strange. But if I didn't do them that way I'd have to do them with my suit on. I might get creases.

The white shirt goes on first. After all the buttons are fastened I pull on the grey socks, and I know I look like a one-legged stork with a hump. But if I sat down it would take the penance for John Cashin out of it. The socks have black suspenders and so do the grey trousers. To make sure I'm not wasting time I push my feet into the shoes while I'm buttoning the fork of the trousers.

With the top button of the shirt in its hole, I bend up the collar and slip the tie over my head and into its place. The knot on the tie has not been undone since the salesgirl in Seerey's made it for me when I bought it. I had to write out my request for her. They're all Protestants in that shop and I think she thought I was odd. She gave me a strange look when I handed her the piece of paper. She went away with the tie, and I could hear her giggling with another Protestant girl behind a row of overcoats.

After tightening the tie I go to the mirror while bending the shirt collar back into place. I check for symmetry around the neck area, though I know that by the time I get to the mirror everything will be symmetrical.

The pauper boy was crying again, calling out his brother's name. 'Seanie. Seanie. Seanie.' John Cashin could feel the struggling in the boy's arms, little tremors of effort to get free. There was madness in the child's eyes; despair, like the eyes of an animal that knows there's no escape. This is wrong, this is awful wrong, John Cashin thought. Peetie Mahon pushed down on the humane killer, turning the boy's flesh white around the hard metal. The boy screamed and managed to turn his head sideways to get away from the pain. 'Hold the fucker!' Peetie Mahon snarled. I'm glad I'm not holding his head, John Cashin thought. Jack Quinlan pushed his hands down between his own knees and the sides of the boy's head. He clenched an ear in each fist, twisted the face back to the sky; turned the head back to the humane killer. The one at the gate screamed like someone who was mad altogether.

John Cashin was wet with sweat all over and the sun had only been up for a few minutes. He wanted to throw up. He wished he'd known the doctor was going to try to get them away in the cemetery lane. He wished he could whisk this boy up into his arms and run away from there, run up the hill. But the others would kill him. They would say, too, that he was not able to live up to the IRA oath, that he didn't have the stomach for it. But this is awful wrong, John Cashin thought. This is a child who did nothing.

Peetie Mahon snarled, 'Don't let him go again, you eejit!' John Cashin could feel the small struggles in the thin arms, could hear the heart racing because he had to use the side of his head to keep the child's chest pinned to the ground. From where he was sitting across the boy's legs, with the side of his face on the grass, Michael Butler-the-Butcher could see what Peetie Mahon was doing. 'Hurry up, for Chrissakes,' he shouted. If the doctor had been there John Cashin would have taken his side. If only I'd done it in the Bottling House, he thought. The boy whimpered and whispered, 'Seanie Seanie Daddy Mammy'. Cashin was terrified.

The boy wasn't straining anymore. The tears were rolling out of the side of each eye, flowing down the side of the head to Jack Quinlan's clenched fists. The one at the gate could see what was being done to his brother. He kept shouting out, 'Willie Willie,' his thin voice loud in the early morning, far-carrying and forlorn like the cry of a curlew. It was as if he was calling to his brother from a great distance, letting the one on the ground know that he would be found, would be found and freed.

'Willie Willie,' he cried over and over, and the iron gate rattled as he pulled uselessly, trying to pull his hands through the tight rope that had been used to bind him. 'Willie, Willie, I'm tied up. I can't get loose,' the thin voice carrying his torment out into the headstones, out into the fields and up the hill across Miss Bevan's farm. He seemed to be telling John Cashin over and over that he was doing a wrong thing. But John Cashin knew that already and wished the boy would shut up.

Peetie Mahon dropped the gun in the wet grass and said: 'Hold on a minute, lads.' He ran over to the gate where the one was shouting, grabbed him by his Workhouse fringe and pulled his face up against the bars of the gate. 'I'll cut your fucking throat if you don't shut up,' he shouted. He pushed the boy's head away and then jerked it forward viciously, jamming his face on each side against the iron bars. 'Shut the fuck up,' Peetie Mahon shouted again. He ran back to where the other three were holding down the brother, and picked up the humane killer. The boy's eyes were the eyes of a bull being castrated. One side of his face had turned blue where Peetie Mahon had hit him with the flash-lamp in the Bottling House.

Mahon started to wipe the dew off the handle of the gun with the sleeve of his coat. 'Shoot the fucker!' Michael Butler ground out through his teeth. 'Will you shoot the fucker, Mahon, and get it over with.' 'I'm not sure how to fire this,' Peetie Mahon said. 'Do I have to hold it against his head when I fire it?' The boy was squirming, the weak struggle going into John Cashin's body. He wanted to be sick again. 'Just shoot him,' Michael Butler said through his teeth. 'Shoot him, you stupid fucker!' Peetie Mahon put the gun to the boy's head. The boy at the gate screamed. The body heaved uselessly against the side of John Cashin's head, the heart in the boy's chest gone mad. But the boy pulled his ears out of Jack Quinlan's fingernails.

'*Camarán! Camarán!*' Michael Butler roared. 'You stupid fucking *Camarán!*' He jumped to his feet and shouted at Peetie Mahon, 'Give me the gun and I'll do it, you stupid fucker. And you, Quinlan! Hold his fucking ears, you great bloody woman!' When Peetie Mahon gave him the humane killer, Michael Butler hit him in the chest with the heel of his hand. 'Sit on his legs, you arsehole, and see if you can do that right.'

The boy jerked his head from side to side, evading Jack Quinlan's grasping fingers. Michael Butler kicked Quinlan on the shoulder so that he fell over into the stones. He slammed the heavy humane killer into the side of the boy's head, stunning him. The boy at the gate screamed and clanged the gate with his pulling.

'Now, hold him, Quinlan,' Michael Butler snapped. Jack Quinlan, pushing himself off the gravel, picked up a stone and flung it, with the anger he was feeling for Michael Butler, at the boy tied to the far side of the gate. The boy at the gate stopped screaming.

'God damn your fucking eyes, Quinlan,' Michael Butler shouted. 'Get over here, you fucking *Camarán*, and hold the bastard's head.' Jack Quinlan plopped to his knees on the grass and, without effort, turned the limp head to the sky. Michael Butler brought the humane killer down on the forehead. The moment the metal touched the flesh he pulled the trigger. Bang.

I never look at my own eyes in the mirror when I shave, nor when I check my tie and collar. Even though everything is invariably symmetrical, I always move the knot of the tie, move it out of line and back again. After the tie I lace my shoes without bending my knees. The pain is offered up in reparation for John Cashin's sin. Next it's the suit coat off the hook at the back of the door. I fasten the buttons and check the pocket flaps to be sure they're out.

Whether it's for the Half-Seven Mass or the Holy Hour, I follow the same course when I'm getting ready. The only time it's diferent is when I put on a clean shirt and socks for Sunday Mass. As I stand at the bedroom door, ready to turn the knob, I check my pocket for the folded white handkerchiefs – one for kneeling on to keep the knees of the trousers clean, the other to take care of a sudden sneeze. I take a deep breath and leave the room.

So far, I don't think there's any odd things creeping in. The alarm clock should be going off soon. It's still as dark as it was.

Down the narrow stairs I go, my back as straight as a soldier's on parade. The hat and raincoat are hanging on the hook in the front door, always ready and nearby if the weather demands. On the hall wall, beside the light switch, hangs the holy water font. A coloured picture of the Children of Fatima is covered in plastic above the tiny water container. Lucy, Jacinta and Francesco are in a state of ecstasy, as they gaze upon the Virgin in a tree, blue scapular over a full-length white dress. To keep the holy water from evaporating too quickly, I have a small piece of sponge in the dish.

Every time, before I unlatch the door, I put my right index finger in the water and make the sign of the cross. I always perform this ritual exactly as Sister Xavier taught me in First Babies in the Convent. Exactly! I hate the way the men do it in the Church, as if they were impatiently brushing a horsefly away from their faces. But who am I to throw the first stone, Lord Jesus!

First, the left hand is placed on the stomach over the navel, the fingers straight out, the thumb pulled in tightly to the side of the hand. The right hand, after dipping the fingers in holy water – if there is some around – is brought to the centre of the forehead while saying, 'In the name of the Father.'

What finally made John Cashin throw up were the tiny spasms in the boy's arms, as the flesh contracted and collapsed. He twisted away from the twitching body. He had killed a boy. On all fours, he watched the vomit splashing into the grass, saw the blotches jumping onto his hands, felt the greasy sweat oozing out of all the pores, the acrid sharpness of the spent gunpowder at the back of his nostrils. He was so weak he didn't think he'd ever get to his feet again. His body heaved by itself and made noises. Then a shudder took hold of him and the nausea was suddenly gone. Strength surged back into his limbs, and with it, the knowledge of where he was coursed back into his brain. Still on all fours he turned his head.

What he saw jolted him. Michael Butler had inserted a piece of strong wire into the hole in the boy's forehead and was twisting and turning the wire, stirring the brain of the dead child the way you would stir a bowl of porridge. Jack Quinlan had moved out of the way, but was still holding the head so it wouldn't fall over. The boy's eyes were open, falling around in their sockets. As John Cashin jumped to his feet – tottering as the world swayed beneath him – he shouted without even thinking about it, 'No! No! There's no need for that, Michael!'

Peetie Mahon went over to see what Michael Butler was doing, then said, 'That fucker won't talk, anyhow.'

'There's no need to do that!' John Cashin turned to leave.

Someone said, 'Don't go away, John. We have the other lad yet.'

He turned around and roared, 'I'm finished with all of this! This wasn't supposed to happen. That's a child, not a barrel of porter.'

'Fuck you, John. We're all in this together. You took the oath like the rest of us.'

'Fuck the oath, Peetie!' John Cashin roared because he was afraid. 'Fuck you, too, Peetie. I'm leaving.'

'You could be shot for this, John', Michael Butler said.

'Then shoot me, Michael! Shoot me now, here! Here!' John Cashin went over to Michael Butler and bent his head forward. 'Here, Michael!' and he put his finger to the middle of his forehead. 'Do it now.'

He pushed Butler, who tumbled onto his arse on the grass, and then swung a kick at Jack Quinlan's arm. When Quinlan's hand came off the dead boy's face, the head fell over to one side; the eyes stared, unmoving.

'What the fuck's wrong with you?' Peetie Mahon gripped John Cashin by the arm roughly.

'It's enough! It's enough!' he shouted into Peetie Mahon's face. 'Let go of me!'

He tried to wrench his arm out of Mahon's hands. Mahon held on, tightening his grip. 'What the fuck's wrong with you?' he roared.

Without thinking, without knowing he was going to do it, John Cashin tore free and smashed his fist into Mahon's mouth. As he spun away, Michael Butler was standing there waiting for him. He hit John Cashin in the two shoulders at once with the heels of his hands, sending him stumbling back into the body of the dead boy. When he fell, his feet were on one side of the body and his arse on the other. His knees were a sharp-angled arch over the body. For the short moment he was sitting there he realized it was not the desecration of the dead boy's body that he should be fighting about. It was the boy tied to the gate he should be trying to save. This made him jump to his feet. Jack Quinlan was still kneeling on the grass near the dead boy's head, his mouth open, trying to grasp what was going on around him. Michael Butler's body was tensed up, like the bristling body of a dog suddenly face to face with a badger. Peetie Mahon's eyes were on fire with murder, bloody spittle on his chin, both lips split. 'You fucking bastard!' Peetie Mahon said, and he leaped at John Cashin.

Sister Xavier brought her left hand down slowly from her forehead. Because she was facing us, all the children in the classroom did the same with their right hands. The nun touched her black habit just above the right hand on her navel. She dragged out the word 'and' until we joined her: 'Aaaaaand of the Son.'

Sister Xavier brought her left hand to her right shoulder. She waited for those children who brought their right hands to the wrong shoulders. When everyone was ready she said: 'Aaaaaand of the Holy Ghost.'

Slowly she took her right hand off her navel. As the left hand descended from the right shoulder it met the navel hand in front of her chest. The hands came together with the outstretched fingers pointing at the ceiling. 'Aaaaaamen. Keep your elbows in to your sides, children. And I told you already, only the devil blesses himself with his left hand.'

Most people in the Town perform a broken-down version of Sister Xavier's perfect model. People who do the crossing according to her directions are jeered at for their perfection. I wonder what they say about me, some of the gossipy ones.

I stand in front of the ecstatic Lucy, Jacinta and Francesco and perform the blessing according to Sister Xavier's rules. If I think I make a mistake, even a slight one, I do it again, even if I have to bless myself twenty times.

Before I go out I bend down to look at the Church clock through the small pane in the door. If it's morning, I step out into the Town at exactly twenty-nine minutes past seven. In the evening I wait for the last stroke of six to ring. Then, like a swimmer taking a deep breath before diving into water, I open the door and step into The Town.

On my way to Half-Seven Mass I know, because of my timing, I will not have to talk with anyone, beyond greeting them with a nod of the head. On my way to the evening Holy Hour the first stroke of the Angelus rings out as my

171

foot touches the pavement outside the front door. Everyone between the house and the Church will be praying the Angelus, so a distracted wave of the hand or a nod is all that's expected.

The Angel of the Lord declared unto Mary, I pray as I stride the short distance to the Church. *And she conceived of the Holy Ghost.*

Hail Mary, full of grace, the Lord is with thee, blessed art thou amongst women and blessed is the fruit of thy womb, Jesus. Holy Mary, mother of God, pray for us sinners, now and at the hour of our death. Amen.

I have to sit up to bow my head at the mention of the holy name. The hard boards hurt my flesh in reparation for John Cashin's sin. Purposefully I whack the back of my head against the boards when I lie down again. The alarm should be going off soon. The monks in Mount Mellary are getting up now, getting ready.

I always pray the words of the Hail Mary slowly. No rushing, no running the words into each other to make the prayer sound like one word said in one breath.

Behold the handmaid of the Lord; be it done unto me according to thy word.

This is my most repeated declaration to God: be it done unto me according to thy word. If I am working on the farm and rain begins to fall, I interpret this as my being done unto according to God's will, and I will not seek shelter. I continue to work as if the rain does not exist.

The next Hail Mary of the Angelus is always finished just as I arrive at the gate of the Churchyard.

And the Word was made flesh and dwelt among us.

With the dwelling of the Word among us, I strike my breast with closed hand. I don't punch myself in the navel with my fist, like half the Town does.

I always have the next Hail Mary said before I reach the Church door, and have already begun the ending prayer to the Angelus.

Pour forth, we beseech thee, O Lord, thy grace into our hearts that we, to whom the incarnation of Christ thy son, was made known by the message of an angel; may by his passion and cross be brought to the glory of his resurrection. Through Christ, our Lord. Amen.

The Angelus prayer ends with the sign of the cross, Sister Xavier's version, no matter who I think is looking at me.

The first thing to do in the Church is dip the fingers in the big, black, marble holy water font. This is followed by the devout touching, with wet fingers, of the feet of the life-sized crucified Christ hanging above the font, and then the performance of Sister Xavier's blessing.

I once had a problem with this. The signing of the cross at the end of the Angelus always coincided with my arrival at the holy water font. Should I bless myself twice? Every day, when I went to do my Holy Hour, I was distracted by this problem so much that I had written to my Spiritual Adviser in Mount Mellary to ask his opinion. I was advised to begin praying the Angelus before I left the house so that the two blessings would not coincide.

Since then, as I approach the holy water font, I bless myself with dry fingers. Then I do the entrance ritual. Of course someone noticed this double blessing. Paddy Lennon once asked me if I blessed myself before dipping my fingers to protect myself from all the little things growing in there. He said that Jimmy Fox had never cleaned out the font since he started working as lay sacristan in 1921; that it had been peed into many times by those scallywags from the country, competing with each other as they stood around the back of the Church at Sunday morning Mass, cow dung on their boots. I didn't answer Paddy's question – my vow of silence.

It was the rage on Peetie Mahon's face, as much as his own determination to free the boy at the gate, that jerked John Cashin into action. As Mahon lunged at him, he ducked under his hands and ran to the gate, trying to get his right hand into the pocket of his flapping jacket for his penknife. Glancing up, all he saw was a featureless face behind the bars. He looked back down: he couldn't get the hand into the knife pocket. As he ran the last few steps across the gravel he grasped at the flapping coat with his left hand, pulled it against his body and plunged his right hand into the pocket.

'Get ready to run, get ready to run,' he shouted at the face on the far side of the gate. As his fingers clutched the knife he felt a sharp pain in his head, and wondered for a second how he could have bumped into something. He hadn't seen anything.

When his eyes opened by themselves he saw a straight brown line across a white page. He thought he was in a dream until he felt the pain in the side of his face. When he moved his hand to relieve it, he remembered what he was trying to do and pushed himself onto his knees. Blackness slid across his eyes like a black cloud covering the sun on a March day. He put his hand to the back of his head to where the split was. But there was no split, just a bump. The blackness ovecame him again and he plopped back down into the gravel.

Then a jumble of sounds thinned out into Peetie Mahon's voice; then the crying voice of the boy; then the sound of feet in the stones beside him. He squinted up. Jack Quinlan was standing there with a knife in his hand, the peak of his cap twisted to one side, almost over his ear. Quinlan's boots were within inches of his face, huge in his eyes. In the ravine formed where the soles and uppers were sewn together was dried-up cow dung.

It wasn't until the boots moved in the loud gravel that John Cashin's mind flipped back to what was happening around him. Peetie Mahon's voice was behind him, angry, demanding. 'Hurry up you little fucker, of I'll kick you off the fucking thing.' John Cashin rolled over in the gravel. Peetie Mahon and the boy were at the top of the stile, the boy's head twisted at an unnatural angle. As John Cashin looked, Peetie Mahon said, 'What the fuck!' and gave a push. The boy fell the eight feet from the top of the stile, and landed on his feet. A pain cried out of him and he sat where he landed on the gravel in the cemetery. As he came down the stone steps after him Peetie Mahon growled, 'Get up! Get up, you little bastard.'

John Cashin sat up, the helplessness of the situation drenching him all over again. He bent over, put his hands on the gravel and pushed himself up. Wide bands of blackness flew across his eyes but, once he was on his feet, he leaned against the gate. Beside him, Jack Quinlan was gaping back to where Michael Butler knelt at the head of the dead boy. But Quinlan wasn't looking at Michael Butler. A big red-headed figure was emerging, resurrecting, from behind a broad white headstone. Doctor McKenna, his smooth-soled shoes slipping on the damp grass, was past Michael Butler before he could be intercepted, and was bearing down on Peetie Mahon, yelling, bellowing, 'Run Seanie! Run Seanie!'

When Michael Butler started after Doctor McKenna, John Cashin pushed himself off the gate and set out to meet him. He knew the butcher would level him, would run over him. Michael Butler had been wrestling fully grown animals onto the floor of his uncle's slaughterhouse since he was fourteen, had inherited the slaughterhouse when a maddened heifer impaled the uncle on one of her horns. As he pushed off the Cemetery gate, and headed for a certain battering, John Cashin said to Jack Quinlan, 'Be on our side, Jack.'

After dipping my fingers in the polluted holy water I touch the worn feet of the crucifix. When I bless myself I kiss the blessing fingers, despite what Paddy Lennon said about the water. I believe it's an act of faith to do the same thing as the volunteers who lower the diseased bodies of the faithful into the waters at Lourdes, then drink from the same water when they're thirsty.

With the taste of the water on my lips, I go to the men's side of the Church. Whether it's for the Half Seven Mass or to do my Holy Hour, there are few people scattered about the long brown pews. There is never anyone in my place.

When I reach my pew I genuflect, the way Sister Xavier showed us. Standing erect, I bring back the right foot, sink the right knee to the floor beside the heel of the left shoe, while bringing the two hands to rest – the right on top of the left – on the left knee. When the right knee touches the floor I hold myself in this position for a few moments while

I look at the tabernacle door, gleaming like gold in the candlelight or reflected sunlight. Devoutly I say, 'I adore thee, O Christ, and I praise thee.'

I step into the pew and sit down, take out a handkerchief, unfold it along its ironed-in crease, and lay it on the kneeler. Next I slip forward on the shiny seat and kneel. Mentally I review how I look and, after making some small changes, slip into my devotions. The first thing is the examination for hints of strangeness, unless, of course, God wakens me up in the night to do it so I'll have more time to praise him during my Holy Hour.

For two months after the killing of Willie Doolin, John Cashin lived in a world where he found it hard to know the difference between his nightmares and the terror of his memories. Awake or asleep, the fear of banishment to hell for all eternity was like a black cloud of sulphur around him. He confessed his sin over and over. When the priest shouted at him not to mention that sin anymore, he went to the Queentown church on his bike every Saturday to confess it there.

'Bless me, Father, for I have sinned. It's a week since my last confession. I held down a boy while another man killed him.'

'When did this happen?'

'A year ago.'

'Did you confess it in your last confession?'

'I did, Father.'

'Why are you confessing it again?'

'I don't feel God has forgiven me.'

'You have to forgive yourself.'

'I can't, Father. I see his eyes.'

When the priest in the Queentown church grew tired of him, and eventually told him not to bother him again, John Cashin decided to become a Cistercian monk in Mount Mellary in County Tipperary. He left the farm in the care of Paddy Lennon and set off one Saturday morning. Once in the monastery he would write and tell Paddy Lennon the farm was his to keep.

Over mountains, along unpaved roads with pot-holes deep enough to drown a dog in, through rain and wind, through a countryside in the throes of civil war, John Cashin pedalled his big bike, offering up the pain in his backside. When the front wheel slammed into a water-filled pot-hole, slamming his face onto the handlebars, he offered up the cuts and bruises for his heinous offence. That was his favourite word for it: heinous. It reminded him of a hyena sticking its snout into the rotting cavity of an abandoned carcass and sucking out the liquid rottenness with careless slurping sounds. Heinous. It was a heinous sin. He was a heinous sinner.

In the dark he arrived at the gate of the monastery. As he stood there, waiting for the bell to be answered, he pulled the seat of his trousers out of his bruised arse, all the time offering up the pain in reparation for his heinousness – liquid corruption dripping off the hyena's hairy jaw.

The monks fed him, gave him a bed for the night, and sent him on his way the next morning when they discovered his vocation was based in guilt.

'This is not the French Foreign Legion, young man,' a kindly old monk had told him. 'Go back home and take care of the boy who survived. That is God's will for you.'

The monk's name was Father Damien, and he became John Cashin's Spiritual Adviser.

On Sunday, the day before Mrs Sheehan was buried, he arrived home, after riding the last eighteen miles off the saddle. His shin-bones felt as though they had been hammered on a blacksmith's anvil, and his buttocks as raw as a fresh steak.

Out of the agony of that journey had come the great idea. For twenty-five years I have kept it to myself, never once mentioning it to Father Damien, nor to Father Joseph, who took over as my Spiritual Adviser when the old man died. Not one person in the Town, not even Father Quinn, not Mister Sheehan or Doctor McKenna or Paddy Lennon, has discovered the great idea, even though it is there for everyone to see. It is such a source of glee that I often confess to the sin of pride without mentioning what I am proud about.

John Cashin had become a home-made Cistercian monk. He had become Brother Dismas, but everyone in the Town still sees me as John Cashin, the shell of my old self.

I sent to the Mount Mellary gift shop for a copy of St Benedict's Rule. Applying the rule to myself, I left out only those things that would draw the attention of the Town gossips. In the privacy of my own house I observe the Canonical Hours, rising every morning at two to read Matins and Lauds. At five I'm up again, standing at the bookstand reading Prime. This is followed by an hour's meditation, and then it's time to wash in the cold enamel basin in preparation for the Half-Seven Mass.

From the picture of the Cistercian monk on the cover of the Rule, I designed and made a monk's habit. To get the material, I had to go to Queentown, where no one knew me. The habit is not perfect – it's tight under the arms and the cowl has no point – but I love slipping it onto my naked body when I prepare myself for bed at eight o'clock. The cowl is very satisfying, even if it has no point. When I draw it over my head it slips forward until I'm looking out through a tunnel. It's as if I have gone into a dark place, have cut out the rest of the world. The home-made leather belt pulls the habit into my body, the roughness of the cloth a source of penance.

To observe the rule of silence, I speak only when it is absolutely necessary. Besides timing my journeys out to the Church so that silence is seen as normal, I organize all my trips into the world so that the least amount of talking is needed.

Part of the farm runs up to the back door of the house so it's not hard to avoid people when I'm working. At first when I went for the groceries I left a list with the shopkeeper and came back later, when I knew everything would be ready. After some years the shopkeeper told me not to bother with the list, since it was the same every week. I time my visit to the grocery store for when I know it will be empty, put the exact money on the counter, pick up my box of provisions, nod to the shopkeeper and leave.

Over the years it has become accepted in the Town that I have a speech impediment, but I know that, behind my back, children called me the Dummy Cashin.

Paddy Lennon told John Cashin one time after Jack Quinlan's explosive exposure at Michael Butler's grave that the people swore he lost his voice the night of the killing. They said John Cashin once had a beautiful tenor voice, that he had sung the songs of Thomas Moore better than any McCormick. Of course, they were wrong about the two things. John Cashin couldn't sing to save his life, and Paddy Lennon knew it was two months after the killing of Willie Doolin that he lost his voice. It was on the day Caithleen Sheehan was buried, the day after John Cashin came back from being away someplace for a weekend, that his voice started giving him trouble.

At the graveside, Paddy told me, when all the people had drifted away to visit their own family plots, John Cashin had a long talk with Mister Sheehan. Even though Paddy had been within three feet of them, he couldn't make out what they spoke about. But it was during the following week that John Cashin had started bringing food up to Miss Bevan's field near The Cemetery to leave at the foot of a tree for Blindeye Doolin, that time he went quare in the head and lived wild in badger burrows and cowhouses for two years, and it was then, too, that he either started losing his voice or stopped talking, one or the other. It had nothing to do with the night they killed Blindeye's brother. It was from the day of Caithleen Sheehan's funeral that, when John Cashin wanted a handyman's job done, Paddy Lennon started finding notes stuck under the knocker of his door in the early morning. By the way he talks to me, I think Paddy sees me as Brother Dismas.

I have just finished my examination when the alarm clock rings – another sign that God woke me to do it. It is two minutes to two on the morning of the day when the new wing of the Church is to be consecrated. It's going to be hard to keep my vow of silence today with all the people around. Maybe I'll go to the Church early and leave late. But it would look odd if I didn't join the parade. Which comes first, my vow of silence or the need not to give myself away? I always chose not to give myself away. Imagine the jeering if they knew about Brother Dismas.

The moment the clock goes off I turn back the blanket, swing my feet out onto the floor and turn off the alarm. Across the uncovered floorboards I trot in the dark, to the light switch at the door.

The light from the sudden naked bulb illuminates a scene that I love. I am able to go out of myself and look at the room from the outside. With its hand on the light switch stands the habit of a Cistercian monk, two bare feet showing, a black hole where a face should be in the cowl. On the scrubbed wood floor is a large enamel basin, three-quarters full of clear water, a bucket full of water beside it. Both are on blue towels, tightly stretched and lined up so their edges and the lines of the floorboards are symmetrical. Beside the bucket is a folded white facecloth on which is a bar of yellow soap, its lines at ease with the lines of the towel and the floorboards.

The black-painted, iron-framed bed stands starkly against the white wall across from the door. There is no pillow on the narrow frame, no mattress. Parts of the four boards, which stretch from foot to head, are visible where the thin blanket does not cover them. The lines between the boards run across the lines of the floor at right angles. Above the bed, exactly half-way between head and foot, a crucifix hangs on the wall. The crucified Christ is still alive, the racked face appealing to the sky for relief. Beside the head of the bed, on a small table, is the alarm clock with a short slat of wood propped against it, the words VOX DEI burned into its surface by an awkward hand.

Another table, painted glossy brown, is just big enough to hold the base of the shaving mirror. The mirror, anchored to its stand at the middle, catches the naked bulb and casts a patch of oblong light on to the wall where the crucifix hangs. On the base of the stand, almost hidden by the angled mirror, are lined up the lather brush, the razor, the shaving mug – all spotless, as if they have never been used.

My eyes swing over to the home-made bookstand near the foot of the bed. After twenty-seven years I still get excited when I'm about to approach the bookstand. Sometimes I am aware of a slight movement of the flesh. And now, as my hand slips off the light switch, I see the rows of monks in their chapel in Mount Mellary; flickering shadows and the chill of the clean morning air; silhouettes in the stained-glass window against a weak quarter-moon. The cantor's voice will soon slice through the silence and bear praise for God; the ghostly voices of two hundred monks will respond, shattering the silence and the darkness.

On the stand is an English translation of what the monks chant in Latin. Bowing from the waist I go forward to join, in spirit and sentiment, my brothers in the Rule of St Benedict. Just as I stretch my hand out to pick up the breviary, I think I hear someone knocking at the front door. I stop my hand on the book-stand. The monks are about to start Matins. My hand moves to the breviary, fingers touching the soft calf leather. The cantor is standing, opening his mouth to intone the sacred words, to fill the monastery chapel with praise, to lift the minds and hearts of the monks up to their maker.

But already, the sound I think I heard has distracted me from my holy endeavour. The monks have gone ahead without me.

There it is again. I must put aside my annoyance at the interruption. The knocking at the door is merely another expression of *vox Dei*.

SEANIE DOOLIN

Willie! Don't make a sound. Don't breathe. They're across there, Red and Peetie Mahon. Turn your ear to me so I can whisper. Oh! Willie, it's over at last. I'm free after all this time. Across the street, *across the margent of the world I fled, and troubled the gold gateways of the stars, smiting for shelter on their clanged bars.* In the shelter of this shadow I'm safe from them. In the back seat Uncle Enda whispered in my ear to run when everyone got out of the car. To run and run. To run anywhere. But Peetie Mahon held me, and he only held me because all this time I thought he could hold me. But look at me! I did it, Willie. He had me by the ear, pulling me and pushing me. He never thought I'd do it. That's why it was so easy. I surprised him. He had beaten and kicked and slapped me, and he never thought I would jerk my ear out of his hand and run.

If you could only have seen me running with Red coming after me, pretending again about Uncle Enda. He's always doing it, always saying it. 'Uncle Enda. It's Uncle Enda, Seanie.' I ran so fast he didn't even try to follow me. I'm free and they don't know where I am.

We must be quiet. Now I can stop the whole thing from happening. I'm going to twist the story when it comes around again, even if it breaks my wrists, breaks every bone in my body. I'll stand there like Merlin, and I'll stand there twisting it and twisting it, even though I know they will throw stones at me and anything they can find to throw, but I'll stand there and twist and twist till the story starts going my way. Once it starts, once I twist it out of its track, it will go where I want it to go.

I will save you, Willie. You won't be killed anymore, nor

frightened. All I have to do is stay free. If it doesn't work the next time around then I'll make it work the time after that. It will be like standing at the end of a mile of thick steel rope and giving it such a sudden, strong twist that the whole length of it, even the other end of it a mile away, turns over.

Shush! They're talking across the street, across the margent of the world. Red smelled like the porter in The Workhouse when he sneaked up behind me, when he thought I wouldn't be able to get up after falling, after jerking my head away from Peetie Mahon. 'Uncle Enda,' he said. 'It's Uncle Enda, Seanie!' Uncle Enda! and he's over there across the margent of the world talking to Peetie Mahon. They're talking to each other, and there is the voice of the woman above that keeps saying, 'What's going on down there? What's going on down there?' Over and over and over. 'What's going on down there? What's going on down there?'

It's a long time before Peetie Mahon steps out onto the footpath and looks up. He says 'Miss Lalor' twice. Then there is a window closing, like the Guard and Hubey Sherlock's daughter's window. 'Miss Lalor, Miss Lalor,' is what Peetie Mahon says with his face turned up, the light from the shop door lighting the skin of his throat, that is all taut because he is looking up, the way he looked up when someone said, 'Look. Look.' That's what I'll say to him and point. 'Look. Look.'

The light from Peetie Mahon's door goes out on the footpath, and Red goes away in his motor. I love the sound of the motor car in the middle of the night. You can hear all the soft little bangs coming out of its pipe in a steady flow. The car, you would think, should have to draw in a deep breath, but the flow of soft bangs keeps coming and coming without stopping for anything. When I imitate it with my lips I run out of breath.

The red lights at the back of Red's car get smaller.

I'll walk into the shop when he's not looking and I'll suddenly say, 'Look. Look,' and I'll point. When the side of his neck is stretched tight I'll stick it with the Priest's knife. I feel in my pocket to make sure I haven't lost it. It's there.

I knew I could get free the minute I grabbed his coat and he couldn't make me let go until he choked me. He won't get the chance to choke me again, because the minute he looks away when I shout, 'Look. Look,' I'll drive the knife as far as it'll go, *drive my dead thoughts over the universe like withered leaves, to quicken a new birth.*

I'll wait till tomorrow, Willie. I'll get the two of them tomorrow. The two with the gun, the Priest and Peetie Mahon. I'll have to leave the knife in Peetie Mahon's neck when I drive my dead thoughts over the universe, drive it in and run away so he won't have any chance to get me. I'll have to get another knife for the Priest. I'll ring the doorbell – but she'd only come out and she might try to peck my eye out. The River! I'll wait for him at the River and push him in; creep up behind him after hiding in the blackberry briars. If God couldn't find me when I fled him down the labyrinthine ways of my mind at the River, then how will the Priest know I'm waiting for him!

Shush, Willie! Give me your ear again. A car is coming. There's nothing to fear. It's only a car passing in the night, two big lamps in the dark like two bright eyes just shining there. Shush! my illie illie buddah, there's nothing to fear anymore. I am free and when I kill Peetie Mahon and the Priest there will be no reason for the others to hold you down any more. Shush, the car has stopped and the man is out and walking this way. He won't find us in the shadow, my buddah. I am going to get you free. Hold on, my illy buddah. He's going back to the motor car. O gentle Willie. Now he's coming back again and he has a flash-lamp. Oh, gentle baby, I have to go. He's going to light up my shadow and find me. Come with me *gentle child, Beautiful as thou wert, why dids't thou leave the trodden paths of men too soon?* Oh Willie.

He will never find me. No one will ever find me again. It's Red! It's Red, Willie. Do you hear him calling me, the way he says my name? Shaw-nee. Like Ban-shee. Female ghost. I'm a he ghost.

Plumtree Lane is all one shadow. It's so dark down there the only way to find where to go is to watch the tops of the walls each side. You have to know the pot-holes, where they are, because if you step into one, when you're going along looking at the tops of the walls, your head snaps as if you got a rabbit punch. Red is following, calling Shaw-nee, the flash-lamp light going from side to side, looking at the walls.

The minute I step out into the grass of the Playing Field I get wet feet because of the dew. I love the dew in the morning when the sun shines on it. You can see every cobweb in the world, all lit up like the diamonds in Hubey Sherlock's shop window, only there's millions of them hanging from bushes and trees and flowers and grass and weeds. Red comes out into the field and he's calling louder now. I move off to the left. His weak flash-lamp is going towards the other goal-posts, so I stop and wait and listen. Then he calls your name, Willie, calls yours and mine.

'Shaw-nee, Will-ee.'

The flash-lamp is gone out, but I stand still in case it's one of his tricks. He calls my name again and says, 'I'll help you.'

Help me what? How does he know? He can't know! I haven't told ... Willie, Willie! Did you tell him I was going to kill them? He wouldn't help me. He's trying to trick me again, capture me to tie my hands on the other side of the gate. I'm free.

I'M FREE!

No one will ever catch me.

Now he's crying your name again, Willie. Don't go, Willie. Don't go!

I think he's standing still. I can escape back up Plumtree Lane! Through the grass, as silent as a mouse, I move, raising my feet to step above the grass-tops, so he won't hear my swishes. Just as I reach the lane Red calls out my name at the top of his voice.

SHAW-NEE!

The nee part shrills into the air *like a wind that shrills*

*all night in a waste land, where no one comes or hath come
since the making of the world.* Around in the air it shrills
and shrills – nee ee ee ee – like the sound you would think a
Banshee would make when someone is going to die.

Once I'm in Plumtree Lane I stop to listen, to make sure
no one is coming towards me. Red is not shrilling anymore.
Before I start again I look behind me, and there's his flash-
lamp, the light swinging around wildly as if he had no idea
where he was or where he was going. But then it comes in a
straight line towards the lane and I set off, walking where I
know there are no pot-holes. When I'm back on the street I
go right. I'm going to Mister Sheehan's house, to sleep, to
hide from them. Maybe they're all looking for me. They
know I'm going to kill Peetie Mahon and the Priest, and
they're out looking for me.

Back on the street I start to run. There's no place to hide
between here and the Four Streets, not if someone has a
flash-lamp and is looking for me. How did he know? Past
the Monument I run, so fast. So fast. I remember one time
with you, Willie, running with our heads back, running
across a field along a path made by cattle, running so fast,
with such effort that we left the ground and sped through
the air, our running feet barely touching the tops of the
blades of grass. Willie, you have lain heavy *upon the sighful
branches of my mind* in the long green grass. But it's over,
my baby Illy.

The Monument whizzes past me, and when I'm nearly at
the Four Streets I slow down to a walk, skipping from
shadow to shadow. When I look back, there is the dim flash-
lamp back at Robin's Corner, appearing and disappearing,
sweeping back and forth from one side of the street to the
other, searching for shadows.

Then everything becomes like the night in the Bottling
House. There are people coming from the direction of
Mister Sheehan's house. I hear the voices low, low like they
were that night before they found us behind the crates, sit-
ting in the flowing porter. Well, no one will catch me again.
Red is behind me. Voices are coming from my left, so I go

right. Willie, I'm going right. There's lights on at Butler-the-Butcher's. I'm running again, running like we ran over the grass-tops. I have to run through a piece of the light where The Four Streets meet. The very minute I go into the light I hear behind me a roar, and I know it's the Guard.

'BLINDEYE, BLINDEYE! COME BACK HERE!'

Even his voice cuts me, from all the times he has beaten me. He is broken glass and barbed wire. I run like a deer, as quick as a deer out of Walter Scott.

'HEY BLINDEYE, YOU CROOKED FUCKER! COME BACK HERE!'

I'm not going back there to be cut. I am free now and I have a knife, and Willie, if anyone cuts me again or touches you again, I'm going to stick the knife in him. I'd stick it in The Guard's big belly, too. When I stop and look back, I see him walking beside his bike in the street-light.

'I'LL GET YOU, YOU LITTLE FUCKER! I'LL ARREST YOU!'

Like the deer leaping forward at the sound of a dog's yelp, I take off again.

There's two lights on at Butler-the-Butcher's, the two of them on the outside walls. Once I pass the lights I'll go over the gate and into the field where Butler keeps his fat ones. That way I'll come back through the fields to Mister Shee-han's house. The gate is on the left, but as soon as I think of it I see two lamps up there, up at the very gate I was going to climb. It's as if every time I think of some place to go, there's someone there before me. I was going to Mister Sheehan's and the Guard appeared, I was going to jump over that gate and two lights appeared.

They're not flash-lamps the ones in front have. They are carrying lanterns, like a farmer uses at night around a farm-yard. I know by the way they're swinging.

It's the night of the Bottling House again, Willie. Red and the Guard are behind me and there's two in front. Daddy Daddy they're killing our Willie!

I don't like Butler-the-Butcher's. Behind the shop there is a house where they kill animals. I have heard the sounds sometimes, terrible sounds, Willie. There's a concrete path, the width of a cow, and a high wall all around the shop and the killing house. What else can I do, Willie? I know it's the same. It's the very same, but there's no place else to go. They're behind me and before me. Oh God, it's going to happen again.

I move to the edge of the road and, just as I'm about to pass, I slip into the space between the shop and the wall, slip into the lane that goes up to the gates of the Cemetery. Oh, Willie! I have to keep going. I know! I know! The sounds of the men's boots in the gravel on the lane! Uncle Enda has gone someplace.

When we tried to run away after getting out of the car Uncle Enda tried to stop the men from running after us. One of the men caught us by the arms and held us. Peetie Mahon and the Priest pushed Uncle Enda against the motor, and they beat him with their fists. I had never seen men fighting. There was the noise of their hard boots on the hard road at the end of the lane. When Uncle Enda would try to stop one of them, the other one would hit him. At first they beat him in the face and belly. Then they did his arms above his elbows. They beat his arms until he couldn't hold them up, until they hung down at his sides like sausages. Uncle Enda would say sometimes, 'Let them go, Jack. Let them go, Jack.' Every time he said it, the man holding our arms would squeeze, and I wished Uncle Enda would stop. Peetie Mahon pulled him away from the car and pushed him into the lane and began kicking him until Uncle Enda started to run, all bent over. Peetie Mahon kept saying things.

'We'll kill you too, you fucking eejit,' he said.

There was a stick at the side of the lane and when Peetie Mahon hit Uncle Enda across the back it broke. But Peetie Mahon used the piece left in his hand and was beating Uncle Enda's head. Uncle Enda ran off up the lane with Peetie Mahon after him. Peetie Mahon shouted back, 'Bring the paupers.'

The Priest pulled Willie away from the man who had been holding the two of us. Willie's face was all black and blue and swollen on one side, where Peetie Mahon had hit him with his flash-lamp in the Bottling House. The men's boots made hard noises in the gravel on the lane and Willie was whimpering like a little pup that wants to get out.

The sun wasn't up yet but it was light, but dark in the lane with all the high bushes on each side. It was like being in a tunnel full of the sounds of stones moving against each other. It was because I knew they were going to kill us that I was so weak. It was because, too, that I knew there was no one in the whole world to save us, only Mister and Mrs Sheehan and Uncle Enda. And they couldn't. No one else in the whole world would miss us. I was so weak that the man holding my arm had to drag me along.

Going up that lane, Willie, I wanted to tell you in real talk that I loved you, that no matter what happened there was one person in the world who loved you. But I couldn't say it in real talk and I said, 'Illie illie oi uv yooo.' Over and over I said it until the one dragging me squeezed my arm and said, 'Fuck up.' Did you hear me, Willie? And then I shouted out, 'I love you, Willie!' and I knew that you loved me, and I didn't mind that I was going to die only I was afraid of how they were going to do it to me. And I was terribly sad for you, my illy buddah.

Did you answer me back, Willie? Did you say back to me that you loved me? You must have, because I knew you did. My illy illy buddah. I felt so sad for you, you were so frightened. The sounds of the boots in the stones made it worse, all the footsteps falling unevenly and making that hard noise in the gravel.

Peetie Mahon was waiting for us all at the gate. There was no sign of Uncle Enda. Peetie Mahon waved us on and said, 'Bring that one first.' He pointed at you, Willie.

Down between the killing house and the high wall I go, walking as fast as I can, as silently as I can. There are big gates and little gates all over the place, but I have only to go through one to get behind the killing house. It's black dark back here. I slide the tips of my fingers against the high wall, and stop when I think I'm at the middle of the killing house at the back. If some men come from the two sides at the same time I'll be trapped.

It takes me a long time to get the knife out of my pocket. I can't open the blade with my nails. I opened it before with a bent nail I found on the road. But I hold the knife in my hand waiting for them to come.

Then the shouting begins out on the road. The longer it goes on, the safer I feel. I get used to it. The raised voices go back and forth for a long time, one voice waiting for another to finish; sometimes they clash like two swords in a sword fight. They clash against each other until one voice goes higher and gets stronger. While I'm hearing, I lie back against the high wall and think of that time we got peed on. Willie, do you remember? – the two of us together holding hands at the wall around the boys' lavatory in the school.

We were only in the Town for two days and you held out your hand and said, 'It's raining.' I looked up at the sky and said, 'There's no clouds.' We stepped back from the wall and we could see several streams of pee arcing over the top, some stronger than others, some falling like the water in a fountain when it's turned off. We never stood under that wall again. We never laughed about that, Willie. It's funny now – the drops of pee splattering onto our bald heads.

Sometimes I remember that we were happy, Willie. I can't remember *times* when we were happy; just that we must have been happy because we loved each other.

The voices on the road suddenly stop shouting and I hear the sound of hard boots on the concrete footpath. My grip on the knife tightens, because no one is ever going to capture me again. The voices are talking now, not shouting, and there is the sound of a gate being swung open on squeaky hinges.

Suddenly a light shines on me. My hand with the knife jerks up as if it was going to kill all by itself. The fright I get makes me shuffle around a bit until I'm out of the light. Then I see it's just a small window in the killing house in front of me that has been lit up from the inside. There is so much chicken wire over the window that the light coming out is dimmed. Slowly I put my head back so I can peep in.

There are three people. I don't breathe. One of them I don't know. The Guard and Butler-the-Butcher are standing together. The butcher is pointing and talking. The other man is standing behind them. I can hear what the Guard is saying.

'That will only dirty me, not keep me clean,' he says.

'Suit yourself,' Butler-the-Butcher says. He walks over to the wall and hangs his coat on a hook.

GUARD McSWAINE

I'd swear to Jesus it's that fucker, Doolin, with his bad eye. I'd swear the little fucker has cursed me or something. Nothing is going right, all of a sudden, since I saw him at the Cinema. I've heard of people like him who can do things to you with a spell. By Christ! When I get him I'll kick the shite out of him. I can't go on like this.

Ploverlegs Dunne was the last straw! – calling me Baggy and laughing like that. The fucker laughed in my face and he knew there was nothing I could do about it. I'll get the fucker. You're out of the hure business, Ploverlegs, because I am closing you down. Guard McSwaine closed down the Ploverlegs, is what they'll be saying next week. Wait till the word gets out and there'll be no more laughing at Guard McSwaine. God! I hope I don't run into Sheehan. He must be home by now. If I can just get past Lord Edward Fitzgerald Street I'll be alright. I'll pedal like a hure, and if he's not home yet, I might beat him before he gets to the Four Streets. Here's his house.

'OH JESUS! OH FUCK!'

He's there! He said something. I'm going to fall. Jesus!

He frightened the shite out of me. Thank God, I didn't fall off my bike in front of Sheehan. He – fuck him, hiding like that and then ...

'Are you alright, Guard?' he calls after me, and my brain is all so twisted out of shape with the fright and the fear of falling that I don't even think of answering him. But after a minute, when I know I have a puncture in my back wheel, I want to go back to him and shout in his face, 'No, I'm not alright, Mister Chief Sheehan. Mister High and Mighty Sheehan I am not alright at all because this night has been one bitch of a night, one thing after another since I met that

192

scrawny little fucker of a Doolin, and not the least of the things that has happened to me tonight is riding onto your goddam loose gravel, because you were hiding in the bushes and you frightened the shite out of me and now I have a puncture in my back wheel on account of you and that's how alright I'm not, your Royal High fucking Chief!

All Butler-the-Butcher has to do is make one crack and he'll be sorry. I've had enough shite for one night.

Will you look at that! Look at that! It's Doolin, the hure, and he flapping up the road towards Butler's like a turkey with a broken wing. By Christ! I'll get you now, and I'll beat the living shite out of you, Doolin.

'BLINDEYE, BLINDEYE! COME BACK HERE!' I shout at him, and I start running with the bike. The little hure! I'm going to beat the holy shite out of him.

'HEY BLINDEYE, YOU CROOKED FUCKER! COME BACK HERE!' Every time I shout he sticks to the ground with fright. Will you look at him! He's staring back at me, like he's saying fuck you, Guard. I roar my loudest.

'I'LL GET YOU, YOU LITTLE FUCKER! I'LL ARREST YOU.' I had to stand to roar that, but Doolin takes off again, flapping all over the place. When I get him he'll be sorry. And I'll get him one way or the other, the same as I'll get the Ploverlegs. I'm trotting with the bike now, and I see Doolin against the lights of Butler-the-Butcher's, a scraggled shadow limping along the road. I'll have to keep an eye on him. He's like a leprechaun that way; take your eye off him for a second and he disappears.

There's two lights up the road – two yard lamps. Who's out at this hour of the night! Some old farmer, maybe, up with a calving cow. There's two people, too. The lights are too far apart for one person to be carrying the two of them. Quick thinker. Where the hell did Doolin go? Maybe them two lads with the lamps ... No! If they caught him for me I couldn't do anything with them around.

The lamps are coming this way. Maybe it's Butler himself. What a God-forsaken place he picked to build his shop in. It's a good half-mile outside the Town. It's the smell, probably. People wouldn't like to live around the slaughter-house. Blood and guts and flies. And all those bones in the hole at the back. I wouldn't want to live near the stink. Stink of death.

I'll take my time putting the bike against the wall so I can see who they are. I go through the motions of taking the clip off my right leg, my foot resting on the pedal axle. Then I change feet, all the time keeping the two lanterns in the corner of my left eye. I'm under one of the wall lights, so they will know who I am before I know who they are. Not a good tactical situation, but beggars can't be choosers is what I always say. The lanterns are almost beside me when I put down my second foot, the two clips in the fingers of my left hand.

'I hope you haven't a message from Father Quinn for me.'

It's Butler-the-Butcher himself, and that's a peculiar greeting, and an edge on his voice. Quinlan-the-Blacksmith, who helps out on killing days, is with him. I wouldn't like to get into a fight with Jack. He's as stupid as an ox, and surely as strong.

'As a matter of fact, I do, Joe,' I say, and then, to let him know that I won't be put off by his tone, I say, 'Hello, Jack. How's the Missus and the young lad?' The minute I have it said I hope to God he doesn't say anything about parsnips.

Jack puts his brain into gear to come up with an answer, but Butler-the-Butcher says, 'What's the fucking message?'

'Oh now, Joe,' I say, 'take it easy. Give a fellow a chance to catch his breath.'

'It better not be yes,' he says, his voice getting loud.

By this time, with all that's gone on tonight, the last thing I can endure is someone raising his voice to me. So this gives me great satisfaction.

'It is yes,' I say in my calmest voice. I take a step back-ward when Joe Butler begins to shout but right away I real-ize this is a tactical mistake.

'What the fuck do you mean yes?' he roars at me, as if I was a messenger boy. But it's the Guard he's talking to, and this guard is pissed off. I take two steps forward and I roar back at him.

'YES YES YES! That's what the fuck I mean yes!'

Butler-the-Butcher is like a dog having a fit. 'When the fuck did Quinn tell you to tell me?'

'I'll tell you when the fuck he told me to tell you. He called the Missus on the phone before I got home from the Cinema, and said to tell you yes. So if you want to shout at anyone you can go down to the Parochial House, ring the doorbell and shout at Quinn. Fuck you!' I turn to grab the handlebar of my bike.

'He was supposed to tell you when he got back from fishing.'

'Well, he didn't.'

'Well he told you two hours ago ... '

'He didn't tell me anything. He told my Missus on the phone and I wasn't even home then.'

'What time did you get home, then?'

'That's none of your fucking business!'

'Well, it's after one now and the bullock is back out on the grass after running us half-way around the country. Did it take you two fucking hours to get from the Barracks to here to tell me Quinn didn't catch his salmon, that he needs the meat?' Butler roars. 'Is that it?'

I grab the bike away from the wall. 'Do you see that back wheel? It's punctured! I had to walk half the way here to deliver YOUR message and I'm not a fucking messenger boy for anyone, not even for that frigging priest.'

'If you crawled here on your hands and knees from the Barracks you'd have been here an hour ago,' Butler bellows at me. 'But no! You couldn't come right away. No! It's Tuesday night and everyone in this fucking town, including the nuns, knows where the guard is on a Tuesday night.'

'And where is the guard on a Tuesday night?' I bellow back.

'He's up at the Ploverlegs Dunne's house picking up his hure money. That's where he is!' Butler roars at the top of his voice.

By Jesus! That's one to the solar plexus, a kick in the

crotch. I look at Jack Quinlan. He's looking at the road, the way a man would be after looking for hours at a river flowing by real slow.

'Hure money!' I roar back at Butler. 'Hure money!' I don't know what to say, because I know he knows he staggered me with that last remark. 'Hure money!'

'Aye, hure money,' Jack Quinlan says in a low, slow voice. Butler and myself look at him the way you'd look at a sick cow that suddenly gave signs of getting better after weeks. But Butler swings back to me, still shouting.

'And now the bullock is back on the grass after starving for two days and he'll be full of grass and farts, and his guts might burst.'

'I don't give a fuck.'

'You'd better give a fuck, because, if you don't, Quinn's not getting his boxes of meat to send back to Dublin with the big shots tomorrow, not unless I can replace it for my Saturday trade. When Quinn knows who's to blame you'll find yourself in some little village in the arse-hole of Kerry before you know what hit you. We're going to get that bullock back in, and you're going to help us.'

'Fuck you, Butler!'

'It's not fuck me, McSwaine, it's fuck you.'

God! What's wrong with the people of this town tonight?

'How dare you say such a thing to The Guard!'

The minute I say that I know I'm beaten.

'It's very easy to say it when the guard is an arse!'

I take a step forward and Jack Quinlan looks up from gazing at the deep flowing river.

Butler speaks again, commanding me now.

You're going to help us in the slaughterhouse, too, McSwaine because we sent Jack's son home around half eleven.'

'I have my good uniform on,' I say, 'the one for the parade tomorrow.'

'I'll give you an old coat,' Butler-the-Butcher says.

'I can't let the legs of my trousers get covered with cow-shite,' I say.

'I'll give you a pair of old wellies,' Butler-the-Butcher says. 'Come on.'

What can I do! I put the bike back against the wall and follow the butcher. He's not a big man, not as big as me, but I'd hate to have to subdue him. Down the footpath I go after him, between the shop and the high wall. Jack Quinlan is behind me, dragging his big feet on the hard cement.

'Is there any cowshite around here?' I ask. With all the dancing shadows made by the lanterns, it's hard to see the ground.

'There's cowshite everywhere,' Jack Quinlan says from behind me, in a voice with no ups or downs in it.

Butler-the-Butcher opens a gate on the left and we go into the space between the shop and the slaughterhouse.

'Where the fuck are we going?' I ask, when I suddenly realize we're right outside the slaughterhouse doors.

'The coat and boots are in here,' Joe Butler says.

The thought of being in the slaughterhouse gives me the willies. The butcher opens the door and switches on a light. Oh God! It's a terrible-looking place, all hooks and saws and knives and water and an iron ring in the floor and a hole in the floor with a grate on it. God! the smell of the place. The feel of it. I can feel my eyes bulging. I don't say anything because I'm not sure I can talk. Butler-the-Butcher hands me a coat, one that you'd see those cattle jobbers wearing on a Fair Day, stepping through the cowshites like they weren't there, years of cowshite caked onto the coats. The one Butler hands me smells like a cow's arse. It's stiff with old dry shite.

'That'll only dirty me, not keep me clean,' I say.

'Suit yourself,' Butler says, and he hangs it back on a meat-hook at the wall.

'Boots!' Jack Quinlan says, and a pair of wellington boots clatters onto the loud floor beside me. They're streaked with dried shite, too. There's a thick rope through the iron ring in the floor and, at the end of the rope, there's another ring that I've seen the vet using. You put it in a beast's nose to control it.

The boots are cold when I put my feet in. They are about two sizes too big for me. They must belong to Quinlan.

'Do you see this ring!' Joe Butler says. 'When I get my fingers in the bullock's nose you slip this into him. Do you know how to work it?'

'You pull down the spring,' I say.

Butler-the-Butcher goes to a square hole in the wall and picks up what looks like a gun, a big bulky thing.

'Do you see this!' he says. 'It's the killer. It's heavy, It's always loaded. Come here!'

When I stand beside him he says, 'The minute you put the ring in the bullock's nose you come over here and get this. You pick up the gun like this, bring it right over to me and I'll take it the minute I'm ready. When I give it back to you, bring it back here to the hole in the wall and reload it. First you push that part away, pull out the empty shell with the nails of this finger and the thumb and put the empty shell here. You take a new shell from there and put it in the gun. Push this part across and come back to me. If I need the gun again I'll take it. If I use it a second time you go back and reload it. If I don't need it I'll say, no gun. Here, do it. Unload it and load it.'

I'm standing there in this horrible place with this five-pound piece of metal in my hands, loading and unloading it. I hate the thoughts of what I'm going to have to see when they're killing this animal.

When we're leaving the slaughterhouse to go for the bullock, Butler-the-Butcher says, 'Are you sure you won't be needing the coat?'

'I'd better take it,' I say, because I know for sure that if I don't put it on, I'll get splattered with shite at some stage of this fucking game. Better to smell the old cowshite than to get fresh stuff on me. The Missus would go mad.

Butler-the-Butcher tells me to stand on the road and not let the bullock pass me. I'm to direct it down the path between the wall and the shop when it comes to me. He gives me an ash-plant. Then himself and Frankenstein go off with the lanterns looking for the fucking bullock.

This is a terrible predicament to be in. After one o'clock in the morning and here I am. God! If the Missus could see me now she wouldn't believe it. It's like seeing the end of a story without knowing all the things that went into making it. It's like that old chestnut – how did the two pieces of coal and the hat come to be together in the middle of the field.

I hear the two of them yelling down in the field.

I can't believe all the things that are happening to me tonight, and everything goes back to that blindeyed fucker of a pauper. I'd swear to God he's put bad luck on me. Jesus! I know he did and I know why. It's because I put my hand in his pocket. Stealing out of God's hand, it was like. Only I wasn't stealing, I just put my hand in to see what he didn't want me to see. By God! if that's what's going on I'll have to go to confession and say I put my hand in a pauper's pocket, but I wasn't stealing from God's hand. Maybe that will break the luck. I'd better not touch Doolin till after confession.

Here's the bullock! At least there's a lantern up at the gate. One of the lads is opening the gate and here it comes – prancing in and out of the light of the lantern. It's so dark I can hardly see it. Jesus! I'd better not let it pass me. They'd eat me entirely if it got past me.

'Whoa,' I say, low and loud at the same time. Where's the fucking thing? 'Whoa!' My arms are stretched out, the ashplant in my right hand. Then I see it coming into the light on Butler's shop front; a big black and white lad; no horns. At least that's something. I'd hate to get a horn in the guts.

'Whoa, boy. Whoa, boy.' He's slowing down. He stops. He's smelling and I know what he's smelling. What he's smelling has knocked the prancing out of him. Come on, you big fucker! Jesus! All of a sudden I'm glad I'm here. Come on, you big ugly fucker, and we'll murder you, cut you up in pieces and hang you in bits from the ceiling on hooks, your arse on one hook, your head on another.

God! I wish you were Ploverlegs, you big piece of dumb meat. You ugly bastard. You dirty fucker. Come on down here!

DOCTOR McKENNA

The ring of the Church bell, bonging out the time over the Town, is a reassuring sound. It will be heard for miles around in the dark, all who hear it connected by its commonality for a moment: farmers up with sick animals or calving cows; mothers up with frightened children; the doctor, half drunk, waiting across the street from the Church for John Cashin to open his door, hoping Cashin has a bottle.

I'm never drunk, just half drunk; enough to switch trains of thought across whole yards of tracks without prior notice; enough to oil the switches to hair-trigger smoothness.

When I knock a second time on Cashin's door the Church bell bongs again. Two o'clock. My feet are cold. I should have changed out of the slippers when I went home for the drink, my trousers too. I'm wet to the knees. Come to think of it I'm shivering all over. I wonder does Cashin keep a bottle in the house. Most non-drinkers don't. Even if they do keep a bottle, they never think of offering a drink. I'm not backward about asking if there's a bottle someplace. The doctor can get away with it.

Seanie! That's why I'm here. Though it doesn't seem as urgent to find him now. There's times I think he would be better off dead, better if he'd died with Willie. Do I wish him dead so I could get on with living my life? No, Goddam it, he is my child, although it's hard to keep that notion alive when he hasn't responded once in twenty-seven years. But he's not with us in his head. He's off someplace else. I hope to God he's not living his life tied to the Cemetery gate.

Come on Cashin, you bloody nut-case! Get out of your monk's robe and get down here!

God Almighty! there's this head hanging in Cashin's hall-
200

way, the head of Blessed Oliver Plunkett, only this one is luminescent. It's Cashin, of course, but whatever way ...

'John, I'm shivering,' I step into the hallway uninvited. That's alright. The doctor's rudeness is taken as homeliness. 'Do you have a bottle of anything in the house?' I rub my palms together vigorously to give urgency to the situation. But Cashin is not one to be rushed. He starts at my feet and scans the length of me with unhurried eyes. I make shivering noises with my mouth. Without waiting for his question, and to win his instant sympathy, I say, 'Mahon beat up Seanie, and I've been out looking for him.'

'Where is he?' he asks in that rusty voice of his.

'I don't know. I didn't find him. I'm going out again, but I need something to warm me, a shot or two.' I shiver with my mouth again.

'I have brandy, Doctor.'

'That'll do,' I say, as if to say I'm not used to drinking brandy. I follow Cashin into his kitchen. I haven't been in a cleaner place since the time I was in an operating-room in Edinburgh.

As he's pouring the brandy, Cashin says, 'What happened your shoes, Doctor?'

'My shoes?' I say, hoping he'll leave the bottle on the table. He doesn't, but he has poured a decent drink; a big one like non-drinkers pour, or drunks – half drunks. I take a long swig from the glass and my throat and eyes smart as the raw liquor sluices down my gullet.

'My shoes, John,' I say, 'are at home under the kitchen table. Nice and dry and warm, they are.' I take another big swig. Tears squeeze out of my sockets and I give a loud shudder. 'God, I needed that.'

I look at Cashin. He has a collarless shirt on; wide blue suspenders hold up brown corduroy trousers. No socks or shoes. He looks clean and fresh, as if he had just dried himself off after a swim in chilly water. 'I was in a hurry. I didn't have time to get them on,' I say. 'Miss Dickingson is ill.'

'Oh!'

I swallow the rest of the brandy and put the glass on the

table. 'To tell the truth, John, I came to ask you to give me a hand looking for Seanie.'

Without answering, Cashin takes a pair of spotless wellingtons out of the cupboard beside the back door. A grey woollen sock is hanging over the edge of each boot. Cashin sits down and picks up a sock.

'I was passing on my way to the Parochial House, and I saw Seanie falling into the gutter outside Mahon's shop. When I went to him he ran away. He looked bloody around the face. Mahon was in his doorway. All he did was jeer at me.'

Cashin pulls on the boots. Despite the brandy I'm still shivering. 'What size boots do you wear, John?' I ask him.

'Nines. Would you like a pair?'

'Two sizes too small,' I say.

Cashin opens the cupboard again and takes out a red pullover. He slips it on, his bald head coming out through the top like a baby being born. His hand goes into the cupboard again and comes out with a dark green scarf. He ties a loose knot at his Adam's apple and pats it into position down his front. Then an overcoat appears. Then a cap. I find it intriguing to watch other people indulging their idiosyncrasies in their own domestic settings. Here's Cashin, fastidious as a compulsive brood hen, dressing up to go out in the dark. But he is warm and dry and he's going to stay warm and dry. He takes a flash-lamp off the window sill.

'Give me another shot of that stuff,' I say when he turns to tell me he's ready to go.

By the time we get near Plumtree Lane I've explained to Cashin why my car is parked near Peetie Mahon's shop. I left it there on the way down for him, I say, on the off-chance that I might see Seanie. In fact I walked by without seeing it. Cashin doesn't say much. He only speaks when spoken to. Paddy Lennon told me one time that Cashin's lack of talk is a part of the religious regimen he has adopted. Paddy told me about the monk's habit, too.

He strides along like a man exercising. Beside him, feeling very much his senior, I shuffle along, the slippers flapping against the hard footpath; the wet trousers, and the pyjamas under them, like the cold legs of a suit of armour.

'I think we should look around the Playing-Field,' I say, when we come to Plumtree Lane. And then, just to keep the silence at bay, I say, 'It's twenty-seven years since the Church Building Fund was started.'

Cashin shines his flash-lamp at pot-holes and says nothing.

With astonishment I hear myself saying, 'It's twenty-seven years since Willie Doolin was murdered.'

John Cashin stops walking. 'Tomorrow,' he says, 'it will be twenty-seven years and four months.'

Jakers!

Whatever way he said that makes the hairs move on the back of my neck. I stop, too; turn back to where he is, scramble around in my head grasping for one of my hair-trigger switches. There are none. The silence and the darkness of Plumtree Lane; the first words I have ever heard spoken about That Night; John Cashin's tone of voice – they all immobilize me.

We stand in silence for a long time. I turn off my flash-lamp and immediately, as if he had found himself at a disadvantage, John Cashin turns his off, too.

In silence we stand like skaters, each depending on the other to make the right moves that will save both. As the silence continues I make another desperate effort to touch one of my switches, but nothing comes to mind. The only thing that does come to mind is how did Cashin, without thinking, know to the day when Willie had died. He spoke as if it were the only thing on his mind, as if it had been on his mind for so long that he was impatient with it.

Standing there in each other's presence, together in the presence of what I, for one, have never looked at with another person before, is embarrassing. It is more than embarrassing. It is standing on thin ice, arms out, knees quaking, breath held.

'That Night for me,' John Cashin says, 'is the hole in Willie's forehead and Michael Butler stirring his brain with a piece of wire. Willie's eyes were moving, like the eyes in a china doll's head.'

I'm slipping all over the place myself, arms waving around for balance, knocking at MJ's door, waiting to tell Caithleen; waiting for the constable to come, as I knew he'd come, to bring me up to the Cemetery to pronounce death, pronounce the death of a child whose death I had pronounced while he was still alive; Mahon smashing Seanie's hands between two stones because he wouldn't let go of Willie; Caithleen on the floor. MJ hitting me.

'I still feel Willie in my chest and arms, little ripples of effort. He tried to get free. He had thin arms.'

The helplessness, the sweat, the whimpering, me hunkering down behind that white headstone; the terror after finding them in the Bottling House; the party at MJ's and Caithleen's that very evening when Willie had played Haydn – all wet ashes now.

'How could a simple raid on a bottling house turn into such a nightmare, Doctor?' Before I can begin to formulate an answer he continues. 'Look at us! It's twenty-seven years and four months later and here we are in the dark, still suffering. Look at Seanie! – still suffering, and suffering more than we can begin to imagine. Why is That Night still tormenting us all?'

John Cashin's answer to his own question sends a crack sound ripping across the ice to me. 'The only answer is that it was the will of God.'

My voice grates out of me; a low hoarse sound just above silence.

'The will of God! You fool, John Cashin. It had nothing to do with God. Even if there is a God, John Cashin, he was a million miles away from the Bottling House on That Night. You were there That Night. You were there, and so was I and so was Mahon and Quinlan and Butler. That's who was there. Not God! God, my arse!'

The darkness has not absorbed my sibilation before John Cashin's firm voice comes back at me.

'I'm going home,' he says.

'Because I blaspheme? Was there not blasphemy That Night when a child was desecrated – two children? Well, you go home, John Cashin, and tie yourself up in your monk's robe. Hide in your play clothes till they carry you out, feet first, saying how saintly you were, how holy you were. You are no different than me, Cashin. I deal with That Night by staying half-drunk. You deal with it by playing at being a monk. I curse the God you adore – the God whose will it was that a boy should die! Were you the instrument of God's will when you held Willie down, when you lay across his chest so Michael Butler could shoot six inches of metal into his head? Is that what you were doing? Doing God's will?'

My voice rises with my anger.

'Let me tell you about God's instrument, Cashin, if you want to place an instrument of God there That Night! It wasn't you or any of the others, it was an ordained man of God! You remember An Tarav, the invisible IRA commandant? Do you know who he was, Cashin? Did it ever cross your mind to wonder who was the arse with ears who gave the order to punch holes in porter barrels so the British Empire would be hamstrung? I know who he was because I was his doctor; I still am. An Tarav was the parish priest of Clonbracken; the priest – the instrument of God. And do you know who the parish priest of Clonbracken was when Willie was killed, Cashin? It was the Very Reverend Peter Quinn, who is now your own parish priest. That's how your God was present in the Bottling House That Night!'

'That's not true!' he shouts. 'Father Quinn is a priest. He is a man of God, a religious man.'

Jakers! How I have longed to talk to Cashin about That Night. Who else is there to talk to? Butler's dead. Quinlan's a half-wit. Mahon is sick in the head. Seanie's mad. I'm the one now who's in danger of plunging Cashin and myself down through the ice. But it's all I can do. I don't know any other way.

'Quinn may be a religious man. But they're the ones who hate the best. His hatred for the English was the thing that spawned all the misery for Seanie and Willie and the Shee-hans and you and me and everyone else involved. You've heard him raving about the English as often as I have! He's still spewing it out, and it wouldn't surprise me if we heard it all again tomorrow – a special show for the president and de Valera. I'm surprised Quinn's hatred hasn't caught up with him and swung itself around his neck like a great bleeding albatross.'

Cashin starts to say something but I cut him off.

'God was not there That Night. I was there, Cashin. I WAS THERE! You were there. There were ways the two boys could have been saved, could have been and should have been. But they weren't. Neither of them was saved, but don't tell me it was God's will that they shouldn't have been.'

By Jakers! All these years I have been talking and shout-ing to myself about That Night. I'm not used to having an audience. When I hear his footsteps I ask, 'Are you leaving?'

'No,' Cashin says. He goes to the wall across the lane from me and leans against it. I turn on my flash-lamp and examine the ground at the bottom of the wall on my side of the lane. With the edge of my slipper I move a jagged piece of ancient masonry to one side and sit down. John Cashin switches on his flash-lamp and prepares a sitting place. When he has lowered himself to the ground he turns off the light. In silence we sit for a long time; in darkness. I'm not shivering. There's no breeze.

The clock tower in the Church lays a bong. It floats out over the Town and the fields. Another bong launches itself into the darkness and all who are awake feel the palm of God's hand brushing their cheeks. A third drops slowly onto the sleeping world, hanging in the bushes and the trees of the Playing-Field.

'How did you know about the habit?' John Cashin asks.

I have no idea what he's talking about. 'The what?' I ask.

'The habit – the monk's habit.'

'I don't know. Everyone knows about it.'

Cashin says nothing to that. I draw my feet up against my buttocks and pull the overcoat into shape around me. With my arms around my legs, I rest my chin on my knees.

Cashin's habit!

'Why didn't you join a monastery?' I ask.

'They wouldn't take me,' Cashin answers immediately. 'They said the French Foreign Legion is the place for guilty people, not monasteries.'

There is a long silence, and in my head I see monks and Legionnaires marching together, step by step. Across the lane the top of the wall cuts across the starry sky. Cashin's voice slips out into the silence.

'I would have helped you in the Bottling House. I tried to go outside with you, but Michael Butler stopped me.'

Like a ripple of water the voice rolls over me, and like a rock in the tide I have no feelings about it. I have heard what Cashin said. It would have been important to hear a long time ago. Now, it's not. But it's important to John Cashin that he says it, that I hear him. He probably wanted to say that to me for twenty-seven years. There's things I've wanted to say too, things I've wanted to tell to MJ.

'I suspected either Mahon or Butler got to you in the dark,' I say. 'I knew you were on my side.'

But this is not enough for John Cashin.

'If I'd only known,' he says, 'that the boys were going to run for it when we got to the Cemetery, I could have helped, blocked Quinlan. I didn't know there was any plan until Quinlan grabbed the boys and the others threw you up against the motor car to beat you. They must have known. I stood there when they were beating you; I was terrified. I was afraid of punches in the face with closed fists, hard knuckles. I was afraid they'd punch my arms like they were punching yours. They kept beating you and the boys were crying and saying Uncle Enda.'

Uncle Enda! They saw, they knew I was trying to save them. That gives me a warm feeling. They saw me taking a beating. It didn't do them any good, the fact that I got beaten, but it does me good now, the fact that they saw someone trying to save them. I even feel differently towards John Cashin.

'They were going to beat me, one way or the other,' I say. 'They had it planned. Their plan got off the ground quicker than our escape plan did. When we drove up to get the gun in Butler's slaughterhouse, Butler and Quinlan got out. Before he went for the gun, Butler spoke to Quinlan and then Quinlan waited for Butler to return – he was guarding us with Mahon. They knew if they put me out of action they could frighten you into going along with them.'

'If I had done half as much as you did, Doctor! I was so scared I couldn't get started. Next to the wire in Willie's forehead, the worst part was walking up that lane to the Cemetery gates. It was the helplessness. I was weak at the knees, my belly feeling like I'd eaten lead. Seanie started talking some kind of gibberish and Jack Quinlan told him to shut up. Michael Butler had Willie, dragging him along, Willie whimpering. The noise of the boots in that gravel! It was the loudest sound I'd ever heard. It was like stones were in my ears tumbling against each other, like thunder when we were small. And then, above it all, Seanie shouted out, shouted fast, as if he were afraid someone would clap their hand over his mouth, "I love you, Willie!" O God!'

I think Cashin is trying hard not to cry. There is no sound from him.

What must it have been like for the boys, each not only knowing he himself was going to be killed, but that the other was going to be killed, too. They were probably taken up more with each other than with themselves. Suddenly, Cashin is speaking again, his voice controlled.

'I knew what we were going to do to them, and I hated it. But hearing Seanie telling his brother that he loved him! I put my arm on Michael Butler's arm and I said, "Mr Butler, please!" and before I knew what was happening he had punched me in the chest and I was on the ground. They waited until I was on my feet again. Then Willie began to stammer like he had a terrible stutter and he said, "I'm afraid, Seanie." Michael Butler hit him across the head and said, "Shut up." Actually, he said, "Fuck up." I began to cry out loud and Oh God! Oh God!' John Cashin shouts out the last

Oh God! as if someone had his exposed guts in their mincing fingers. Somehow, the shout dispels the darkness between us. Dimly, I can see Cashin sitting over there, his face in his hands bent to his knees, bawling.

I don't feel uncomfortable. It's as if the crying is a part of the story. It's as if Cashin is telling me this is how he felt, and I think it's the first time he has told anyone about it. Sometimes during his crying it sounds as though he is kicking his heels into the ground, beating the earth beside him with his fists. I wonder at how peculiarly comfortable I feel.

Across the dim lane I hear and see John Cashin leaning over to one side. Then a white handkerchief flutters into the air like a released pigeon. Cashin blows loudly. He keeps the handkerchief in his fist and, like me, he rests his head on his pulled-up knees. His hands are under his chin. I don't know if he can see me. I look back to the top of the wall. It obliterates part of the sky with its blackness.

'It was the helplessness for me, too,' I say to the top of the wall. 'Behind that headstone I was weak with helplessness and from the beating. I couldn't stand up. All I could do was whimper at the inevitability of it all. Mahon had whacked my upper arms along the length of the lane, and when I came to the gate I turned to face him. He stuck the end of the stick against my throat and told me if I didn't disappear in one minute they'd kill me, too. He said, "You're the weak link." Then he opened the gate, pushed me in the back and told me to get lost. I lay down behind the first headstone I saw. Mahon's "weak link" kept going around in my head, because I felt myself being weak for Seanie and Willie.'

'When I heard that shot I jerked up my head. The sun was so white, blinding. I stood up, my arms hanging. I thought I would rather be dead than have to face MJ and Caithleen with the deaths of Seanie and Willie. I was beyond caring anything about my physical self. They could hack me to pieces and I wouldn't have cared. Anything would be easier than facing the Sheehans. I swung each arm up and clutched the opposite sleeve. I was running to get myself killed as much as to save whoever was still alive.'

In the dimness of Plumtree Lane I touch my upper arms at the remembrance. I see myself stumbling over the kerbing around the grave, stumbling and knowing that one of the boys was probably dead already. Then I started shouting, 'Run, Seanie. Run Willie!'

I have been talking for myself. Cashin hasn't heard me. He starts to talk again, as if I had just interrupted him, as if he had been waiting for me to draw a breath so he can recite his lines, lines that he knows by heart.

'When we ran to the motor car, after Miss Bevan came, everyone was trying to get through the gate at the same time. Peetie Mahon was trying to open the gate, but he had you by the hair and the others had you by the arms. I ran up the stile and more or less fell down the other side. Instead of getting up and running to the motor car, I crawled up the bank and out through the hedge. I wanted to get away from Mahon and Butler more than I wanted to get away from Miss Bevan. I was afraid they were going to kill you and me. I lay on the other side of the hedge, too terrified to move.

'After a few minutes footsteps sounded running back up the lane. They stopped at the Cemetery gate. I thought it was Peetie Mahon coming back to look for me. Then they advanced fast into the Cemetery. I edged over to where the hedge meets the stile wall, and peeped out. Peetie Mahon was sitting on top of Seanie, a leg each side of his chest. He was strangling Seanie, and he kept looking up the hill to where Miss Bevan had been near the furze bushes. All of a sudden, she was just the far side of the Cemetery wall on her horse. Peetie Mahon got up and ran back to the gate. Seanie didn't move and I thought he was dead. I heard the motor car going off and then Miss Bevan went away from the wall.'

'After a long time I tiptoed through the gravel into the Cemetery to look at Seanie. He was holding Willie's hand and he was breathing. Then Miss Bevan came galloping up the lane from the road. I ran to the headstones and hid.'

This was new to me – that Mahon had gone back to kill Seanie.

Mahon! That's why Seanie can't talk. Mahon damaged him. I hope he burns forever in hell. I hope he dies in his own filth, dies of hunger and thirst in his own filth.

I take deep breaths to help expel my anger.

'I left you to die in the motor car,' John Cashin says.

'They didn't kill me,' I say. 'Mahon threatened the whole weight of the IRA against me if I didn't protect everyone involved. By the time we got back to Madden's Bridge he had it all worked out. He knew Miss Bevan would go to the constable. The constable would come for me to pronounce death. When they dropped me off I cleaned myself up and put on fresh clothes. But I had bruises on my face and my hands were skinned in several places. I waited for the constable to come. But it wasn't the constable's arrival that worried me. It was having to go to MJ and Caithleen and tell them that Willie was dead. I started to drink.'

'Why did you have to tell the Sheehans?' Cashin asks.

'They were going to adopt the boys.'

'Oh God!'

'That very day – the day of the morning Willie was killed – they were all going to Queentown to have the papers signed by a judge.'

'Oh God!'

'I drank a lot. I didn't hear the car coming up the street. I heard a knock on the door. When I answered, the constable was standing there; and over his shoulder I could see Peetie Mahon's taxi, Mahon at the steering-wheel, looking at me.'

'I never knew about the Sheehans,' John Cashin says.

I can see Cashin quite clearly now, his legs stretched out, his hands in the overcoat pockets.

'It was the going to MJ and Caithleen that was the worst part. Even though I was drunk, I knew the devastation I was bringing to them. The pretending was the worst part. The lies, the obvious lies that they knew were covering up something. What would have been better – an IRA apology along with the truth, or the lies I told them? Would it have made any difference what the Sheehans were told? Willie was dead and no matter how or why he had died, he was dead. Of course, I fucked up the whole thing. It was obvious to MJ that I knew more than I was telling. It was obvious that in some way I had been implicated in Willie's death. Can you imagine what that did to MJ? Here I was, his friend, who the night before had asked if I could be considered the boys' uncle; here I was standing in front of him and he knowing I had been a part of Willie's death.'

'Just before Michael Butler shot him, Willie called out for Uncle Enda.'

When John Cashin says that it's like my brain slips into neutral gear. I just sit there, my chin on my knees, staring in the dark, under a wall, all scrunched up under a coat like a baby inside its mother.

Then, uncalled and unbidden, images waft through my head, silent wavy images at first; the people laughing and talking and listening and looking in silence. Willie sitting at the piano, fingers silently skipping around on the ivories; nothing of the Workhouse about him, except his peculiar haircut; even though he is dressed and shod as a pauper, he is transfigured. Caithleen in a wicker armchair, an embroidery hoop abandoned on her lap, beaming, floating, loving, unaware of anything except Willie playing, her eyes bright with happy tears. MJ, big and awkward, as he always looks, sitting on the sofa, his left arm stretched out along the back, his premature white mane shaggy around his ears, light glinting off his rimless glasses, looking at Caithleen looking at Willie. Seanie beside him, lying back, his bald head touching MJ's arm – the beginning of an embrace – Seanie looking at Willie's fingers, in his eyes the rejoicing.

And then I hear the music, in the distance at first, but even when the music fills my head the people remain still, frozen in a moment of happiness as the piano music pours over us. Over us, because I am there, too. Uncle Enda! Uncle Enda had been on Willie's lips before he died, and I had gone and told them that Willie had fallen and struck his head. In one sentence I betrayed the people closest to me .

'Uncle Enda,' I say aloud in the lane. 'Caithleen is dead and so is Willie. There's nothing anyone can do about that.

Seanie is mad and will stay mad. There's no changing that. MJ is isolated, withdrawn, a lonely old man who must cry at night. And Enda McKenna – town drunk, town doctor, cocooned in his shame. We should be able to reach across to each other. But it's so painful.'

I sit there staring, thinking of MJ, of how difficult it would be to walk up to him and say, 'MJ. We have to talk. I have to talk to you. There's things I have to tell you.'

John Cashin speaks. 'When Peetie Mahon discovered that Seanie was alive, wasn't he afraid he might tell what happened? I was.'

'When we went back up for Willie in the taxi, Mahon pulled Seanie off Willie and threw him aside. Later, when he was bringing me to the Sheehans, he told me no one would ever believe what Seanie would have to say, because, he said, "That fellow's gone mad." But even so, I saw Mahon one day up on Miss Bevan's farm – that time when we were trying to entice Seanie home. I told Mahon that if either Seanie or I died unexpectedly, there was a letter in the bank for Mister Sheehan. I never saw him on the hill after that.'

There is silence again, then again the Church bell. The bongs don't sound as confined as before. Maybe it's the faint light in the east that allows the sound to escape, to travel out farther at a quicker pace. Maybe it's my imagination. Four bongs. The blessing of the new wing is only eight hours away.

'Have you ever spoken to Jack Quinlan about That Night?' John Cashin asks.

A picture of the big, sullen Quinlan pops into my head: Quinlan-the-Blacksmith, hulking over his anvil; the leather apron tied in the middle with binder-twine; the muscled and blue-veined arms bared to the shoulders, glistening; in the big hand the big hammer that strikes the red-hot iron.

'Jack Quinlan spends his life waiting and listening for someone to sing the Ballad of the Bottling House. He comes to life when he hears it because his name is in it. Beyond that, I don't believe he ever thinks of That Night. If it had been anyone else but Jack, the boys might have been saved.'

My legs are beginning to cramp. My bottom is numb. To get up, I twist over onto my knees and hands. By the time I'm standing Cashin is in the middle of the lane. We can see each other's faces now. I rest my hand on his shoulder.

'Maybe we did our best to save them, John,' I say, 'the best we could do at that particular time. It was the Sheehans I betrayed. I'll have to go to MJ. I'll have to.'

We start walking towards the Playing-Field. A white dawn low in the sky behind us gives shape to the world, the hawthorns yield their scent and rustle down their perfumed showers of bloom on the dewy grass.

'If we find Seanie,' John Cashin asks, 'do you think he'll come with us?'

'I don't think he will,' I say. 'Maybe somewhere in his head, someday, he may see us as people who don't hurt him. As well as that, looking for him allows me to think I am doing something for him. I will probably look for him till one of us dies. I would like to hold him in my arms once before I die.'

PADDY LENNON

You'll have to put the chair on the other side, so the window's in your back. It's the only way I can see you. And don't forget to put the chair back when you're leaving. Nuns and their rules! She keeps telling me I can do as I like when I go home. But no one who comes in here ever goes home again. It's a place to die, and not a bad place to die, either.

There was a time when no one from the Town would be caught near here – it was still the Workhouse, even with all the old buildings gone and new ones built. Changing the name helped. Once they started calling it St Christopher's Hospital it wasn't shameful anymore. But then, too, Doctor McKenna and Mister Sheehan died in here. Once Mister Sheehan came in there was nothing wrong with the place.

They're all dead, you know, except Cashin. He's in the asylum in Queentown this good few years. Mad as a March hare! They took him away when he started wearing the monk's habit to the Church.

The priest who came after Father Quinn decided to have three masses on Sundays instead of two. The Church, with its new wing, has never been full since That Day. Quinn spent twenty-seven years wringing pennies out of the people, crying and whining every Sunday, so we could have a glorious house for God. Every Christmas he gave the same sermon about how miserable and shitty the place was where Christ was born, 'But we', he would say, 'will build a house worthy of our God.' He was collecting for his own monument, that's what he was doing. When his big day arrived the people were delighted, because they would never again hear the words 'Church Building Fund'. One thousand five hundred sermons is what Slip Carey figured it out to be

– at least that's in one of his songs. He had a song for everything.

I never saw such a happy parade. It was a grand May day. You could smell the Maybush blossoms blowing in from the country. Everyone had their overcoats over their arms or shoulders. The women all looked different in their dresses with no coats on. Everyone was out, except the Protestants, of course. They were out of sight because That Day the Catholics owned the Town.

We all assembled at the Monument. The Pipe Band was there warming up, all of them in kilts – the whole shebang – sporrans and ribbons and brooches and berets. You could see the women giggling behind their hands to each other and glancing at the knees of the lads in the band. The people were organized into sodalities and legions and societies and associations. The children were lined up in two groups as usual, boys and girls. The young ones, who had just made their first communions, were in their white dresses and the lads in their suits with the big white badges on the lapels. Nuns and teachers were prowling around like sheep-dogs, keeping the children in line and quiet.

About fifty priests in black and white, with the little three-cornered hats, were in two rows between the children and the grown-ups. Most of the priests had big bellies and red faces. They did a lot of loud laughing until the big cars drove up at eleven o'clock. There was a hush and everyone could hear the clock in the Church tower bonging away. They must have been waiting around the corner up at the Four Streets, because they couldn't have timed it so well. All the doors of the second car opened together and four big men got out. I've never seen four bigger men in the same place at the same time before or since. They all went straight to the first car and one of them rapped his knuckles on the roof. It was those lads who would shoot Seanie. It was for Mister Sheehan I felt bad That Day. He had always been kind to Seanie Doolin. He even got me to work for him one time making the shed at the back of his house into a snug bedroom for Seanie, because he couldn't get him to

216

come into the house. I wasn't surprised when he buried Seanie in his family grave. Six months later Mister Sheehan got permission to move Willie's body into the same grave. I did all the digging. He had a new coffin for Willie, and strange enough Miss Bevan was there, the only one besides myself, Mister Sheehan and Michael Dalton. When I saw what was put on the headstone I thought the engraver had made a mistake, he had put the same date for the death of the two brothers. Mister Sheehan said, 'The two of them died in 1921, Paddy.'

The first one out of the car was Father Quinn. Then the bishop – a long, thin man whose head was too big for his body. He had those big eyes, as if he thought someone would jump out and frighten him. Then the President got out – Sean T. O'Kelly – a little man in striped trousers and tails and a hat. He seemed to expect everyone to start cheering, but we all just stood there gawking. Then Dev emerged, like a stork unfolding itself after being in too small a box. He was thinner and taller than the bishop, but his head fitted his body. By then he was going blind. I don't know how bad he was, but there was an aide there to steer him.

Quinn was hopping about like a child, the hair combed for a change. He fussed around everyone, helping them all out of the car. You'd feel like going over and hitting him on the back of the head with a shovel to get his attention, and then roaring at him to stay quiet.

Anyhow! The parade got going with the Pipe Band out in front, drumming and piping like hell. The children and priests went first; then Quinn and Dev and the rest with the bodyguards; then the men and then the women – everyone in the best of form. Of course, those of us in the know were excited about Baggy McSwaine. I suppose all the men knew about it, at least the ones from the country did. They never told the women, because you know women – telegraphs! There was a lot of nervous laughing and talking in the men's part of the parade. Someone would lift his coat and point to the bag he was hiding under it. John Glanvil, from the canal, had a sack with a terrible stink. He wasn't laughing at all; he was still mad at McSwaine, who had caught the son without a light on his bike the week before. It was Glanvil and John Joe Grimes who organized the whole thing.

When we got to Robin's Corner some of the men started poking a finger into their necks and squealing like pigs. Everyone was tittering and laughing, and the ones who didn't know were being told. Of course, only a few of us knew at the time that it was John Joe Grimes and his lads who were killing the pigs. They had tried to keep who it was a secret because if something went wrong, Baggy could have time to get his revenge.

One of the guards from Queentown was standing at Robin's Corner with his hands behind his back. Doctor McKenna was talking to him.

'Will you look at McKenna!' someone said, and then you could hear it being passed back along the parade – 'Look at McKenna! Look at McKenna!'

I never saw Doctor McKenna looking as good as he looked then. His hair had a split in it. He was clean and shaved. He had a suit on that looked like a tailor had stitched it onto him. He had a white shirt on and a red tie and his shoes were shining. His hands were behind his back, like the guard, and his back was straight. Of course, we all knew he was going to the Big Dinner and that he had to look good. But we had never seen McKenna like this since he first came to the Town. He said something to the guard and joined the parade. When he stepped in beside Mister Sheehan they shook hands like they hadn't seen each other in years.

Some of the lads started up about Doctor McKenna being all dressed up to make an impression on Miss Dixon – that hatchet-faced bitch! She must have been drunk That Day. The Convent nuns had to cook the Big Dinner. Of all the people in the Town, besides Mister Sheehan, who should have been in the middle of everything, it was the nuns. They had the Church Building Fund for breakfast, dinner and supper for twenty-seven years and, now that the day was here, they had to miss everything and cook for Quinn and his gang.

When we got down near Peetie Mahon's shop, the parade came to a halt and everyone was quiet. That part of the Town is where most of the Protestants and Ditkoff-the-Jew live. No one knew what the hold-up was, and everyone around me was standing on their toes with their necks stretched, like partridges in barley stubbles. Then one bagpipe by itself began to wail out 'Faith of our Fathers'. When the bagpipe got near the end of the verse, some of the women started to sing: 'We will be true to thee till death.' That made it worse. All of us who knew the Protestants well were sweating with embarrassment. When the pipes started the second verse more people joined in, and by the time the verse was over there was enough religious defiance in the air to start a war.

During this singing we were standing opposite Peetie Mahon's shop. The shop was closed on account of the solemnity of the occasion, as Father Quinn put it. But Peetie was standing there in the doorway, wearing his shop apron, letting everyone know, without saying a word, that he wasn't going to the Church; letting them know his shop would be open when the celebrations were over. Some people didn't like Mahon. To tell you the truth, I hated the man. When I heard what happened to him I wasn't sorry. I thought it was just another part of his story, that he was murdered.

Of course they blamed Seanie Doolin for that, too. They tried to blame everything that happened That Day on Seanie. How the hell could anyone think Seanie killed Peetie Mahon? You should have seen Mahon's shop – there had been a hell of a fight! Seanie Doolin couldn't have fought his way out of a paper bag. And as well as that, Seanie Doolin called to the Parochial House that morning looking for Father Quinn. He didn't even know what was going on That Day, that there was a parade. He had already passed Mahon's shop when he rang the doorbell right after the people had gone into the Church. The nun who answered the door said he had dry blood on his face, like his nose had been bleeding a long time ago and he had wiped it across his face with his sleeve. She didn't see any other blood. She told him where Father Quinn was, went off to get him a cut of bread and jam and when she came back he was gone. She looked out and saw him going towards the Church. He had his blanket on. The blanket once belonged to a horse and it stunk for ages. He used to throw it around his shoulders and tie it under his chin with a safety-pin. You'd swear it was a monster when you'd meet him near dark; this terrible head of his – all misshapen and the eye with the scar running through it like an arrow.

The Queentown detectives said Seanie stabbed Mahon and ran away. Then Mahon fluttered all around his shop breaking everything, and falling over stuff, all the while trying to pull the knife out of his neck. The detectives had this way of getting fingerprints, but the handle of the knife had been all daubed with Mahon's blood when he tried to pull it out, his two eyes staring up the arse-hole of the devil. He had marks on his face like someone had scraped their nails from his eye to his chin.

You know who killed him? Tinkers! That whole thing about Father Quinn's knife was pure shite. They said Seanie had stolen it, had broken into Quinn's house. Seanie Doolin never did anything like that, he was too afraid of people. Quinn told Guard McSwaine that he'd lost the knife the night before when he was fishing. That's what McSwaine told the inquest. The tinkers found the knife and when they went in to rob Peetie they killed him with it when he put up a fight. Anyhow! That's Mahon.

McSwaine was next.

The closer we came to the Church the more nervous everyone got. They kept asking stupid questions. As long as they heard John Glanvil talking they calmed down, even though some of his answers were as daft as their questions. When we got past the corner just below Maxwell's, the lads in front all turned around grinning at Glanvil. They had seen Baggy. He was standing by himself in the churchyard, hands behind the back, legs apart and his chest puffed out.

Two of the Queentown guards were standing at attention

each side of the Church door, but the men were more worried about Mister Sheehan than the guards. No one ever liked Mister Sheehan seeing them doing something wrong.

The parade slowed down a bit when the children in front got to the Church steps. By the time the priests were going in, it had slowed down to a shuffle. Then Quinn and his crowd turned into the churchyard and walked, real slow, till they were opposite where Baggy McSwaine was standing. You couldn't hear a sound from the men, only the shuffling boots on the road. Then everyone started getting the stuff out of their bags. You never heard such rattling of paper. No one was to do anything until John Glanvil gave the signal. The whole idea was for Father Quinn to see McSwaine getting plastered.

Just as the big shots reached him, McSwaine brought his arm up to salute, his fingertips trembling at his temple. I can still see him in that last second before his life changed forever, and it changed when a rotten mangel fell out of the sky and burst like a bomb of snots at his feet.

It was like the whole world, and everything in it, turned to statues. The President's bodyguards went on alert. All heads had turned to the plopping noise and there they saw McSwaine at attention, with his shining buttons, and all this rotten stuff plastered to the legs of his trousers up to the knees. And while everyone was looking at him, do you know what this powerful eejit did! He looked down at the squashed mangel and then he looked up in the sky, as if he expected to see a crow or a seagull. That's when the shower of shite came down on him: potatoes and onions and carrots and rhubarb and parsnips and apples and cabbage – most of it rotten. McSwaine tried to make himself small, with his hands protecting his peaked cap and a hump on his back.

A few late pieces were still falling when Mister Sheehan left the parade and strode into the churchyard. He went over and stood beside the guard and glared across at the men. You could see he was fit to be tied. Everyone knew by the look on his face that he was saying, 'This is not the time, nor the place.'

There was a terrible silence. The priests on the steps who hadn't gone in yet had stopped to look around. The two guards were staring. Everyone was still and it was like a spotlight was on McSwaine and Mister Sheehan standing there in the middle of all the rotten fodder.

Then someone moved, started pushing his way out of the crowd of men. Of course it was Glanvil. He got a week in jail for assaulting an officer of the peace and was fined ten shillings. He said, to the day he died, that it was worth it. As he stepped into the churchyard he made a little run and threw a small rotten mangle as hard as he could. It hit McSwaine in the chest and burst open. Then Glanvil roared, 'Fatten your pigs on that, McSwaine!' It became a chant around the Town for years: 'Fatten your pigs on that, Mc-Swaine, as Glanvil said to the guard.'

He stood there glaring at McSwaine, his fists clenched at his sides. Then Mister Sheehan walked over and touched his arm. It was like magic. John Glanvil looked around as if to say, 'What the hell am I doing here?' and at the same time the parade started moving forward. Glanvil went to his place and all the men cheered for him under their breaths. They didn't arrest him till the next day.

When the last of the people in the parade were in the Church, we had to wait while Father Quinn went into the sacristy to get his duds on. There was great excitement in the Church. During the pelting of McSwaine, John Joe Grimes and his pig-killers had come in over Madden's Bridge and had mingled in without anyone noticing. They were busy telling the lads around them what they had done. Putting the pigs in McSwaine's bed had not been part of the plan, but at the last minute John Joe had come up with the idea. They put pillows under the pigs' heads and pulled the blankets up to their necks.

Of course, before the mass started nearly everyone in the Church knew what had happened, and there was a terrible buzz as the people whispered from one to the other. Dev and Sean T. were up there in the front seat, two bodyguards each side of them. They must have thought we were a terrible pack of heathens, with the guffaws and sniggerings and the odd handclap. The bodyguards kept glancing around as if the whispering was part of a plot or something.

Well, at last, the nun playing the organ hit the keyboard a ferocious wallop, and out on the altar came the bishop, dressed up in his mitre and vestments, surrounded by two flunky priests who waited on him, like he was the queen herself. The three of them genuflected and went to the side of the sanctuary to the chairs with the red cushions. Then, with another thump on the organ, out comes Father Quinn and he surrounded by priests and altar boys with smoking thuribles and holy water and crucifixes and candles and big books. The Sunday before, Father Quinn had explained to us how the ceremonies would go. The consecration of the new wing by the bishop would take place after the sermon. So, when Father Quinn arrived on the altar, he started right into the mass. Everything was in Latin. It was a high mass with a lot of singing. Every move Quinn made, a priest on his right and left made the same move, like a ballet.

When Father Quinn got to the sermon, instead of going to the pulpit, he stood at the top of the steps in front of the altar, with the new microphone in front of him. I think he figured the photographers would get a better picture of him on the steps. So, there he was, twenty-seven years behind him, and he standing proudly in the renovated Church and its new wing. He started off with, 'Your Lordship, Monsignors, Right Reverend Fathers, Very Reverend Fathers, Reverend Fathers, Very Reverend Sisters, Reverend Sisters, Mr President, Mr de Valera, Distinguished Guests, My Dear Brethren.' The ones who paid for the whole thing the last on the list.

And then, to the amazement and embarrassment of all, he launched into what we used to call his Foreign Policy sermon. Jaze! We all bowed our heads and put our hands over our faces. We knew it by heart, every man, woman and child of us. In no time at all he had himself riled up, beating the air with his fists, shouting about Partition, Protestants, Henry VIII, Lloyd George, Michael Collins, Extermination,

Annihilation. He wound himself up like a toy with a spring in its back. Tighter and tighter he went and louder and louder, and very few of us noticed Seanie Doolin limping down the aisle on the men's side. While the vaults in the ceiling rang with hate, Seanie silently made his way towards the altar rail. Everyone who saw him must have been as surprised as I was. He was wearing his blanket and, in the distance for a moment, he looked like he was wearing one of those vestments they call a cope, that the priests wear at Benediction.

Then, all of a sudden, everyone could see Seanie when he stepped into the sanctuary on the side where the bishop was sitting. That is, everyone except Quinn, because if God himself had appeared in front of him, Quinn wouldn't have seen him. He had worked himself into a trance. He was inspired.

Everyone watched as Seanie walked towards the sacristy door, which was behind the altar and a bit to the side. But instead of continuing, he turned right and climbed up the side steps to the altar. He stood behind Quinn and swung his two hands up from under the blanket. From where I sat I thought he had a big piece of metal in his hands.

A whole lot of things happened at the same time.

Three people stood up in the Church: Doctor McKenna, John Cashin and Mister Sheehan. Cashin was sitting off by himself and only later I heard that he stood up, held out his hand like he was going to stop something and shouted, 'Seanie!' Doctor McKenna and Mister Sheehan did exactly the same. I was two seats behind them and to the side. For a split second Father Quinn stopped ranting. Seanie's name was going around and around the Church in big echoes.

SEANIE SEANIE SEANIE

Father Quinn pointed his arm down towards Mister Sheehan and Doctor McKenna, and into the microphone said, 'I'. Then there was a bang in the microphone like a shot from a howitzer, and Quinn fell down the altar steps – a marionette that's had all its strings snipped at the same time.

For an instant there was silence: Seanie standing up there on the top step; Quinn down below him on the floor like a bundle of old clothes. Then Seanie shouted and nobody knew what he said, but most people agreed it was, 'Illy illy yuf ree naw. Illy illy ...' As he said it he began to swing up the humane killer – that's what it was, of course. He swung it up with his two hands, as if he was going to throw it up in the sky like a man would throw his hat in the air in gladness. One of the President's men jumped to his feet and fired, because he thought Seanie was going to shoot at Sean T. or Dev. Then another eejit jumped up and he began to shoot too. Then, so help me God, a third one started. And they shot and shot and shot and you could see they were hitting Seanie .

He was a terrible sight – up there at the altar with all the lights on him, and the big horse blanket swinging all around him. Every time a bullet struck him he'd be jerked around like he was dancing on the red carpet, but he stayed on his feet, and they shot and shot and Mister Sheehan shouted out, 'Go down, Seanie! Go down!' and he was bawling like a child and he kept shouting and Doctor McKenna too: 'Go down, Seanie, go down!'

The poor little bastard!

He finally fell back against the altar, his arms splayed out, supporting himself, his poor disfigured face flung up as if he was looking straight into the face of God. I have never heard such a silence in a full church. It was like in a nightmare, all of us paralysed while someone we were holding slipped inch by inch out of our grasp over a cliff. Seanie crumpled onto the floor right in front of the tabernacle door.

You know how many times they hit him! Fourteen! Fourteen bullets. Big stupid eejits they were. Fourteen bullets.

Doctor McKenna got out into the centre aisle and ran to the altar. Of course, some of the bodyguards had already turned around and were sweeping their guns back and forth across the Church waiting for, hoping for, a conspiracy to show itself. When McKenna ran up the aisle one of them aimed his gun at him and shouted something. McKenna said: 'I'm a doctor, you fool!' and kept running, the bodyguard swinging around, keeping the gun aimed at him.

The doctor vaulted over the altar rails and, when he came to Father Quinn, he jumped over him like you'd jump over a bag of spuds that's in the way. He went up to the top step and knelt beside Seanie. After a few seconds he stood up and when he turned around he had Seanie in his arms; Seanie's funny-looking head hanging back and down over McKenna's arm, the mouth open; the blind eye, with the arrow through it, looking at nothing; the matted hair sticking out in every direction; the horse blanket tied at the neck with the safety-pin, a bullet-hole in his jaw.

When McKenna turned there wasn't a sound. It seemed like no one was breathing as he came down the steps and walked over Quinn again, one of Quinn's feet twitching. When he got to the altar rails Mister Sheehan was there already and had opened the little gate. They spoke for about a minute, the two of them looking down at Seanie; then Sheehan put his hand on McKenna's shoulder and they looked at each other.

They walked together down the centre aisle, Mister Sheehan holding up Seanie's head with his two hands, so it wouldn't be hanging down over the doctor's arm. They were crying. I saw his face as they went by, Seanie's. The eyes were half closed. There was a drool over his lip and the scar through the eye was white.

The little things we remember! The flowers on the altar. The schoolchildren from the country had picked dog daisies That Day – bunches and bunches of them.